MEMBERS ONLY

Richard Seymour

Paperback Edition April 13, 2024
ISBN 9798322695981
© Richard Seymour.

To my mum and dad.

THE PROLOGUE

Eric lay dead. He had not known what had killed him, either. This was a shame. For while his death had been painless and, in his ignorance, without trauma, he had always wondered how his end would come. Now he would never know.

He had not heard the tell-tale screech of brakes or the words, 'I am afraid it's terminal', either of which would have heralded his fate. Nor had he had the time it takes to hit the ground from a top-floor window to make his peace with God. A bullet had entered his body through the back of his neck, splitting his cerebellum in two and killing him instantly.

Since the gun that fired the bullet was discharged from a distance, his death had been mostly silent. Indeed, his girlfriend, Amber, continued along the high street, talking to herself while responding to a message that had just come through on her phone.

"This doesn't make any sense," she said, shaking her head. "Predictive text is useless. She'll ball me at good?" She repeated the phrase several times, under her breath, until the words rearranged themselves into something more likely.

"She'll call me at home!" she said, the penny dropping at last. *Going nut*, she replied, *Pee you newt vine you are fred*.

Chuckling at her own joke left her only partially fulfilled, so she offered the phone to Eric for his approval. On finding him absent from her shoulder she stopped and turned to find him face–down on the pavement–a pool of blood expanding from his head.

She screamed.

An elderly lady rested her hand on Amber's arm and asked her what the matter was. Amber pointed. The lady stared just beyond her trembling finger and the colour flushed from her aged face. The driver of a bus, which was taking on passengers, leapt from his cab and crouched beside Eric's body. He had no previous experience with the dead and dying, but he had spent the formative years of his working life in London's 'Gang Land'. His duties involved nothing more sinister than delivering crates of fish to restaurants in east London on a cash only basis and looking baleful from behind dark glasses at the funerals of colleagues. (His photograph once appeared in a tabloid newspaper. The caption underneath described him as a 'Heavy'. He was so pleased, he made a clipping of it and slipped it in his wallet behind his driving license.) But he liked to think of himself as having a Past and he pressed his fingers to Eric's neck wearily for signs of a pulse as if he had done it all too many times before.

He caught Amber in his arms when she fell to her knees and pressed her hand to Eric's bloody skull. "Come on, love," he said, building his part. "He's gone."

Amber wailed into his blue London Transport pullover as her phone beeped twice in her hand. He peered over her shoulder at the screen. "Surf no spoc?" he mouthed and furrowed his brow.

He encouraged Amber to her feet and led her away. A crowd was beginning to gather. A few minutes later, two police officers arrived on foot. The older of the two, PC Dodd, strode with no discernible sense of urgency through the onlookers speaking into a two-way radio, which was attached to his lapel. The bus driver had often wondered how police officers could act so casually. He imagined that they had been patrolling the town centre, letting sixteen-year-old skateboarders know they had their eyes on them, when a call came through that a violent murder had been committed on their patch. He assumed they called them patches, unless that was just on the telly.

But they had not removed their truncheons and sprinted through the shoppers, blowing their whistles, as he would have. Nor had they commandeered a car in the name of His Majesty, leaving its driver at a loss by the road, scratching his head. No. Instead, they could not have appeared more care free if they had strolled in and said, 'Allo, allo, allo. What's goin' on 'ere then?' The killer would have had time to escape on a pogo stick. If he had one handy.

PC Dodd was a man of later years, with a moustache and rosy cheeks. This gave him the appearance of being jolly. In fact, PC Dodd (or 'Doddy', as he disliked being called) was nothing of the sort. He had rejected offers of promotion for thirty years, believing instead in the notion of the Officer on the Beat. He had seen his loyalty repaid by a reduction in the numbers of his colleagues, a disdain displayed to him by the general public, whom he had genuinely once wanted to protect, and, worst of all, with the fact that his superiors, who were almost all younger than him, considered him a harmless throw-back to the past and patronised him, constantly. This placed him in a foul mood, which he had stopped trying to conceal many years before.

"Colin!" he yelled at his partner.

Colin was in his mid-twenties and had no intention of remaining an Officer on the Beat for a day longer than he had to. His head had become drunk on a dream of becoming a ruthless detective in the drug squad who didn't mind bending the rules if it meant 'banging up scum dealers' and the like.

He had inflamed the ire of PC Dodd on this occasion by peering too closely at the bullet hole in Eric's head.

"If forensics find just one of your follicles on that body," he warned, "you'll go down for twenty years."

"I've got an alibi. I was with you the whole time."

"Really?" replied PC Dodd, who was busy urging the crowd back. "Well, there was the two minutes when I was stuck inside that Super-Loo. Start looking for witnesses or I'll tell the jury I saw you pull the trigger."

Colin stretched to his full, unimpressive height, and did his best to look important while his partner arranged for a cup of sugary tea for Amber from a small sandwich shop. The bus driver gave his statement and was allowed to leave with his passengers, who had congregated on the top deck and were pressing their faces against the windows for a better view.

As the bus pulled away, leaving behind a plume of

diesel smoke, a police car with its siren wailing and blue light flashing screeched to a halt at a forty-five-degree angle to the kerb. The occupants leaped from their seats, their only regret being that they had no guns with which they could duck down behind the open doors and poke through the rolled down windows.

"So what's going on?" they asked, together.

"There's a cat stuck up that tree there," replied a tired sounding PC Dodd.

The two officers looked up at the tree, then at each other and finally came to rest again on PC Dodd. "We were told there was a murder."

"What do you think scared the cat?" The brief silence that followed was broken by an excited Colin.

"All right, boys?" He placed his hands on his hips and went on as casually as he could manage. "White, Caucasian male. Approximately thirty years of age-"

"He was thirty," interrupted PC Dodd.

"Yeah?" gawped Colin, impressed. "How can you tell?"

PC Dodd sighed. "His partner told me." He pointed his finger at Amber, who was seated upon a white plastic chair outside the sandwich shop and draped in a red blanket. "Oh, and if he's Caucasian I think we can safely assume he is white, Colin."

"This is a murder scene, Doddy," replied Colin, gravely. "Never assume anything."

PC Dodd closed his eyes and counted to three but when he opened them again saw Colin was still there.

"Don't call me Doddy."

The paramedics, who PC Dodd had always harboured a professional admiration for, arrived next. A young girl, pretty, with bright blue eyes and blonde hair bouncing behind her in a ponytail, hopped from the cab and crouched beside Eric's body with a medical kit.

"There was no pulse when I arrived on the scene," offered Colin.

"Thank you, Colin," cautioned PC Dodd, "and you can put that tongue away before someone trips over it."

Her partner, an older but healthy-looking and agile man, pressed his ear to Eric's back. A more sophisticated test confirmed what was obvious to everyone and solicited renewed wailing from Amber. "He's dead."

Some hours later, when Eric's body had been photographed from every conceivable angle, it was zipped up inside a white plastic bag and taken away for further examination. The forensic officers in their overalls and hair nets finished collecting what little evidence they could find—mostly discarded chewing gum and cigarette butts—and Amber was driven to her parents' house. Eric's blood had congealed in pools and stained the pavement where it dried. A strong chemical cleaner was deployed and the only remaining sign that Eric had been there at all was a section of pavement that was conspicuously cleaner than the pavement either side of it and a yellow sign, balanced up against a lamp post that appealed for witnesses to come forward. The tape that had been strung up to keep people back was pulled down and the high street was reopened.

They never did catch who did it.

ONE

Eric stood in a room with white-washed walls that had yellowed with age. Strips of electric light buzzed and blinked from a false ceiling and a bare, wire leaflet rack which had not been restocked for years, hung beside the door. He had no idea how he had got there, but the interesting thing about that was that this fact did not seem to bother him particularly. He knew, somehow, he was supposed to be there, and that was good enough for him it seemed.

Narrow windows, spaced at regular intervals, lined the opposing wall. Above each shone a bright red number on a liquid crystal display. Between Eric and the windows, a metal handrail, placed there to organise a large volume of people, switched back on itself several times. Three of the nine positions were manned and only one of those was serving a customer. Other than a single gentleman stooping to make himself heard through the slot at the base of one the windows and the assistants behind the glass, Eric was alone. Snaking his way along the handrail when he was the only person in the 'line' seemed unnecessary, so he by-passed the formality and presented himself at window number three.

"We put the Human Filtration System in place for a reason, you know," said the assistant, nasally.

"I'm sorry?"

The assistant, whose name was Bryan, pointed over Eric's shoulder to the metal handrail.

"Oh, I see," said Eric, then, after an uncomfortable pause, asked, "What reason's that then?"

Bryan sighed. "We get vast numbers of people through here each day. Were it not for the handrai- the Human Filtration System, there'd be chaos."

Eric looked around the room. "But there is no one here."

Bryan conceded this point.

"So, what are you saying?"

"What I am saying is, I will not serve you if you don't follow the proper procedure. If we make a concession to you, we'd have to make concessions to everybody, then where would we be?"

"You want me to join the queue?"

"Yes."

"What queue?"

"The one you jumped to the head of."

"The queue which is made up of just me?"

Bryan nodded. Eric, knowing logic was on his side, somewhere, questioned Bryan that since he had jumped to the head of a queue of one, had he not, therefore, also joined the back?

"It depends on which way you look at it," replied Bryan.

He thought about it, and Eric rather supposed it did.

"And the way I look at it," continued Bryan, "is that you

jumped in at the front, which is very unfair to those at the back."

"Unfair, in fact, to me."

"Then you know what I am talking about."

Eric was reminded of something his mother used to say: "The world is run by stupid people," she had told him when he was a young boy. "They can't do anything about being stupid, so it's up to the rest of the world to learn to stoop."

Eric 'stooped'. He walked to the back of the room and made his way through the Human Filtration System, around its hairpin turns, like a single head of cattle on its way along the slaughtering process and arrived back at window number three.

Bryan shook his head.

"No?"

"No."

"What did I do wrong this time?"

Bryan pointed to a sign behind Eric that read *Please Wait Here*. Eric, head hung low, returned to the sign and waited. Bryan made a movement with his hand, which Eric took to mean that he should stand further back. He looked down at the tiled floor and realised his indiscretion: his toes were an inch over a painted white line. He shuffled back and waited. Bryan rolled his eyes, heaved his head off his fist, on which it had been resting the whole time, and pressed a button on the counter.

"Window number three, please," chimed a clear female voice. Eric looked up. Bryan nodded, permissively, and he stepped forward.

"How may I help you?"

"I really don't know," Eric replied. "I am not entirely sure how I got here or even where here is."

Bryan removed a document from a drawer and stamped it with red ink. He pointed to a door. "Take this to room eight, last on the left."

"Yes," said Eric, as he took the sheet of paper. "I was wondering if-"

"Window number three, please," chimed the voice once more at Bryan's command. Eric looked behind him but saw no one waiting. "The thing is-"

"Window number three, please. Window number three, please. Window number three, please," came the voice in quick succession.

"Look, I am terribly sorry but-"

"Window number three, please."

"If you'll just-"

Bryan thumped the red button on the desk beside him again only this time there was silence.

"And now you've broken it," said Eric.

Bryan placed his fists on the counter and, with what was as much a force of will as effort, lifted himself to his feet. However, once off his perch, he was shorter than he had been sitting. Then, pausing after each word so Eric could be left in no doubt: "Window. Number. Three," omitting the 'please'.

He left Bryan to struggle back onto his stool, passed through the door as directed and walked along a narrow, poorly lit corridor. Room eight. Last door on the left. A piece of lined paper pinned to it revealed the occupant as a Mr Kyffin. He cleared his throat and knocked. There was no call to enter. He knocked again, this time with a tuneful rhythm, but still no one answered. He turned the handle, opened the door slowly, and poked his head through.

The room was small. A dry mop, propped up inside a silver bucket in the corner, gave a clue as to its former purpose, but a set of shelves, sagging beneath the weight of heavy books and a desk squashed into the far corner revealed its primary use as an office. A short man, whose toes floated above the ground as he sat in a swivel chair, continued to write, maniacally, and did not look up.

"Mr Kyffin? I was told to see you," said Eric.

"Take a seat," said the man, pointing to one. Again, he didn't look up, but he knew where his chairs were if nothing else.

Eric pushed the door open further and walked in. The seat was a hard-back wooden chair, buried beneath a stack of books and folders. He lifted the stack and set it down on the floor, at which moment it chose to topple over and sending books sliding across the floor and under a table. He muttered an obscenity, then an apology, and knelt down to gather them up.

"Leave them," ordered Kyffin and pointed once more to the now empty chair. Eric sat. Kyffin finished writing, slipped the pen into the top pocket of his tweed jacket, and looked at Eric for the first time. His hair, which to him was a thing that just happened to grow in a haphazard fashion from his head, was black and greasy. His eyes were soft, but his face was taut and set into a permanent expression peculiar to the overworked. Eric handed over the sheet of paper Bryan had so gracelessly given him.

"I see," he said, after a brief moment scanning the page. "And what was the cause of your death?"

"Excuse me?"

"Your death. How did it happen?"

Eric grinned, slowly. But the smile vanished, like breath from a mirror, as he realised the question was a serious one. "But I'm not dead."

"I am afraid you are."

Always cautious of existentialist debate, Eric struggled to prove, in simple terms, that he was, in fact, alive and well.

"Well, if I am dead," reasoned Eric, "how can I be talking to you now?"

This, he felt, would serve as proof enough.

"Precisely!" replied Kyffin, with a note of triumph, which Eric had not been expecting.

"Look," pleaded Eric. "Can you just be serious for a moment?"

"I am always serious. And you're still dead."

"Stop saying that!"

Kyffin, who had been in his job for a long time, had seen all this before, of course.

"You're in a great deal of denial," he said.

"I am denying I am dead, yes," admitted Eric. 'But that isn't the same as me being in denial."

"It sort of is."

Eric massaged his eyes then exhaled heavily. "All right, I'm dead."

"You're just saying that."

"Well, of course I am just saying that!"

"What makes you so sure you're alive?"

This was a sore spot for Eric. A housemate at university had asked him that very same question once. His inability to offer a convincing argument for his own existence had haunted him for weeks after. It was never death that stalked Eric, as it does many, but the uncertainty of anything being real in the first place which had kept him awake at night ever since. He could only repeat the answer he had given his housemate: "I feel alive."

"That will pass," said Kyffin without hesitation. He leant back in his chair, swivelled, and launched himself to his feet. "What's your name?" he asked as he opened the top drawer of a filing cabinet.

"Eric. Eric Pickles."

"Pickles, Eric," he muttered as he searched for Eric's file. "Ah, here we are." He opened the file, shut the draw with his elbow and returned to his chair. He slid his finger down the document, frown lines deepening as he read. Licking his finger he flipped the page, started nodding and smiling knowingly. "I see."

"What do you see?"

"What is the last thing you remember?" he asked, ignoring Eric's question.

"Being taught the etiquette of queuing by Bryan."

"No. Before that."

Eric's eyes edged closer together as he concentrated. He was disturbed to discover that he could not remember anything. Where memory of his life once was there existed now only a white wall of doubt.

"I'm sorry. I must have hit my head. I don't remember how I got here."

"Close your eyes and relax. Breathe slowly."

Eric did as he was told. Except whenever he became aware of his own breathing, he ceased to be able to do it unconsciously. Each breath would then require a conscious effort and he would worry that it would never return to normal. So relaxing was never made easy for him.

"Are you married?" asked Kyffin, with a now gentle voice.

"No, but . . ." Eric frowned. Kyffin knew better than to speak at such a delicate moment. "I have a girlfriend." Then, opening his eyes and exclaiming loudly, "Amber! Her name's Amber!"

"Close your eyes again and tell me what else you re-member."

Eric did his best to allow his memories to come to him, but he had never been very good at trying to not try. He didn't really understand the concept.

"I was meeting her for lunch."

"Go on."

"We had lunch and we talked."

"What about?"

Eric ceased all effort and waited for the memory to reveal itself. Just as a forgotten dream suddenly presents itself when triggered by an object or a passing comment, so the missing moments burst to the forefront of his mind when he cycled through everything he and Amber might have been talking about and he then he remembered.

"A holiday" he said, his eyes suddenly eager. "She's been going on about wanting a nice holiday somewhere hot. It has been years since we'd been anywhere. We went and booked it."

"Where was the holiday?"

"In a travel agent's window."

"No," said Kyffin patiently. "Where did you book to go?"

"The Maldives," he replied, after a few moments where he struggled to remember.

"And then what happened?"

"We left."

"And."

"We were walking." The skin on Eric's face pulled tighter across his eyes. There is a moment when the past becomes the future. Many have tried to isolate that moment. Those who succeeded were those who realised, suddenly but after many years of searching, neither the past nor the future existed. They were just thoughts. Once those thoughts are allowed to unravel no sooner than they are woven, the answer doesn't become clear: the question disappears. That was the space Eric's mind occupied for an instant. And then, like another thought, for that is what it was, it was gone.

There was a long silence, broken by Kyffin, who spoke in barely a whisper.

"And then?"

"Then I was here," said Eric, opening his eyes, but a final desperate idea occurred to him, which rather rendered Kyffin's satisfaction at a job well done premature.

"I've heard about this. I'm in a coma."

Kyffin felt his internal organs sink.

"You're not in a coma, Eric."

At this point, something unseen appeared to startle Eric. He pulled his right shoe and sock off and examined the sole of his foot, closely.

"What are you doing now?" asked Kyffin.

"I felt something," he said, vaguely. "I think someone's tickling my foot."

"I beg your pardon?"

"It must be the doctor trying to get a response from me. They do that, don't they? They tickle your foot to see if you react." Eric leapt to his feet and started waving his hands in the air and yelling out above him in the manner of a man marooned on a desert island who has just seen a passing ship. "I can feel it! I am still here! Don't switch me off!"

"Mr Pickles," said Kyffin, pinching the bridge of his nose, but Eric was still hopping around the office with one shoe on, warning the doctors off his organs. "Mr Pickles," he said again, this time a little louder, at which point Eric stopped moving, placed a finger over his lips in a plea for silence and stood completely still.

"Can you hear that?" he asked.

"Hear what?"

"Someone's saying my name," he whispered.

"Mr Pickles, I-"

"There it is again!"

"Mr Pickles!" Kyffin had by then decided he had quite enough. "That's me calling your name."

"Are you my doctor? Like, you know, if you fall asleep listening to the radio you start to dream that the DJ is in the room with you?"

Kyffin disabused Eric of this notion and asked him to sit down. Eric sat slowly but could not take his eyes from the ceiling.

"I realise this is very difficult for you to accept, but accept it you must," he said.

"Why?"

"You'll find it is not so bad once you get used to it."

"Being in a coma?"

Kyffin, defeated, but with the air of a man who knows he will be proved right in time, told Eric to have it his way.

But Eric did not need any encouragement in that direction. He had already begun to form an idea, which he would flesh out later, that he was more than just dreaming. He was, he was on the way to deciding, constructing a reality based on his own psyche and rich with symbolism—a riddle he would have to solve if he were ever to wake up again. So, he was happy enough to go along with the pretence. "What happens to me now then?"

"That all depends."

"Depends on what?"

"On whether you are a member or not."

"A member?"

"Well, are you?"

Eric didn't know what to say.

"Yes, I am."

Two

Eric left the room through the same door by which he had entered. However, the corridor outside, instead of ending at a wall decorated by a dusty pot-plant as it had before, now gave way to a golden, ascending escalator. He approached the moving stairs, as he always did, self-consciously, attempting to match his stride to their speed, and with a wobble back and forth, took hold of the rubber handrail. This was moving at the same pace as the stairs, meaning he could support himself and not spend his skyward journey imperceptibly, but very definitely, leaning forward at a diminishing angle to the horizontal.

He squinted but could not see to the top of the escalator. It continued till it disappeared into a distant vanishing point. He looked behind him and the same was suddenly true for the bottom of it. Small billboards glided by advertising performances by artists that were long dead. Elvis was in residence at the Afterlife Astoria; Bach was headlining at a concert in Bethlehem Park that night; Judy Garland was going to be closing her long run of one-woman shows of stories, surprise guests and songs at The Virgin

Mary Arena. Signs, passing at regular intervals on his left, warned anyone tempted to look over the side that they were probably better off not to. Of course, Eric peered over, but there was nothing there. It would be more accurate to say there was a total absence of anything at all. If you ask a physicist what the universe is expanding into if the universe is everything, you'll be told, pretty much, that it isn't expanding into anything and that your question was wrong in the first place. That was what Eric was looking at now. This caused in him a sensation that he would later reflect on and describe as his mind being pulled from out of his nose and snapping back like an elastic band. He reeled, clasped his stomach and spent some minutes fighting back waves of nausea. The signs changed to read 'We told you so'. He sat and waited for his sense of being located in space and time to be returned to him.

He wondered, if he were in a coma, what had just happened. Perhaps they were operating on his brain and had touched the area that dealt with that sort of thing. He was not sure that was how brains worked though. After a few more minutes, he stood and looked up in time to see the steps levelling out into a vast hall, not so much constructed from bone-coloured marble as carved out of it. It was the sort of space that drew your gaze up to the ceiling and kept on going. Rays of sun, like spotlight beams, coloured by the tall stained-glass windows criss-crossed the chamber, picking out motes of dust as they passed through them, wafted up on columns of air, warmed and churned by the thousands of people below. Returning to ground level, Eric struggled to take in the sheer clambering, heaving mass of humanity that surged forward. Men, women and children of all ages, cultures and heritage, confused, scared and pleading. They looked like penguins huddling against the Antarctic wind. Their voices rose and bounced from the walls and ceiling, mixing with each other and with every other voice that had ever spoken there for many, many thousands of years till it was now a single drone that could have shattered crystal. Voices that would never fade, but would linger for eternity, growing louder with time, calling out for loved ones, and at the same time scared and hopeful. If you paused for long enough and closed your eyes, it was possible to isolate individual voices. Those who had would tell you, with sad eyes, that it was not a good idea to try.

Against the smooth walls, tables had been set up. Some sold food. Others offered help and advice. A small group had gathered around one table that catered for atheists who were naturally concerned and eager to get their stories straight. One was arguing, rather loudly, that since God apparently existed why had he provided so much evidence to the contrary and absolutely none in support? He was handed a leaflet, which he was told would answer any questions he had. He snatched it away, asking if it had anything in it about bone cancer in children, and marched away to read it. Farther along was another table, set up for those who had taken Pascal's Wager. Blaise Pascal, a French philosopher, who was, helpfully, present to answer questions, had once suggested that if you did not believe in God, then it would perhaps be a good idea to act as if you did. If there really were a God, then your efforts would not have been in vain, and if God really did not exist, then, what did it matter? You were dead anyway. The trouble was, as it turned out, that saying you believed something with your fingers metaphorically crossed behind your back, was not enough to fool an all-powerful entity that was everywhere at all times and knew all things. In fact, even trying to get away with something like that would only result in annoying him. You would have been better off simply not believing and being up front about it. Pascal himself was attempting to placate a small gathering of angry philosophers by saying he could not apologise enough. This led one of the philosophers to quip that that was the only true thing he had ever said, adding, "That doesn't help us now, though, does it?" Eric looked for a table that might help him, but even he didn't know what that might be. He had been born to an Irish mother and an Anglican father, baptised a Catholic to appease his mother's family, gone to a Catholic school, then stopped attending church when he was too old to be forced to go. After that, he had not given it much thought at all. He never prayed, wasn't sure he believed in God but thought vaguely there was something; some sort of vague force. Plus he'd led a good enough life that would not have been too different to the one he would have led had he been devout.

It was at that moment that the first brick of acceptance was laid. Perhaps he was not lying in a hospital bed, after all. What if he were actually dead? The evidence against was that if he really were, then the afterlife was not at all like anything he had been told to look forward to. He didn't think it should be so much like a central European railway station during a workers' strike. But he could feel the breeze on his arms when he moved, the first stirring of hunger and could smell the aroma of thousands of fearful people. He didn't remember any dream being quite so vivid. Alive or dead, though, he couldn't just stand around all day doing nothing.

Not knowing what else to do, he made his way forward and, like a good human, joined the crowd. He eased himself through gaps that opened and closed behind him, until the bodies barring him formed too solid a barrier. Now closer, he could see that they were edging their way toward an arch. Swung open on either side were gates. These were tall, cast from a heavy, dark metal, which disappeared as if into a mist, but there was no mist. He tried to see through the gap to what was on the other side, but it felt like trying to remember a word which was on the tip of his tongue. Everything he saw just slipped through his attention, very much the way directions, when you're lost in an unfamiliar place, when explained, are instantly forgotten. Hanging in the air between the giant pillars was a sign: *Members Only*.

Eric tried to get the attention of those nearest him but was ignored. They heard him, but they had more pressing concerns of their own. The crowd had closed in behind him and he was being forced forward against his will now, too tall to be actually lifted from his feet, but no longer in control of where they took him. The anxiety which was rippling through the crowd reached him and he began to panic too. They were all just primates now; all responding to each other's cues, now more like a murmuration than people with their own wants and desires. Everyone else in the great hall may have wanted to get closer to the gates, but all he knew was that he wanted to get as far away from them as he possibly could. He could not have told you why if you had asked. He turned and forced himself against the motion of the people and pushed his way free. Once he had regained his composure, he made his way to a uniformed man who was leaning against a pillar.

"What's through those gates?" asked Eric, pointing. He was normally a stickler for good manners, but his recent experiences had got the better of him and he neglected to add 'please'.

"The Other Side."

His hearing not keen enough to detect the capitals, he asked, "The other side of what?"

"Just *The Other Side*."

THREE

Carmine Craxxi was running, which is something he had not done for many years. He was fifty now, but when he was nineteen he had run from the police, having just been spotted by them climbing out of a business premises with a bag full of cash he had stolen from it. They had caught him. Of course, he had not let them take him without a fight, and the punches he had managed to get off before the handcuffs were clasped onto his wrists had only added to his sentence. That he probably should have given himself up more easily never occurred to him. He was a fighter. When cornered, he came out, arms like a windmill. Those days were behind him, however. Other people did that sort of thing for him now. Not that he didn't miss his days as a young man on the streets. It's just that he had a family now, one not built on blood but loyalty, fear and respect, and rolling around in the road with uniformed officers was bad for business. He was not running from the police now, though.

Just thirty minutes earlier, he had been in the Great Hall. The mass of people that had consumed Eric had not been a problem for Craxxi. He had a Gold Membership: a shining card with his name on it that had not come cheap. Centuries earlier, young men who went to war in medieval Europe had a problem. They killed people. They were very good at killing people too, being well-trained from an early age and brought up to actually enjoy it. They fought on behalf of barons, whose deal with the king was that they would, in exchange for land, provide an army should he ever need one. And in medieval Europe, kings needed armies a lot. Killing people, itself, wasn't a problem. As has been established, they *liked* doing it. The problem was they were Christian, and Christianity had a policy on the killing of others that made young men, who wanted to go to Heaven, uncomfortable. Fortunately for them, there was a ready solution. The monks of the time could, they said, use their powers of forgiveness to let young men who had killed other young men (and often women, and children, who sometimes had other things done to them before they were slaughtered) off the hook. Forgiveness didn't come cheap, however. That was okay, though, because in addition to being very good at murder, the same young men were adept at plundering, too, so they could afford it. In a short space of time, monasteries in Europe became ludicrously wealthy and powerful, and young men could keep killing and plundering till they were either killed themselves or simply grew tired of it.

The paying of indulgences, as it was called, you'd think would be a relic of a more ignorant time. Such a practise couldn't still be taking place. Among the extremely wealthy and powerful, the exchanging of money for forgiveness still very much goes on. The world still has barons. Today they own oil, mining and logging companies; they run banks, control pharmaceutical companies, launder money, rule as kings, queens, presidents, dictators and prime ministers. They own the world, and they let everyone else live on it–for a price. And as regularly as their annual health checkups, they make a donation to the church and get the all clear for another year of obscene wealth grabbing. Carmine Craxxi, through his many connections, and like many others like him, made such regular donations himself. Sometimes they were in the form of cash. Sometimes they were in the form of favours. Over the years, he had made a lot of donations and had rendered many favours. He had paid for his Gold Membership several times over. So, when he had died, which he didn't want to think about at that exact moment, he at least had the consoling thought that he wouldn't have any trouble taking his place in paradise.

Except he had lost it. It had been in the top pocket of his suit jacket, and now it was no longer there. It wasn't until he had bypassed the crowd and presented himself at the smaller gate to the Gold Lane that he realised it was gone. He turned his pockets inside out, removed his jacket, looked on the floor around him, cursed, threatened and generally became more and more enraged until a man from security pushed a box into his ribs, pressed a button to release forty thousand volts of electricity, and he collapsed to the floor. He came round a few minutes later in the sort of room he had seen the inside of often. He knew he was in trouble. He rubbed the side of his body that had taken the bulk of the electricity and flinched. His head hurt, too, and he was terribly thirsty. A bottle of water stood on the table in front of him. He tore the cap off and swallowed half of it in just a few gulps, before wiping his wet lips with his sleeve and pausing to gather his thoughts. Before he had time to do even that, the door opened and in came a woman, dressed, he thought, like someone who might work at an airport. She sat opposite him, opened a file she had been carrying, and read. Craxxi waited till she had finished reading and slapped the file shut.

"Mr Craxxi, you claim to be a Gold Club member but that you have lost your card," she said, somewhere between a question and a statement.

"If you could just issue me with another, I'll get out of your hair."

The woman, who had not introduced herself, but would have said her name was Naomi if she had, shaped her face in such a way as to communicate to Craxxi that that would not be quite as simple as he hoped.

"That won't be quite as simple as you might hope," she said. (Craxxi was very good at reading expressions.) "The selling of indulgences may well be going on still in the mortal realm, but we up in the afterlife take a dim view of it.

"The gold lane is one we keep open grudgingly. If you can prove you are a member, then so be it. But if you turn up empty handed, you'll find that we have very little sympathy. As you can imagine, we get a lot of people claiming to have lost their cards. You're not the first to have the idea."

"Idea?" Craxxi clenched his fists. "You think I am scamming you?"

"It's been tried."

Craxxi started reeling off names. People he knew. Peo-

28

ple Naomi should have heard of. Those he had paid and who had promised, well, not the Earth, but certainly Heaven. She was not at all impressed. He began to think.

"You must have my name on record."

"Do you have any photo ID?"

Craxxi had died without his wallet.

Then there was nothing more that Naomi could do. Not that she had tried very much. He was going to have to take his place in line with everyone else and hope for the best. From what she had seen of his file, though, he should prepare for disappointment.

"And what does that mean?"

Naomi pointed at the ground in short, stabbing motions. Hell wasn't actually in any direction, least of all down, but everyone always knew what was meant by the gesture. As did Craxxi. His life had not flashed before his eyes at the point of his death; it did so now. He didn't stand a chance.

Craxxi stood up and pointed at Naomi, who, to her credit, did not seem in the least perturbed by the aggression directed at her. That may have had something to do with what she knew was about to happen in three, two, one . . . the door to the room opened suddenly. Through it came two large guards. Craxxi, like a wild animal, was always coiled, ready to fight at any moment, however. He punched the first guard in the middle of his face. Craxxi enjoyed that. The guard's legs were the first part of his body to become unconscious. He teetered for a moment, then collapsed straight down, like a pile of tossed laundry. Naomi pressed a button under her desk and stood up. The second guard didn't have much more success than the first. Craxxi used his forward motion against him, directing him face down onto the table, which broke in half. The guard lay between the two splintered pieces and didn't move. Craxxi turned his red-eyed gaze to Naomi. He was not an indiscriminate man, though. If she tried to stop him from leaving, he would do what he had to do. But as she was backing away from him, he saw no reason to pay her any more attention. He ran from the room, expecting to see more guards closing him down, but he was alone. He didn't know which way to go, so he kicked open the door closest to him. That led through to another corridor. For want of a better option, he ran. He forced open another door and hurled himself down the stairs on the other side, skipping several at a time and vaulting over the banister at each turn. At the bottom of the stairwell was an emergency exit, which he made short work of. That was when he found himself outside a grey-coloured building, with high walls, not unlike a prison. In front of him were rolls of barbed wire and beyond that, trees: a dark wood, which looked as if it existed in a perpetual winter. An alarm began to sound from inside just as he was deciding what to do next, making his mind up for him. Throwing his jacket over the sharp wire, with its barbs and hooks, he climbed across it. The jacket offered little protection. The skin at all points of his body became snagged, and he had to pull himself free repeatedly. Had he perhaps paused and negotiated his way through more slowly, he'd have come off better, but he was in full flight mode and, adrenaline coursing through him, he was feeling no pain.

Behind him, half a dozen guards streamed out of the emergency exit, guns held out in front of them. Naomi joined them a moment later. She saw that Craxxi was more than halfway across the barbed wire moat. She considered sending some of the guards out to retrieve him, but she could sense their unease at even being outside the protection of the walls. The sense of dread that oozed from the woods was already causing them to take half a step back, but to keep their weapons held aloft. She didn't like losing souls that way. It did happen sometimes, though, and it wasn't as if he were heading anywhere she wouldn't have happily sent him anyway. They waited and watched until he made it, bloodied, to other side and disappeared into the woods before she ordered her men back inside. An order with which they eagerly complied. They didn't want to spend any more time in the Pale than they absolutely had to.

Now very much beyond the Pale, Craxxi kept running. Although he didn't know the guards were no longer chasing him, it wasn't from them he was running now. He was running from the wood itself. This is difficult, of course, as he was now in the heart of it. The moment he had entered its damp shade, a feeling of profound dread had gripped him. There are those who, when standing at the top of a high building, have the urge to jump. No one quite knows why that might be. Some think that the very rational sense of caution that accompanies being so high is interpreted by some other part of the brain as 'I think I'm going to jump'. That's what the wood beyond the Pale did to a person. It made them worry about worrying. Or rather, it made them absolutely terrified of it. Dodging trees and ducking below low branches, Craxxi ran. Once a high-school athlete, he was no longer built, like Richard III, for sportive tricks. He was tiring yet compelled to run. Then, through the trees, he saw a squat, wooden hut. Black smoke curled from its chimney. Not that he was in a state to notice such details. Instinct now fully in control, he made straight for it. As he approached it, still at speed, he turned his shoulder to the door and entered without knocking. Suddenly sprawled inside the hut, the door beneath him, he closed his eyes and went to sleep. From the next room, a man entered silently on bare feet to where he lay. He stood over him for a moment, not seeming to mind the damage done to his property, and he had the look people have when they walk into a house they've just bought that needs a lot of work and wonder where on Earth they are going to start.

Four

Eric took a step toward the guard, who himself stood a little straighter, as if to prepare himself to be assaulted. Eric stopped, softened his posture and asked again.

"And what's on the other side?"

"*The Other Side*, is on the other side," the guard replied.

Eric realised that this could go on perhaps indefinitely, so he approached the problem from a different angle.

"What's it like there?"

"Oh, it's very nice."

Eric was beginning to feel hungry – a development he didn't like. He had never felt hungry in a dream before. Perhaps his drip needed changing.

"How do I get to the other side?"

"You'll have to present your pass at the Pearly Gates."

Eric didn't recall the gates looking very pearly and re-marked upon the fact.

"Everyone says that."

They had in fact been named after Josiah Pearly who had designed them, but the guard kept that part of the answer to himself.

"If I don't have a pass, what then?"

"You go to the other place," said the guard in a low voice, the capitals now notably missing.

"And what's that like?" Eric asked, feeling sure he already knew the answer.

"It's horrible."

No surprise there then, thought Eric. He thanked the guard, though he was unsure for what, and moved away. It was then he noticed a figure lurking behind a marble pillar. Instinctively, Eric glanced at the guard, but he was already attending to his fingernails. There was apparently something beneath one of them that required mining. The figure gestured him over. Not knowing what else to do, Eric attempted a saunter. Those who were not used to sauntering should never attempt to pull it off, and Eric had never knowingly sauntered before. Still, no one was watching, and no harm was done.

"Need a pass?"

The figure, now Eric was closer, had resolved into the shape of a hefty man. Eric scanned him from pole to pole and wasn't greatly encouraged by what he saw. Eric was quite tall, but this man was big. There was a difference. A cruel critic would say he was no such thing; he was overweight. That meant little to Eric. If punching one's own weight meant anything at all, Eric knew he was not in the same division as the man looming over him now. But why would Eric worry about being punched at all? It's not as if being smacked, thumped, clobbered or whacked was a constant concern of his. There was, though, something about this man. We all know what Eric meant by that. Some people just ooze menace, and this man was standing in a puddle of it.

"I'm sorry?"

Eric had heard, but he needed more information.

"A pass. To get in."

The man spoke with a strained voice, not much more than a loud whisper, if you can imagine such a thing. He was from London, though. Eric could tell at least that. He went on:

"I've got yer basic membership. That'll get yer in. After that, you'll get what yer given."

"Right. And what's above basic?"

"I've got a couple of silvers. With them you'll get a nice little place, but you'll be stuck with yer dead relatives. Some people don't mind that. It's up to you."

Eric was happy enough to see his deceased aunts, uncles and grandparents again, but he was curious about what else was on offer. If this really were Heaven, of course, which is was still not ready to admit.

"You're in luck. I've just acquired a gold membership. Very rare these. Full VIP status, luxury accommodation, you get to meet anyone you want from any time period, all your pets will be waiting for you too and relatives are optional."

Eric thought immediately about the dog his family had when he was a child. Her name was Daisy: a mix of several breeds, which led to her looking like she had been put together from spare bits and pieces left in a box. But she was fiercely intelligent – often outsmarting the young Eric – and often demonstrated a subtle sense of humour. She had died at a good age when he was twelve, and in the twenty years since, there hadn't been a day when he hadn't thought of her at least once. Except, he wasn't dead. Not yet anyway. At least, that's what he was still holding onto. He was in a hospital bed, surrounded by loved ones and beeps. On the other hand, he could be in a coma for a long time. He couldn't just stand around in that hall forever.

The man produced a gold card. It had a name on it.

"Who's Carmine Craxxi?" Eric asked.

"You are, at the right price."

"Let's just say I accept that I am, you know, dead."

"You are. We all are round here."

"All right, well, just supposing, how much would a gold membership be?"

The man looked Eric up and down, much as Eric had done to him a moment before. He made a swift judgement.

"You can't afford it, mate."

"What makes you so sure?"

"You had to ask."

Eric considered this for a moment. The man was right. Not least of all as he didn't have any money on him.

"All right. The basic membership. How much is that?"

"Hundred."

Eric was not up to date on which currency Heaven used. He hoped it wasn't dollars. It was always dollars.

"Prayers."

"You want me to pray for you? A hundred times?"

"No. That's not how it works. I want you to buy a hundred prayers for me. From a saint. They're the only ones what count."

"Why don't I just give you the money and you buy them?"

The man couldn't have known at that point that he was involved in a purely academic exercise now. Eric didn't have a single penny on him. He was simply curious.

"You can't buy prayers for yourself. Someone else has to ask for yer sins to be forgiven. I don't know why. That's just how it's always been."

The man pointed to a saint who was, at that moment, slouching on a chair behind a stall smoking. He was wearing a filthy tunic, which was either authentic, or there to please the tourists. Eric couldn't work out which. His features were sharp and hard – the sort of face that's shaped by the weather. His eyes were dark, matching the blackness of his beard. Eric could easily have imagined him herding yaks, but he would never have said so.

"He's not busy."

Eric approached the saint. Propped on the table was a notice, which explained who the saint was and what he had done to reach such a status. His name was Jerash, and he had lived in what is now Syria about three-hundred years after Jesus' death. He had a particular talent for farming. One day, a man he didn't recognise passed by, remarked on the plumpness of his lemons and, without asking him if he would be okay with it, asked his name and said, "You are from this day forth, St Jerash of Lemons." He never saw the man again, and it wasn't until he had died a few years' later that he gave it another thought.

"You were made a saint because of your lemons?"

The man took a drag on his cigarette – a habit he had picked up since his death – and exhaled slowly.

"In those days," he said, with a thick accent but perfect English, "They handed out sainthoods for anything."

"Really?"

"Yeah, Christianity was still trying to get off the ground.

It really needed more saints. Once they had elevated the obvious ones, it sort of dried up. So, they sent people out looking for them. I think they got paid for every saint they made, if you ask me." He pointed with the tip of his cigarette to a saint three stalls along who appeared to be doing good business. "That's Harry. He was known in his village for being able to fart the Lord's prayer. Someone heard about it and, just like that, he's a saint."

"Of what?"

"Farting. You won't have heard of him. Nothing was made of it at the time. Just like with me. But they all got logged up here, you see. So here we all are. More saints than you can shake a prayer stick at."

"And you sell prayers?"

"That's not all I do," replied Jaresh, a little offended. "But yeah," he admitted, reluctantly, "I sell prayers too. What are you after?"

"A hundred prayers for that man standing over there."

Jaresh exhaled more smoke.

"He'll need more than a hundred prayers him, but fair enough."

"And what will that cost?"

"A merit per prayer."

Eric didn't know what a merit was. He hoped it was something to do with depth of character, but upon further questioning, he learnt it was just what they called their currency. He also found out you could change whatever money you had for merits at an official booth, or, for a better rate, at an unofficial one, but you were likely to be left with a wad of counterfeit merits and no one to complain to.

"I don't have any money on me."

"No money, no prayers."

"Who dies with money?"

"Get a job. They're always looking for porters or cleaners. You should earn enough for a basic pass in six months or so."

Eric stepped away. What was his brain trying to tell him? Was this all just symbolic of his need to fight if he ever wanted to wake from the coma? He was still betting that he was in a coma: nothing else made sense. What was on the Other Side? Would he wake up if he stepped through, or would he slip away and die? *Really* die, that is. There was only one way to go, though, and that was to follow the crowd.

He returned to the man behind the pillar.

"Look, can't you just give me a pass. I'll pay you when I get through."

The man made an about turn and marched away. Eric caught up with him and gripped his shoulder.

"Look-"

But that was as far as he got. Placing his hand on the man's shoulder had awakened a reflex in him. He spun around and punched Eric right on the nose. The man had one of those meaty fists at the end of a thick wrist that seemed to form a single piece that went up to the shoulder. And it was true about fat people punching their weight. Eric sat down as if his legs had been swiped away by an invisible gladiator, jarring his back and neck. His eyes filled with water. He waited for another blow. Perhaps a kick to the ribs. But through his blurred vision, he made out the shape of the man leaving the scene. He stood up and dabbed his eyes with his tie. He looked down and noticed spots of blood on his white work shirt. That would need a hot wash, and quick. It was then he noticed it. A little distance in front of him, on the floor, was a gold card. He picked it up and read the name *Carmine Craxxi*. The man must have dropped it when he hit him. He thrust the pass into his back pocket and looked around. The man wouldn't take long to realise what had happened. He'd be back soon, wanting it back. He wiped his eyes with his sleeve and blood from his face with the back of his hand and made a decision.

The Gold Lane had two people already in it. Eric joined them, looking behind him, and urged those ahead of him to hurry. He was British, though, so did so entirely in his head, of course. Then it was Eric's turn. The lady at the gate was the same who had turned Craxxi away previously. However, when she saw the name on the card, far from having her suspicion aroused, she felt satisfied that she had been right to suppose the man who had claimed to be Carmine Craxxi before had been lying. That sort of thing happened to her all the time. It was a wonder anyone thought she'd ever fall for it. She smiled and typed something into a computer. Eric glanced over his shoulder. The man had realised he was missing a gold pass and had worked out where he had most likely lost it. He was looking around for Eric. And then he saw him. Eric turned back to the woman, who smiled back politely. She was waiting for her screen to change. The man had by now covered half the distance to Eric, who turned back to the woman with a stiff grin. The woman's smile broadened as something appeared on the screen. Eric couldn't see what it was, but she seemed satisfied for she handed Eric his pass back and released the gate. Eric took one more look over his shoulder. He wasn't going to make it. The man was too close. He made for the gate and was bracing himself to feel that heavy weight crash into him, when he heard the sound of a great deal of air escaping from something very quickly. Once safely through the gate that clanged shut behind him, he saw the man gasping for breath under a pile of guards. He looked up, saw Eric, pointed with an unsteady finger, said something Eric was glad he couldn't make out, and was dragged away.

"This way, sir"

Eric jumped. A young man with a shiny face, dressed very much as a flight attendant might, beckoned him forward and smiled.

"Welcome to Heaven."

FIVE

If Eric had been honest, he would have told you he expected more from paradise. He'd have agreed that it was pleasant enough, but then so was north Wales. He had a distaste for clichés so was pleased to not be walking on a low cloud or be greeted by trumping cherubs, but was this really it? He was in what appeared to be the lobby of a very expensive hotel. A middle-aged lady on towering heels walked expertly by, followed by a tiny, yapping dog at the end of a taught lead. The dog was wearing knitted shoes, which may well have been the source of its irritation. On sofas, set out squarely in the middle of the vast, marble floor, men comfortable enough to wear pullovers draped around their shoulders and tied across their chests, lounged sipping coffee and laughing loudly. A set of revolving doors led out into a bright, white light. On the other side of the echoing hall, an opening led to a bar. He was tempted to head straight there, but he decided a drink, however welcome at that moment, would have to wait. He presented himself at the reception desk, which spanned an entire wall and waited. The mundanity of it all pleased

Eric. He had always lacked imagination. Had he found himself in a more fantastical place; something he could not have thought up himself, he'd have worried. That the afterlife was so ordinary gave him comfort that it was probably being generated by him in a coma dream. A young man in a red waistcoat appeared from a door behind the reception and apologised for keeping him waiting. He was in his early twenties, with tanned, smooth, shining skin, carefully trimmed eyebrows and slick, gelled hair.

Eric slid his membership card across the desk and waited while the young man typed his name into their system.

"Ah, Mr Craxxi," he said.

"Sorry, what?" asked Eric, happy to be snapped out of his troubling thoughts.

"Your name. Mr Carmine Craxxi?"

"Oh!" he exclaimed, "Yes, yes, that's right. Mr Crack-see. That's me. I'm Mr Crack-see."

Why Carmine Craxxi? he wondered. Of all the names his subconscious might have invented where did it dredge that one from?

"Okay," said the young man, uncertainly, returning to his screen.

"Yep," Eric went on, puffing his cheeks out and knocking rhythmically on the counter with his knuckles. "Mr Crack-see. Call me Carmine."

"If it's all the same to you, sir, I'll go on calling you by your surname," he said, reading an attached note on his screen that appeared to put a whole new complexion on matters. "They hate informality round here. Unless," he added, overcome by a sudden attack of nerves, "that would offend you. I mean, if you want me to call you Carmine I will."

"No, no, that's quite all right. Wouldn't want to get you into trouble."

He scrolled to the next page on the screen and looked alarmed.

"Because I'm sure they'd not mind as it's you," he said.

"Me?"

"Yes, well, I mean, you know, they wouldn't want to appear disrespectful or anything."

"Oh," said Eric, loosening the frown on his forehead, "you mean the customer's always right?"

"Yes, sir."

"Oh, I see, well, you know, I don't think we need make a fuss. Mr um . . ."

"Craxxi?"

"Crack-see! Yes, Mr Crack-see will do."

The young man smiled nervously and tore a print-out from under the counter.

"If you'll just sign at the bottom there, Mr Craxxi."

Eric untangled a pen from the chain that was securing it to the counter and let it hover over the dotted line while he wondered to himself how to spell his new name. Eventually he settled for his doctor's signature as a safe option, which was notoriously difficult to decipher. The young man called for a porter, whose uniform was the same as the desk clerk's, except for a hat shaped like a cake tin. Seeing that Eric had no bags with him, he led him away to the elevator. The young man behind the desk exhaled with relief. He looked down at the signature Eric had scrawled.

"Dr. Granger?"

Left alone in his suite, Eric did what all men do in such circumstances: he opened and shut all the drawers and cupboards to see what was inside them. The cupboard at the foot of his bed was empty but for a set of wooden hangers. One walk-in closet, however, was fully stocked with suits: some pinstriped, some not, but all black. He took one out and held it up against him. It seemed to be about the right size. He put it back and wandered over to the piano on which gifts and flowers had been apparently left for him.

He reached into a bouquet of white lilies and remove a card. It read: *My respect and loyalty in death is as it was in life* – Benito Mancini. The others were of a similar sentiment and signed by men with Italian names. Some were from judges and others were from United States senators, although at the time Eric could not have known that. One, however, caught his eye. It was from an Earl van der Gilt. Eric recognised the name as belonging to an FBI agent who had been murdered on his doorstep by the mafia not long before he himself had . . . well, whatever it was that had happened to him. What made Eric remember him in particular was the fact his daughter had witnessed his murder and, traumatised, had not spoken a word since. It had been in Eric's newspaper the day he died. The message from him read simply: *Heaven welcomes Don Carmine Craxxi.*

Perhaps Carmine Craxxi was involved somehow. Maybe he had read his name in the same report and his brain, possibly suffering from a trauma, had remembered it and, for some reason, used it. Why, though?

He dropped the cards on the table and turned to inspect the bedroom. A king-size bed with draped curtains was pushed against the wall. He tested the springiness of the mattress by taking the height to which he could bounce off it from a running jump as a rough measure. In this way, he found that the mattress was very springy indeed and struck his head against the lampshade, itself clattering to the carpet. He climbed back on, kicked his shoes off, and lay flat on his back, staring at the bone-white ceiling. He was suddenly so very tired. His limbs grew heavy, and his eyelids became increasingly difficult to keep open, but he was worried that if he fell asleep in his coma-induced dream he would not wake up, either in his dream or in his hospital bed.

He thought for the first time of Amber, his parents and his sister. He imagined them sitting around his bed, his mother reading the sports results from a newspaper, his father droning on about the road works at the corner of their road and his sister saying nothing at all. What would Amber do? Would she wait for him to wake up? And if he did wake up, would she want to look after him? Would he even want her to? He felt fine as he lay there in what he was still sure was a dream, but in the waking world he might be a vegetable: a burden to his loved ones. His parents would always look after him. That was expected. But Amber was young, attractive and ambitious. He did not want her to waste her life feeding and bathing him. The thought of that spread inside him like an infestation of crawling insects. Perhaps, he thought, he and everyone else would be better off he did die. He fell asleep with this morbid thought, not knowing if it would be his last. He dreamt of his family and of Amber and snored deeply. Could this be a dream within a dream? Eric had not had one of those before. Even in that state, he wondered if such a thing were even possible. Amber was sitting by his bed, holding his hand. The next moment she was dressed in black and standing by a hole in the ground. It was raining and she was bent over, crying so hard she wanted to scream. Then she was standing by a buffet as people they both knew, and a few he didn't, told her how sorry they were. That image was washed away and replaced by another of her shopping for one at a supermarket, looking older, more tired and sadder than he ever thought possible. He tried to speak to her. She reacted as if she thought she had heard her name called, before dismissing it and carrying on.

Carrying on.

That's what they were all doing, wasn't it. Soon enough, she would be expected back at work as it would be decided that she had grieved for long enough. When asked how she was, she would lie and say she was fine. Then, after an appropriate passage of time, they'd stop asking. It's not as if she were the only one to ever lose someone, even if that is how it felt.

He called out to her, but she didn't hear him. And then he stopped dreaming at all.

He woke, several hours later, in an oblong of sunlight, hot, wet. He took a few moments to orientate himself to his unfamiliar surroundings and discovered that waking and remembering you are in a coma or possibly even dead is at least as wretched a feeling as realising it's Monday.

If he were dreaming and it was true he had constructed a reality based on his own psyche then it might be interesting to explore. There might even be something important for him to learn, without the knowledge of which he could never wake up. But he could do that later. He was still tired, and his bed felt like a womb.

Less than a minute later, his eyes popped open. There are some things that even the luxury of never-ending tomorrows will not allow you to put off for very long. He heaved himself from the bed and, scratching himself in that way of men in the morning, walked flat-footed to the bathroom. He lifted the lid of the toilet and relieved himself — mostly — into the sparkling white bowl. The door to the cabinet on the wall before him was open. Inside, on the narrow shelf, was a pack of razor blades, three bars of soap, shaving foam, five sachets of shampoo, bubble bath and a tub of moisturiser. He closed the door and what he saw in its mirrored surface appalled him.

Several days' worth of growth cast its shadow across his features. He had never known his whiskers to grow in his dreams. Were they not shaving him as he lay in his hospital bed? His eyes were blood-shot and his hair, flattened on one side, shone with grease. He peeled back his lips in a grimace to reveal two rows of yellow teeth and a furry tongue.

He opened both taps in the bath and, sitting on the side, poured, squirted and squeezed the entire contents of the cabinet (minus the razor blades) into the steaming water and stirred. He dumped his clothes into the waste disposal, slipped into the tub and lowered his head beneath the frothing surface.

More than an hour later, a shrivelled Eric emerged from the bathroom amid bellowing steam, clean-shaven, pink-faced, wrapped in a fluffy, white towel and smelling absolutely divine. Of Eric's very many habits which Amber disapproved, it was that of leaving a trail of wet footprints between the bathroom and their bedroom which she disliked the most. Nor, for that matter, did she particularly approve of his not drying his hands after washing them, his unerring habit of leaving half a potato on his plate then declaring that he was full and the inexplicable – and often violent – sniff he never failed to emit in bed at the very moment she was about to drop off to sleep. And despite this perhaps being his dream and that he could do what he liked in it, Eric looked back at the soaking wet carpet with a deep sense of unease of what she would say if she were there.

The wardrobe was a room that was bigger than his first flat had been. He stepped into the gloom and switched the light on. He walked among several rows of suits of black and beneath half a dozen tie racks that revolved from the ceiling, took a suit arbitrarily, plucked a tie from one of the racks, laid them on his bed and started to dry his hair, roughly, with a towel.

There then came a knock at the door. A young man in a red suit that appeared at least one size too small for him stood in the corridor beside a trolley, upon which Eric eyed three silver platters, a basket of crusty bread and a tea pot.

"Good morning, Don Carmine," chimed the boy, courteously.

Then, glancing nervously down the corridor, he pushed the trolley past Eric with a single shove and without pausing for a tip, nodded his head respectfully and scurried off in the opposite direction with obscene haste.

He had not eaten since first feeling hungry at the Pearly

Gates and the smell of bacon and eggs set his stomach rumbling.

When he had cleared his plate, he wiped the last smear of grease from his lips with a piece of bread and popped it into his mouth. After washing it all down with his third cup of tea, he stretched his arms above his head and his legs beneath the trolley, whereupon he felt something square with his toes. He reached down and removed a small bundle, which was gift-wrapped and finished with a bow. The card that dangled from it read simply, 'Don Carmine. Salute.' He placed the bundle to his ear and noticed that it ticked. Assuming it was a carriage clock, he placed it carefully on the table with the rest of the gifts and began to dress.

Eric did not know very much about bespoke tailoring, but, as with anything, there is a level of quality that is impossible for even a layman to not recognise. He dressed in one of the suits left for him – black with a blue tie – and faced the full-length mirror. Unlike the suit he usually wore for work, the lapels on this one were not dog-eared. Nor did the pockets sag open lecherously. This suit was heavy, but comfortable; it rested gently on his shoulders and seemed to move when he moved. He didn't know he had such a taste for the finer things. If he were not careful, he could get to used to this fantasy world and not want to go back. However, he could not help but feel more and more that he was not dreaming at all. He shook this defeatist thought from his head, straightened his tie and set out to explore the highways and byways of his mind.

Six

Carmine Craxxi awoke gently. He was aware that he was in a strange place, but he was too tired to worry about that now. The shoulder he was sleeping on was stiff, so he attempted to turn onto the other, but this started his head throbbing and brought him more to his senses. Suddenly, the vulnerable position he was in alarmed him. He sat up suddenly, regretting the violence of his action and wincing at the sharpness in his back and neck and skull.

He cleared his eyes and, blinking, took in this unfamiliar environment. For the first time he realised he was inside. He had tumbled through a world of wood and confusion and had no memory of finding shelter. He was in a hut. In one corner grew a tree, too broad for him to have wrapped his arms around, should the idea to do so have occurred to him. He was not a tree-hugger, however, so this was unlikely. A thick branch grew sideways from the tree, about high enough from the ground that had Craxxi jumped, he might just have brushed it with his fingertips. Again, that was an unlikely scenario. From that branch, someone had fastened long beams of wood to form the skeleton of a roof, with the space between them packed with thinner branches and clay. The rest of the structure seemed to be supporting itself, with heavy branches driven into the spongey forest floor. There was a single window of dirty, cracked glass, but most of the light was being provided by a fire. Its orange light forming a dance macabre of shadows on the walls. There was not much that could be called furniture. Whoever lived there seemed happy to sit on the ground.

His first instinct, as it always was, was to look for a weapon. He patted his pockets, but they were empty. He stood uncertainly and hunted around for a suitable tool. There was very little in the place that any ordinary person would see as an offensive weapon. But Carmine Craxxi was inventive. Against one wall stood a broad shelf, which passed for a counter top. He searched there among tiny bowls of what looked like spices but found nothing to protect himself with should the need arise.

His brain, now more fully alert, suggested the idea that perhaps it might be better for him to escape while he could. However, his stomach had ideas of its own. He was hungry. A pot hung from a construction of thick twigs above the fire which cracked and spat in the middle of the room. He took the ladle hanging beside it and scooped out from the rising steam a sample of what was boiling. It smelt fine. He was just about to put it to his lips when the door to the hut swung open and in came the old man. He passed Carmine Craxxi, still with the ladle to his lips, and disappeared into the next room.

Craxxi dropped the ladle into the pot and moved to the still open door. Shafts of sunlight beamed through the high tree canopy and illuminated hundreds of tiny flies which buzzed about in their warmth. Relaxing somewhat, he turned and, carefully now, entered the second room.

Sun Yu was of an indeterminate age. He looked old. But there was an energy about him that made you doubt the years his face suggested. He was Asian; Craxxi thought Chinese. His long hair, white and thick, flowed most of the way down his back, and a white goatee beard, along with tatty grey robes, completed the sage-like look.

"Who are you?" asked Craxxi.

"My name is Sun Yu," replied the old man as he picked bottles and jars from a shelf and began mixing their contents together in a bowl. Craxxi didn't know it then, but that was the last straight answer to a straight question he was going to get for some time.

"What's that?"

Sun Yu did not answer. Craxxi would, with some struggling, get used to that. He stood beside Sun Yu and watched his dexterous hands at work. A green liquid was added to an exact measure and the whole thing was poured into a wooden beaker and stirred vigorously.

Sun Yu handed it to his new guest.

"Drink."

Craxxi sniffed the concoction. He opened his mouth to speak by Sun Yu had already departed silently. Craxxi followed him.

"What's it for?"

"You will feel better."

Craxxi was unsure. But such was the state of his body, which felt as if it had been trampled on by a marching army, that he was willing to take the risk. He held his breath and drank the bitter medicine down in three noisy gulps. He threw the empty cup down and made an ungracious hacking sound with the back of his throat.

"That's disgusting."

Sun Yu made no reaction. He merely sat cross-legged on the ground and appeared to be smiling at something funny that had happened a long time ago but which he had just been reminded of. Craxxi straightened his back and, pausing when he felt no pain at all, gave Sun Yu a curious look. His head had stopped hurting too and his hunger, for now at least, had been satisfied.

He thanked Sun Yu, cautiously, and, seeing no point in hanging around any longer, stepped toward the door to leave.

"You are going the wrong way," said Sun Yu without looking up.

Craxxi paused in the doorway. "You don't know where I am going."

"Every way is the wrong way."

Craxxi was not a man well equipped with patience, and he had even less for the cryptic musings of Eastern philosophies. He turned his back on Sun Yu and ventured out into the forest. But all he could see were trees. He had expected to see a path between them, but the tall grass that surrounded the hut in its clearing yielded none, not even where Sun Yu must have trampled through just minutes before. His mother would give him a look when, as a child, she sensed he was about to do something naughty. It was never accompanied by words. It didn't have to be. It was that same look that the forest gave him now. His defiance left him, as it would with his mother. He re-entered the hut.

"Where is this place?"

Sun Yu did not answer. Instead, he tended the fire and resumed his posture.

"How do you get out of here?"

With an unnatural spring for a person of any age let alone his, Sun Yu was instantly on his feet.

"Come with me," he said.

He walked swiftly but still, somehow, with no rush, into the second room. By the time Craxxi caught up with him Sun Yu was standing, ready, beside a cauldron that had been collecting rainwater from a hole in the roof. Craxxi was puzzled but said nothing.

"Look," said Sun Yu, pointing at the surface of the water, which was very nearly at the brim.

Craxxi had no idea why, but he felt unsettled. He took half a step forward and, angling his body slightly, peered in.

"What am I looked at?"

"Closer," ordered Sun Yu kindly.

Craxxi stepped closer to the cauldron and did as he was told.

"I don't see anything."

"Much closer."

Allowing frustration to get the better of his unease, Craxxi rested his hands on the side of the iron bowl and moved his face above the water.

"Closer," again, urged Sun Yu.

Craxxi's nose was now almost touching the water and he looked for some object or other at the bottom. He was about to protest that there was nothing there when he felt

Sun Yu's hand on the back of his neck. With a force that astonished Craxxi, the old man thrust his head into the water and held it there.

Craxxi was a physically powerful man. He gripped the side of the bowl and attempted to forced himself up out of the water, but he was unable to overcome Sun Yu's strength. He lashed out with his fist at where Sun Yu had been standing last, but he could only find empty air. He could feel pressure building up behind his eyes and his chest began to ache. His struggling took on a new ferocity, underpinned by panic and the primal urge to breathe. In a futile effort to save himself he punched hard at the outside of the bowl, hoping to break it open, but although he could hear the dull, muffled sound of his fists striking the metal, the action served only to weaken him. He fought the desire to breathe, a wave of nausea rose in him, his eyes felt as if they were about to pop from his skull and he felt the fight leave him.

At that moment, Sun Yu lifted him from the water and dropped him to the ground. Craxxi gasped and rolled over onto his stomach to cough and spit out the water he had inhaled. It took him a minute to find his voice but when he did, he already had his speech prepared.

"I'll kill you!"

But Sun Yu, if the words spoken in anger had worried him, did not show it.

"You crazy old man!" Craxxi added between heavy breaths. "You're dead."

"When you were drowning," asked Sun Yu, betraying no emotion, "what did you want more than anything else?"

"What?" Craxxi's terror had subsided and was being

replaced by fury, a feeling he was more accustomed to. Sun Yu repeated the question.

"Air!" he screamed as he rose to his feet and moved toward Sun Yu, his fists rolled into balls.

"When, even at the point of death, you desire the truth more than even air to breathe, then you may leave this place. Not before."

Craxxi halted his approach and Sun Yu walked calmly into the next room, leaving his damp guest dripping behind him.

"Don't give me that Yoda crap," Craxxi replied, chasing him. "I'm going to kill you."

"You cannot."

"You don't think so?"

"You may render my body lifeless, but you cannot kill *me*," he said, with special emphasis on the last word.

Craxxi had faced more formidable men before. But there was something about the old man standing before him that frightened him. He knew from experience that you cannot bribe a man who is not greedy; shame one who is not proud; flatter one who is not vain; threaten one who fears nothing; steal from one who does not value possessions; tempt one who has no desires; or break one who is unbending, but everyone had at least one weakness. Even the bravest of men were scared at the thought of something happening to their families. Craxxi could see in a moment that Sun Yu was none of those things. He had made a career from threatening, exploiting, flattering and bullying men, but Sun Yu was like an unblemished surface with no cracks to widen. He made one last attempt to intimidate him, but his baleful stare fell from its target like arrows from a castle wall.

"And where do you get your strength?" he asked, calmer now. "What are you, a hundred-and-twenty?"

Sun Yu let that pass. He sat down again beside the fire, cross-legged, inviting by implication Craxxi to do the same, which he did. His former defiance, since it had nothing to push against, had left him.

"I paid a lot of money for my place in Heaven," he said, gripping his ankles and forcing his legs into the crossed position. His knees made a sound a lot like the crumpling up of a chocolate wrapper.

For the very first time, Sun Yu seemed struck by what he had heard. Or at the very least, he raised one of his eyebrows ever so slightly.

"I have heard of such a thing, though I didn't know it continued to the modern day."

"Sure, why not? Nothing's changed. Every catholic kid who goes to confession buys into the fact you can do what you want, but that a priest has the power to make it all okay again."

"I believe that the only person who can forgive you is yourself."

"Yeah, well, it doesn't hurt to have a little insurance." Craxxi looked around him and settled his gaze back on the old man. "So, who are you?"

"My name was Sun Yu."

"Was?"

"I have left many things behind."

Craxxi didn't know what to make of Sun Yu. He didn't like how that felt. He had made a career out of judging the character of men, but Sun Yu was revealing nothing.

"What are you hiding, old man?"

"I am hiding nothing."

After a moment, Craxxi asked, "What was that in there?" gesturing toward the cauldron of water in the next room.

Sun Yu shrugged.

"Your first lesson."

Craxxi stretched out his legs and propped himself up on an arm. He had held men's heads under water himself a few times. The lesson was always simple: pay me or you're dead. This was different, though. It was then he first began to wonder: if he were already dead, why did being drowned feel so much like his life was being extinguished? What could possibly be so terrifying when you don't have a life to lose?

"Is this Heaven?" he asked after a long silence.

"What is Heaven?"

Craxxi had always been such a simple man. If he asked a question, he wanted to know the answer to it. If that answer wasn't forthcoming, or if he didn't believe you, or if he simply didn't like it, he hurt you. If you answered a question with a question, he really hurt you. He suppressed the urge to beat the answer out the old man this time, though.

"It's where your soul goes when you're dead."

It was a Sunday school answer, but it was all he could think of.

"If you're dead, why did you struggle when I forced your head under the water?"

This had already been bothering Craxxi.

"Are you saying I'm not dead?"

Sun Yu was not a man who spoke much. That had not

always been the case. As a young man, he had been curious. He wanted to know not just how everything worked, but why. He didn't so much ask questions as interrogate. Every answer led onto another question. He felt that if he kept going, at some point, he'd find the ultimate answer. He did, but it wasn't at all what he had been expecting. And first, he had to stop asking. These days, he saw silence as the peak of a mountain in that every step you took from it would lead you away from it. In response to Craxxi's question, he just smiled and said, "There are some answers to which there exist no questions. The subject of death is one of them."

"How can you have an answer without a question?"

He shifted his weight so that he was facing his host.

"Come on, what aren't you telling me?"

"There is nothing I am not telling you."

This, though infuriatingly enigmatic, was true. By his very manner, Sun Yu was showing Craxxi everything he needed to know. But he knew Craxxi would need to stop looking and start seeing if he were to learn. And not just from him. He regarded his new pupil with an incisiveness of vision that could slice peaches.

"This," he said, "will require patience."

"I am not a patient man."

Sun Yu smiled.

"I don't mean you."

SEVEN

The elevator returned Eric to the ground floor. Its doors parted silently. The reception area was quieter than it had been when he first arrived. As if everyone who was going to check in that day already had. People, looking very much like tourists, sat on sofas, flicked through magazines and glanced at their expensive watches. An Italian-looking gentleman in a black suit and dark glasses sat with one leg over the other reading a newspaper. He wondered how he could make out the print in the low light. Eric had travelled in his early twenties and knew from experience that you can tell a lot about a culture by the quality of its beer. It was in this spirit of inquiry that he made for the hotel bar.

The bar was brightly lit and expansive. There was a lot of wood in the room, from the panelling on the walls, the heavily varnished tables and the bar itself. Comfy sofas squatted about the room and booths lined the walls. The bar itself gleamed with empty glasses that hung upside down above the barman's head, who was chatting with a lone customer seated on a stool. Was everyone in the bar dead? Eric wondered. If they were, they seemed to have come to terms with it well. He made an effort to recognise any of them, for if he were dreaming, they would likely be people he knew, but none looked familiar to him. He saw a couple who he was certain were on a first date: he was one moment this person, the next moment that person, doing his very best to present himself in different ways until she spotted one she liked.

"I think dying came at a really good time for me," Eric overhead him saying. "I needed to just stop so that my life could catch up with me. It's been a great opportunity to reassess and work out who I really am, you know?"

Whether she did or didn't know really didn't matter. She had made her mind up about him within thirty seconds of sitting down. He couldn't have known that, though, so off he went onto another version of himself, hoping it would bring him more luck.

Eric presented himself at the bar and scanned the pumps for something cool and refreshing: Angel's Ruin, Forbidden Fruit, Armageddon, and Monk's Sandal all looked appealing, though he settled on Lucifer's Regret – a 'crisp and hoppy ale with lingering notes of honey, 4.5 % ABV'.

The barman broke away from his conversation, pulled a perfect pint from the tap and placed it down gently in front of him.

"That will be two-pounds twenty-pence." Eric had not been expecting this. What need was there for money in Heaven? He patted his pockets, but they yielded nothing. Then he had an idea.

"Could you charge it to my room?"

The barman took a notebook from his top pocket and a pen from behind his ear. "Certainly, Mr . . ."

"Craxxi," said Eric. "Carmine Craxxi."

The barman looked as if he had just stepped out onto the road only to notice, a moment too late, the number 38 bus bearing down upon him.

"Oh, Mr Craxxi!" He seemed quite flustered, thought Eric. "I apologise. Please, have the drink on me."

Eric didn't mind this at all.

"Thank you, I will!" He raised the beer to the barman and added "Cheers!" before putting the frosty-cold glass to his lips. The barman retreated backwards to what he perceived to be a safe distance and started drying glasses nervously that were clearly already dry. As he drank, he noticed, from the corner of his eye, the barman stooping over in whispered conversation with the customer he had been chatting to before, only now, the amiability had vanished. The customer he was confiding in followed the barman's nod in Eric's direction and stared for a moment. Without finishing his drink, he stood and walked unevenly to his coat that was hanging from a stand in the corner and left.

Eric was not really a drinker. He liked a beer, and had lied to himself, as many men who make the claim do, that he actually liked whisky, and he enjoyed a nice red, but he didn't drink very often. This meant that when he did, he got drunk fast. That was okay, though. He wasn't a surly or emotional drunk, and definitely not a violent one. He just got very happy, then philosophical for a bit, and then he'd fall asleep.

Eric drained his glass and sought the barman out for another, waving it discreetly at shoulder level. Some hours later the barman could be seen leaning towards Eric in confidence and urging his shift to be over as Eric, at the philosophical stage of being drunk, held court.

"I mean, really, what is it all about?"

The barman shook his head and was unwilling to even venture a guess.

"They say I'm dead," slurred Eric, "and what am I doing? I'm sitting on my own in a bar getting drunk. Is that," asked Eric, "what they want me to believe happens in Heaven?"

The barman was, once again, reluctant to commit an opinion.

"Thirty years alive and here I am in a dream, with a drink in my hand, wondering why I bother," at his point he suppressed a belch, "which is where I left off really."

This was unlike Eric. Alcohol never made him maudlin. However, he had been through a lot and felt that he was allowed the self-indulgence of feeling a little sorry for himself.

"I worked in IT. I work? I worked?" Eric was struggling with the past tense, but that level of grammatical detail was beyond him as he was. "It's not the job I wanted, but I thought . . . fine . . . I'll do this for a few years, then retrain as something I really liked. But if I am really dead, then what was I waiting for? I just wasted the last ten years of my life when I could have been . . . I could have been . . ."

This was where Eric ran aground. While he regretted not having done more with his life when he had the chance, he didn't know what he would have done differently if he could go back and start again. He had no real passions. No hobbies he could turn into a job. They say that if you do what you love as a job then you'll never work another day, but what did he love? He loved Amber. That's where he had put all his passion and his dreams and his hope. They had met at university. He was studying business, while she studied psychology. He graduated and got the job he was still doing when he supposedly died, and she got her degrees and became a child psychologist. She loved her job, and it was enough for Eric to see her so happy. He went to work, he came home. He left everything about it at the office and was able to devote the rest of his time to Amber. He didn't know it at the time, but that was enough for him. He knew it now, though. If he woke up in a hospital bed right at that moment, he'd be happy for the rest of his life. Except, of course, that was not the human way. He'd slip back into being tired, frustrated and unhappy; but he hoped that he'd be able to catch himself sometimes, look around him at what he did have, and realise how lucky he was. If he ever did wake up. Perhaps it was the alcohol, but he was beginning to wonder if perhaps he was dead after all.

Eric closed his eyes and appeared to be falling asleep. The barman started to back away as slowly and as quietly as he could, but his progress was arrested by a suddenly alert, but no less incoherent Eric, who was not yet finished.

"Am I still missing some sort of subtle point? Is the answer staring me in the face and I still can't see it? And why?" asked Eric, the first signs of drunken anger and frustration rising, "does it have to be a game of hide and seek anyway? You're either dead or alive. Why all this in-between stuff?"

"Maybe," said the barman, before he had a chance to stop himself, "life was the dream and now you're awake."

Eric looked up, earnestly, from his beer.

"What did you say?"

"Oh, nothing!" said the barman, backtracking, nervously, "don't take any notice of me. I'm nobody!"

"No," said Eric, "that's brilliant. I'm awake!"

"It might not be, I was just-"

"I think you might well have hit the head on the nail . . . the nail on the head! I mean, think about it. How do you really know? Perhaps that's my problem. Perhaps I am still just waking up and trying to work out where I am."

"Perhaps!"

"Am I awake?" Eric asked himself, "or am I asleep? Or somewhere in between?"

Eric's look of triumph melted from his face, and he dropped his head into his hands.

"I'm dead, aren't I?" He looked up for confirmation. "It's okay, you can say it."

"You'll be all right," said the barman, softly. "It hits everyone hard at first."

"God I'm lonely," said Eric, suddenly, grasping the barman's arm. "Everyone I know is alive. All my friends, healthy."

"Josh! Sorry I'm late, pal." Joshua's relief breezed through the door and a relief it most certainly was. Josh said a quick but respectful goodbye to Eric, peeling his fingers away from his arm, and stared at his replacement in a way more evil than you would expect to find in Heaven. Then he was gone. Eric looked up at the stranger in front of him who smiled back at him, naively.

"Who's Josh?"

Eric did not notice the explosion that rocked the hotel, although, the state he was in, he would not have noticed a firework if it had gone off in his trouser leg.

EIGHT

Eric emerged from the bar – his brow furrowed in deep concentration. Three hotel staff ran past him to the sound of a ringing alarm. From the sofa in the lobby, the Italian-looking gentleman he had seen before stood, adjusted his suit and walked casually from the hotel with a newspaper tucked under his arm, apparently unconcerned by the unravelling emergency. Whatever was causing the commotion, Eric was oblivious to it. He was too busy wondering how he was going to negotiate the broad reception with nothing to hold on to. After swaying for some moments in the manner of a man on a boat in heavy seas he leant, more by accident than design, against the outer wall with his shoulder and slid along it, knocking paintings from their hooks and plants from their pots.

Upon reaching the windowed front of the building he attempted to continue forward, perplexed at his lack of progress, like a house fly frustrated by what is, to it at least, an invisible force-field between it and the outside world.

He continued in this way from pane to pane until he reached a set of revolving doors. He followed them as they swung by with great oomphs of displaced air and began to prepare a well-timed leap into the maelstrom of metal and glass. Even sober, Eric found revolving doors intimidating. He always felt, somewhat illogically, that the door to his rear would somehow catch up with him and gobble up his ankles. And he would always exit with a panicked skip as if an unseen hand had reached out and grabbed his posterior. He took hold of the brass handle of a passing door and ran as close behind it as he could until he had completed a full revolution and was flung, in a sling-shot action, back inside the hotel lobby, across which he staggered at an uncontrollable speed until he came up against the door to the hotel bar, back exactly where he had started.

"Mr Craxxi, you are alive!"

The manager of the hotel, a short man with a thick moustache and a French accent, raced up to Eric and started patting his body for injury.

"Oh, thank goodness! We were so worried!"

With all Eric's brain's run-time devoted exclusively to keeping him upright, this unexpected encounter was a touch more than he could cope with. Through tightly pursed lips he began to laugh uncontrollably. Then, as if hit over the head by an invisible assailant, he collapsed to the floor and passed out. The manager clicked his fingers and two porters shimmered into view.

"Help me get him to my office."

The porters heaved Eric's limp body onto a luggage trolley and wheeled him away, banging his head against a door frame and sending him toppling off when they cornered too quickly. Eric was faintly aware of being manhandled, but he was unable to connect current events to anything that was any of his concern. Even the sounds of vases shattering and waste bins being sent clattering out of the way left him untroubled. He heard a door click shut and there followed the sensation of being carried and dropped onto something soft.

"Mr Craxxi!"

Eric could hear someone's name being called, and he wished whoever it was would just answer; he had a terrible headache and would appreciate some quiet.

"Mr Craxxi!"

This was really beginning to irritate Eric now.

"Mr Craxxi, please, wake up!"

Yes, wake up, thought Eric. Then perhaps the rest of us can get some sleep.

"Mr Craxxi!" shrilled the manager, with an increasing note of panic in his voice. "The doctor will be here soon, but you must wake up."

Mr Craxxi?

The parts of Eric's brain that had lain dormant since his excessive thirst quenching in the bar began to light up and ask one another what was going on. They had all heard the name 'Craxxi' before, but between them, they could not remember where.

"Mr Craxxi!"

Something in the back of Eric's brain raised a tentative hand and cleared its throat.

"Err, excuse me."

"Not now. Can't you see we're thinking?"

"Yes, I can see that. Actually, that's what I wanted to-"

"Later, okay? We're right in the middle of something here."

"I see. But, the thing is, it's just that-"

"Oh, for the love of . . . WHAT?"

"This Mr Craxxi."

"What about him?"

"Well, isn't that us?"

Eric's eyes opened.

"Yes?"

"Oh, Mr Craxxi, there was a terrible accident. You were almost killed!"

The two porters exchanged glances. They could smell the beer on Eric's breath and even see some of it down his shirt from the back of the room, and they knew exactly what was wrong with him.

Eric sat up and pinched the bridge of his nose but could not remember any accident.

"There was an explosion in your room," the manager explained. "You don't appear to be injured at all, but we called for the doctor just to be safe. We have a new room for you – every bit as nice as your old room."

Eric wondered who this strange little man was and stared at him, squinting.

"Nicer!" added the manager, nervously. "Please accept our apologies."

Worried that Eric might be in shock, he poured some brandy and pushed the glass under his nose. The smell went straight to his stomach. Eric took a few quick breaths and his face shone with sweat.

"I think I'm going to be-" he said, but that, unfortunately, was as far as he could get before vomit projected from his mouth – some out of his nose – and over the manager who was squatting far too close to get out of the way in time.

The manager stood and turned, slowly, with his arms spread out and lips tightly shut like a man emerging from a vat of vegetable soup and glared at the porters who had to hide their smirks behind their hands. Then, mustering as much Gallic dignity as he had remaining, said: "Would one of you be so kind as to fetch me a towel."

~

Several storeys above the manager's office, Eric's room smouldered, quietly. A fire had gutted the entire suite. The heat had been such that the water from the sprinklers had evaporated before there was a chance for it to douse the flames and they had raged unchecked until the fire fighters arrived.

What remained of the piano was lying on its side up against a wall where it had been thrown by the force of the blast. The table, upon which the gift-wrapped bomb had detonated, was unrecognisable among the puddles of sooty mush that was once the carpet. A team of experts had taped off the room and were busy dropping items into plastic bags as evidence as to what might have caused the devastation. The team leader, Henry Winston, dressed inappropriately for the occasion in a bone-white suit, stood aloof in a pair of rubber boots while his men got their hands dirty.

"I found this, sir."

A young officer, keen to make an impression, held a wet rag, singed at the edges, in front of Henry's nose from the end of a pen.

"What is it?"

"A pair of underpants, sir." Then, for added clarity, "Y-fronts."

"And you're showing me because?"

"There, sir. Scorch marks. Should I bag them?"

"Those aren't scorch marks, son. Best put them in the laundry."

"Yes, sir."

Henry crunched his knuckles and wiped his forehead with a handkerchief. Embers still glowed red, and the air was hot and damp. Water from the fire fighters' hoses dripped from the ceiling. The sooner he could be out of there, he thought, the better. He reached into the inside pocket of his jacket and removed a boiled sweet, which he unwrapped and popped into his mouth and, since his wife was not around to scold him for it, proceeded to crunch loudly.

"So, what do you think, Henry?"

A short, fat, hairy man named Bob, with a New York accent, waddled over to Henry. He removed the paper mask from his mouth, let it hang around his neck and stood with his hands resting in the small of his back.

"A discarded cigarette?" replied Henry.

Bob, though no expert, was doubtful.

"Really? Do you think so?" he asked, looking about him at the wreckage.

"Oh yes, definitely. We haven't concluded our investigations, but I am confident that that's what they'll turn up."

"A cigarette, huh?"

Bob rolled his lips and looked at the blackened candle stick holder that had been driven into a marble pillar to the depth of about half a foot by the force of the blast.

"Well, whoever it was, he'd better start smoking lights, that's all I can say."

Henry was constitutionally opposed to Bob and his like. He found him coarse and vulgar and, frankly, was disappointed that someone like him should be in Heaven at all. He had written a letter to the relevant authorities asking if, perhaps, there could be a section of paradise reserved for those with, as he had put it, more delicate tastes: a private, gated community where new residents would be required to be nominated and appear before a selection committee. He was a member of a prohibitively expensive country club and a number of other discerning societies. He had made every effort to distance himself from the 'Bobs' of Heaven, with their crass humour, cavalier table manners and lax personal hygiene but, it seemed, had to reluctantly accept that contact was sometimes unavoidable. He looked down his nose at Bob, like a pigeon regarding a freshly polished car from the air.

"What do you mean by that?"

"Well, I don't know. It's just that if this was caused by a discarded cigarette then it must have fallen into a box of TNT."

Henry narrowed his eyes, suspiciously.

"I don't follow."

Bob removed one hand from the small of his back and curled it into a fist in preparation for counting off the salient points.

"Henry, witnesses reported a loud explosion. A guest nine floors down said that the water in her bathtub slopped over the side. A porter who happened to be walking past at the time wants to know if someone will 'answer that damn telephone' and this penthouse suite is now the in the basement!"

"What are you suggesting?" asked Henry, barely re-straining his contempt.

Bob slipped his hand over his thinning hair in exasper-ation.

"I am suggesting that you consider the possibility that something else other than a cigarette ripped this room apart."

"Such as?"

"Such as a bomb, Henry!"

"We're in Heaven," replied Henry, not willing to sound Bob's name. "The fact may have escaped you, but there are few if any bombs around here. We're not in the Bronx or whichever hideous place you might be from. This is a respectable neighbourhood.

It was true that crime was relatively rare in Heaven, but it was not as if nothing of the sort ever happened. Not everyone adjusted well to being dead; the transition would sometimes have side-effects. If a person had left a whole-some life then, once dead, they might be tempted to cut loose. Especially once they found out that sins weren't counted in the afterlife once you were there. This omission was something the original architects of Heaven regretted. They really didn't think it necessary at the time. Surely, any deserving entrant would not, by definition, cause any trouble. They failed to account fully for human behaviour, however, discovering them to be endlessly strange and im-possible to predict. Henry did have a point, though. At least as far as bombs went. There had not been any previous cases of an actual bomb going off in Heaven. What he hadn't considered was that Heaven would be around for an infinite amount of time. And the thing with infinity that a person dealing with it needs to get clear very early on is that everything that can possibly happen will happen, over the stretch, an infinite number of times. Failing to grasp this, Henry took a deep breath, straightened his posture and rolled his shoulders.

"When I presume to tell you your job, whatever that is" he said, resolute in his ignorance, "then you may presume to tell me mine. Until such time I suggest you leave matters that are clearly beyond you to me."

"Have it whichever way you want," said Bob. "But before you write your report why don't you find out who this room belonged to. It might make you think twice."

With that, he tore the mask from his neck, threw it to the floor and stormed out, slamming the door violently behind him. There then followed a creaking, proceeded, moments later, by the penthouse suite crashing down onto the floor below, that had, thankfully, been vacated as a precaution.

Out in the corridor, a door opened, and black soot bellowed out. Emerging from it like a geriatric chimney sweep, Henry, unrecognisable but for his superior manner, coughed a black wisp of ash, straightened his jacket, said a polite "good evening" to the open-mouthed couple who had emerged from their room to see what the noise had been, and went home to his wife who, for she knew better, simply did not ask.

NINE

Eric woke in his new room early. He sat up and rubbed
the sleep from his eyes. An invisible hand turned a crank
in the side of his head and made his brain throb. He was
still fully dressed: his shirt, stained with dry vomit, was
twisted round his body and the bottoms of his trousers
were crumpled up around his knees. He rubbed his chin
and found it had the coarse consistency of the side of a box
of matches.

He was beginning to consider the possibility that he
was dead after all. This was like no dream he had ever
had before. True enough, he had never been in a coma
before, either, but he was now having difficulty keeping up
the belief that he was lying in a hospital bed somewhere
being read the football results to by his mother. It felt as if
his heart was filling with mercury. He lay on his side and
hugged his knees. He was dead. Was he dead? He closed
his eyes. He thought of Amber, his mother, his father,
his sister. He thought of them all until his heart cracked
and he sighed, partly with sadness, but mostly with relief.
Holding on was proving to be exhausting.

There came a knock at his door. He considered pretending he wasn't in, but whoever it was was persistent. He opened the door onto a short, hairy man.

"Hi, Robert Decker," he said with a New York accent, holding an ID card out in front of him for inspection. "But call me Bob. Can I come in?"

Eric stood to one side and let Bob in.

"Do you mind if I sit?" asked Bob, pointing to a white, leather sofa.

Eric didn't mind at all. In fact, he was quite keen to sit down himself. He wasn't quite ready still to conduct himself while upright. His new room was much the same as his old one. Except this was bigger and had a sunken hot tub by the glass doors. Bob sat forward and, his elbows on his knees, looked hard at Eric. He thought for a moment, appeared to make up his mind about something, and began to speak.

"I hope you don't mind me coming here like this, it's just that there's something you should know."

He waited for Eric to prompt him. When no prompt was proffered, he continued.

"Look, um, I don't know what you've got yourself into, but I am guessing you don't have much of a clue, either."

"I don't know what you mean," said Eric, although of course he knew exactly.

"All right, have it your way. But you need to know you're in danger."

Eric sat up a little straighter at that word.

"What do you mean, danger?"

"I was part of the team who had a look around your room last night after the explosion. Now, my colleague is going to say in his report it was a discarded cigarette or something like that. I'm sorry to say it, but he's an idiot."

"Right."

"I'm not an expert, but I know an explosion when I see one."

Eric was beginning to wish he had not opened the door to this man. He was still not well, but even he could see where this conversation was going, and it was a bit much for a man with a head like his.

"An explosion?"

"Specifically, a bomb."

That's what Eric thought he was going to say.

"Why would anybody want to-"

"Look, I'll say it again, I don't know what you've got yourself into, but you need to start looking for answers. You should start by finding out exactly who Carmine Craxxi is."

"I'm Carmine Craxxi," protested Eric.

Bob stared for a moment, made his mind up about something for the second time in their conversation, and stood up.

"Okay, chief. I came here to warn you. If you want to know more, go along to the public records office and ask to see your file."

"Why should I do that?" asked Eric, weakly. "I know who I am."

Bob scoffed, waved a hand in a gesture that told Eric he had given up, and let himself out. However, he stopped in the door and turned to face Eric before he left.

"Be very careful," he said.

Now alone in his suite, he placed his hands to his face

and slid sideways to a reclining position on the sofa. He didn't know what to make of this new information. Five minutes earlier he had just been coming round to the idea that he might very well be dead. But if he were to finally accept that that is what he was, he needed to answer one last question: if he were dead, why would someone be trying to kill him. And for that matter, how? Can you die twice? Tears welled in Eric's eyes and a knot of pain expanded in his throat, but he would not — he could not — cry. He rose unsteadily and went about the humanising process of washing, shaving and dressing and, after scooping out the inside of a grapefruit and drinking down half a litre of orange juice, he felt ready to find out exactly who he was.

The reception area was quiet. An elderly couple, recently reunited, stepped hand-in-hand from the restaurant where breakfast was being served. A postman landed a bundle of letters onto the main desk and stayed to flirt with the girl there who had rather hoped she had left all that nonsense behind. Eric loitered for a moment by the elevator and scanned the outside of the hotel through the window for suspicious figures. An olive-skinned gentleman in a brown suit and shiny shoes leant up against a lamp post and read from a newspaper. As if aware he was being observed he chose that moment to look up from the sports section and spot Eric doing his best to look inconspicuous. Eric swivelled to face the wall and started reading from a sign that explained what to do in the event of an emergency. When he turned around, the man had folded the newspaper under his arm and was watching Eric, intently.

Eric strolled as casually as he could to the restaurant

and, once out of view, dashed into the bathroom where he shut himself in a cubicle and sat down to gather his thoughts. While the idea of being killed in Heaven seemed absurd to him, until he knew more, he was not inclined to take any chances. He looked behind him and saw a narrow window, hinged at its top edge, that he decided might just be big enough for him to fit through. He stood on the toilet cistern and peered out into an alley. Directly beneath the window stood a tin dustbin that, if he lowered himself onto it gently enough, would aid his passage to the ground. He opened the window as far as it would go and heaved himself up onto its sill, knocking with his arm the prop holding the window open, sending it crashing down onto his head. Forcing himself through the gap with a final kick that sent the lid of the cistern smashing to the floor Eric managed to squeeze through as far as his waist. However, having reached this critical juncture, he discovered that there was not enough space for him to swing his legs through. This meant that he was going to have to drop onto the dustbin headfirst. Unfortunately, he no longer had the leverage to force his backside through. Nor the lithesome waist required to go back the other way.

Eric was weighing up his options that, owing to the facts already presented, were reduced to remaining where he was, when he heard the door to the cubicle behind him creak open and then shut.

"I say," came elderly, but robust British voice. "The door was unlocked. You don't mind, do you? It's just that there is something ghastly floating in the one next door, and I am quite fastidious about these matters."

"No," replied Eric, insouciantly. "No, not at all."

"Thanks awfully," said the man as he dropped his trousers and proceeded to conduct his business with Eric's feet dangling either side of his head. A minute or so later, Eric could hear the toilet tissue being unrolled followed by the sound of flushing water. When it had settled down, the man spoke again.

"I say, are you quite all right there? You look terribly uncomfortable."

"Now you come to mention it, it is beginning to lose its flavour."

"Are you trying to climb out or in?"

"Out, actually."

"I see. Would you like a hand?"

"If you could perhaps give me a shove, I think that might do the trick."

Eric could feel the man's hands settle on his rear.

"Brace yourself! I am about to push!"

With that the man, who had played rugby for his school, brought his shoulder into play, lifted himself up underneath Eric's backside and cried, "Heave!"

Eric's rear squeezed through the gap followed very quickly by his legs and feet. There was the sound of a toppling dustbin and that of a dustbin lid rattling to a halt like a spinning coin.

"I say, are you all right?" called the man.

"Yes, I think so," echoed Eric's voice from inside the upended dustbin. "Thank you."

"Not a problem, old boy. Glad to have helped. Cheerio!"

"Yes," replied Eric, weakly, "Cheerio!"

The man washed his hands and rejoined his wife at their table.

"Pervert in the gents," he said when he sat down.

"What was he doing? One of their sordid games I suppose."

"All good clean fun. Got himself into a spot of bother. Didn't see his friend anywhere. Probably scarpered and left him there. Poor form."

"You didn't get involved, did you Reginald?"

"Can't leave a chap compromised like that. Had to do the right thing." Reginald had tried many times to explain to his wife the importance in cricket of playing with a straight bat, but she had merely responded that if your bat was not straight, you should just take it back to the shop you bought it from. Thus the convenient metaphor for life that this basic cricketing skill provided had always been lost to him when reasoning with his wife – as it was now. His wife considered the matter for a brief moment.

"Well," she said, buttering another slice of toast, testily, "I just hope you washed your hands."

~

Eric stood up and cleaned himself as best he could. He righted the dustbin, replaced the lid and, upon spotting a hole in a chain-link fence opposite, squeezed through it and made his way to the main road. He found himself on a wide boulevard, paved with red bricks upon which were scattered tables and chairs that waiters and waitresses buzzed between like bees among a bed of flowers.

Every effort had been made by the town planners to recreate a typical Parisian street scene. What the town planners had failed to understand (what every town planner everywhere has always failed to understand) is that you cannot recreate Parisian café society anywhere other than Paris. No number of cheeses the shape and size of wagon wheels in shop windows is going to be enough to fool anybody.

Eric made himself small and cowered against the thick trunk of a tree. He scanned the roofs of the buildings opposite but did not see the giveaway gleam of sunlight bouncing from the telescopic sight of a rifle. No one loomed in shadowy doorways or walked with violin cases tucked under their arms. A couple, sitting on a table outside a café, sipped frothy coffee and ate crumbly pastries. Children played in a nearby park, watched over by their parents who were chatting idly with other mothers and fathers and an elderly man fed seeds to a flock of pigeons from a brown paper bag.

Eric took a map he had taken from his room from his back pocket and, after turning it round in his hands several times, finally found his bearings. According to the key, the building marked by a red number six on the map was the Public Records Office. Every piece of information ever gathered on you over the period of your life, he had found out, could be obtained from its vaults and it was there that Eric intended to find out exactly who Carmine Craxxi was and what, as Bob had said, he had got himself into. Rather than walk round the full perimeter of the park, Eric decided to take a short cut through it. He could see the Public Records Office looming tall beyond some wooded trees and headed off in its general direction. The wood was thicker than he had imagined and the path that he followed into it had disappeared into tangled brambles. He could still make out the Public Records Office through the dense canopy of leaves, but no matter how hard he tried, he could not get any closer to it.

He climbed over fallen trees and stooped beneath low branches; he snagged his clothes and scratched his arms and face on thorns, but still he was not making any discernible progress. He paused for breath and sat down on a tree stump now utterly lost. He wiped the sweat from his forehead and noticed he was bleeding from a cut above his left eyebrow; tiny black flies buzzed excitedly around his sweaty face. He slowed his panting and looked around him. Not only did he not know in which direction he had to go, the vegetation appeared to have closed behind him and he had no hope of retracing his steps. He picked up a stick with which to thrash back nettles and ploughed on.

Forty-five minutes later, he emerged hot, exhausted and with his skin burning from numerous cuts and stings, exactly at the point he had entered the woods in the first place. He raised a hand above his head when he got to the road to hail a passing taxi and got in.

Behind Eric, in the woods and unable to disentangle himself from a particularly aggressive bramble, the olive-skinned gentleman who had been watching Eric from outside his hotel–his stomach overhanging his waistband like a bag of sand–spoke into a mobile phone.

"Boss, I lost him," he said, breathlessly. "I don't know how he knew he was being tailed. He's good. He's very good."

~

Eric crunched along a gravel path, taking a wide birth around a sprinkler and started to relax under the mid-morning sun. Readers sat propped up against tree trunks, their heads buried in books, idly turning pages and swatting flies with absent-minded waves of the hand. Eric could never read in public. He was always unable to shake off the feeling that, the moment his eyes settled on the page, everyone would start staring at him. Either that or he would be plagued by the thought that those around him were quietly judging his choice of reading matter.

He skipped up a set of stairs and entered the main hall of the municipal building, its cool air instantly drying the sweat on his forehead. He ran his finger down the floor plan till he found the service he required and called the lift. A minute later, he was standing at the periphery of a large, open-plan room and a little confused as to what to do next.

"Can I help you, sir?"

A security guard had manifested himself at Eric's right shoulder and, leaning forward with his hands behind his back, spoke directly into his ear. Eric, to his embarrassment, jumped.

"What? Oh! Thank you. I'm just here for my public record."

"Very good, sir," replied the guard with affected politeness. He extended his arm and, looking down its length to the tip of his index finger, as though it were the barrel of a gun, added, "Over there on the wall is a ticket dispenser. Take a number from it and sit over there (sweeping his arm across the room as if he had seen a rabbit) and wait for your number to be called."

"Thank you very much."

"Not at all, sir. Only too happy to help. It's what I'm

here for."

Eric took a number from the machine under the watchful gaze and encouraging nod of the guard and sat down. He looked down at the pink slip of paper in his hand. Number one-four-seven. He looked to see what number was currently being seen. Eleven. He sighed and attempted to make himself comfortable in a chair that had apparently been designed against that very possibility.

He found himself drawn to the book that a lady seated beside him was reading. Discreetly, he read as much as most of the first paragraph before she turned the page. He started again at the top and had barely read halfway down before she turned the page once more. Eric was not an express reader, by any means, but he wondered how she was able to take anything in at all reading at that speed.

Eric was not one of those men who found initiating conversations with women in public natural. No matter which way he approached it, he could never pull the trick off without making the opening remark sound more like a preliminary for some sort of attack–possibly of a sexual nature.

He cleared his throat.

"Fast reader, eh?"

The woman looked up, noticing him for the very first time, and smiled dismissively. All she wanted to do was read while she waited. Why did men insist on trying to talk to her?

"Yes."

Eric clasped his knees with his hands and straightened his back.

"Good book, is it?" The woman repeated the gesture of

a few moments before.

"What's it about?"

Without looking up from the page. Nor, apparently, ceasing to read at a remarkable rate, she said, with a note of irritation creeping into her voice, "Dhamma."

Eric's eyes widened at what appeared to be a way into a conversation.

"That's a coincidence. I was reading a book about that when I well, while I was still, you know, while I was still alive."

The woman's attitude to Eric softened slightly. If that was what he liked to fill his head with, perhaps he was worth a brief exchange.

"I find it all so difficult to get my head around," she said.

"Yeah, it can be a bit like that," said Eric, taken aback that his efforts to be friendly had paid off. "It's difficult to imagine how another human being could do those things."

"Oh, absolutely!" she replied, suddenly enthused by meeting a like-minded soul. "I have enough trouble comprehending it all. I don't think I could ever actually see myself, you know, in the same place."

"I know what you mean. What would it take? I mean, it's got to all start in childhood, hasn't it."

"I think you're probably right. Perhaps it starts in the womb. Karma."

Eric had never truly understood what anyone ever meant by the word 'karma', but he knew it was something to do with bad deeds being punished. Or at least, he thought it was.

"You can say that again," offered Eric, a trifle uncertainly.

"But I think you can work at it," continued the woman at a similar pace to that which she read with.

Eric frowned. "Well, yeah, I suppose you could, if you really wanted to."

"Oh, yes, of course, it takes a huge commitment, but the rewards are fantastic!"

Eric began to wonder if he would be made to regret beginning the conversation. "Well, I don't know about that-"

"But it's so liberating in the long-run, don't you think?"

"If you like," replied Eric, looking around, nervously, for the guard who was now, of course, nowhere to be seen.

"If you can manage to somehow get inside Dhamma then you can be Dhamma."

Eric shifted in his seat and frowned.

"Look, I'm sorry, I never got your name, but I don't think it's something I want to actually be, you know?"

"Oh, I see," said the girl, disappointed. "You have different beliefs?"

"I certainly do!"

"Like what?"

"Well, for a start, I don't believe you should go about killing young boys, chopping them up and putting them in your fridge, so you can eat them later!"

There was a brief silence, broken, at length, by the woman. "That's Jeffrey Dahmer."

"I know his name!"

"But I was talking about Dhamma," a word she now helpfully spelt out. "The Buddhist doctrine: the Four Noble Truths? The Eight-Fold Path?"

She pointed to the front cover of the book, which was now resting shut on her lap. On it was depicted the familiar figure of Buddha, sitting in the lotus position, smiling in the manner of a man who gets a joke no one else does.

Eric's mouth dried up. "Well, I was talking about the serial killer."

The woman, whose name, for the record, was Erika, replied simply, "I wasn't."

She reopened her book and resumed reading. Eric looked up at the screen for the number being called. *Fourteen*. As soon as the tips of his ears had stopped burning with embarrassment, he rose casually, as if he had felt like a walk all along – just to stretch his legs – and wandered away with his hands thrust into his pockets, waiting till he was out of sight in the stairwell before slapping his forehead in self-reproach. He took the stairs to the tenth floor where the floor guide promised shops and cafés and took a few minutes to browse the newspapers and trashy novels there. He paid a short visit to the bathroom, squirted chilled water into his mouth from a water-fountain and walked back up to the fourteenth floor where he discovered that, in his absence, there had been a terrific–and not wholly unpredictable–flurry of activity. Eric's number had been and gone. He puffed his cheeks out, pulled another number from the dispenser, and sat down, alone, and kept his mouth shut.

Half an hour later his number was called. He leapt to his feet and presented himself, as instructed, at position eight.

"Hello, yes," he began. "I'd like to see my public record, please."

The austere lady behind the counter, her grey hair tied back into a bun and reading glasses hanging from a chain around her neck, shook her head.

"You need to go to one of the other positions."

Before he could protest, she had called for the next number, and he found himself shouldered to one side by an elderly woman. None of the other positions were free, and being English, he did not feel comfortable stepping up to any of them unbidden. He took another number and returned to his seat. When his number was called, he was directed again to position eight. He dropped the ticket in his hand to the floor and allowed his head to sag between his knees. He returned to the dispenser and reeled off a dozen tickets. And one by one, as they were called, he was directed back to position eight.

Eventually, and in desperation, he flung himself against the counter at window eight and pleaded.

"Please," he said. "I've been here for two hours. I just want to see my public record. Don't send me away. I beg you."

"Certainly, sir," replied the woman as though no task could possibly be too much for a humble public servant such as herself. She smiled brightly and took Eric's membership card from his hand as he stood looking dumb. "Take a seat. It shouldn't take very long."

She disappeared through a door behind her. Eric turned and looked about the room in the manner of a man who had just seen a dog walk past on its hind legs and wondered if he was the only one who thought it strange. He returned to his seat and felt like crying.

"Mr Carmine Craxxi!"

Eric was snapped suddenly from a sporting daydream in which he was the hero and stood before the position once more. The lady pushed a thick, brown file stuffed with papers, underneath the window.

"You may not take the record from the premises," recited the lady by rote. "There is a reading room for your convenience. Please return the file to this window by close of business today."

Eric thanked her and shuffled away, absentmindedly, as he flicked through the documents. The reading room resembled a library that had been shorn of books. Long tables with wooden partitions for privacy stood in rows. Each booth had a green reading lamp with a gold chain. Three of the booths were occupied by people–two women and one man–going over their own records. One of the women took a balled-up tissue from her bag and dabbed a tear from her eye. Eric chose a booth away from them, scraped a chair out and opened Carmine Craxxi's file. It was a thick document, but there was a helpful summary page. It was that to which he turned.

Carmine Benini. Also known as Don Carmine Craxxi: boss of the Craxxi crime family and head of the New York syndicate. Born in Brooklyn, USA, in 1955 to Gaetano (a butcher) and Maria Benini–originally from the small Sicilian village of Sutera. He moved to New York with his family at the age of two.

Educated at the Our Lady of the Immaculate Conception school in Brooklyn, the young Carmine Benini rapidly gained a fearsome reputation as a brutal fist fighter. However, while his fellow school friends found themselves embroiled in playground scuffles most days, Carmine Benini put his dubious talents to use for financial gain by organising a protection racket. The fact that Ca-

rmine Benini was the boy the other pupils were most likely to need protection against guaranteed him a steady flow of income. Though the school's principal, Mr Evans, was made aware of the illegal activities of Carmine Benini, he was reluctant to expel him as he had 'never known any teacher who could keep order among the pupils quite as effectively as the Benini boy'.

Benini soon spread his empire beyond the school gates to include much of his local neighbourhood and he employed older boys to enforce his reign. At the age of just thirteen, Carmine Benini caught the attention of a local mafia boss by the name of Don Amadeo Craxxi. Carmine Benini never returned to school but instead was put to work: selling packets of cigarettes from the trunks of cars; serving drinks at the various mob hang outs and – as soon as he was tall enough to see over a steering wheel–stealing cars.

At sixteen, Carmine Benini committed his first murder: Carlo Vinci, an irreverent thug, who, despite repeated warnings, had opened his own gambling den in the heart of Don Amadeo Craxxi's territory. From that moment, Carmine Benini became known as an effective contract killer. Though no man can ever be truly cold-hearted, it is the opinion of this biographer that there were no lengths to which Carmine Benini would not have gone in his efforts to rise through the ranks of the organisation.

Ironically, it was just this ruthlessness that held back his progress. His superiors were wary of him and preferred to keep him safely employed at a distance rather than give him any real power.

At the age of twenty-five, Carmine Benini had not progressed as far as he had hoped. He grew frustrated and bitter. This feeling of being unfairly treated and seeing others less capable and younger than himself leapfrog over him to positions of influence and respect festered within him for a further five years.

Shortly after his thirtieth birthday, and at possibly his lowest ebb, a meeting of the five most powerful families in the city ended in a blood bath. By the time the many dead had been buried, Carmine Benini finally found himself promoted. His Don, Amadeo Craxxi, who had survived the cull, decided that at a time of war the soldier-like qualities of Carmine Benini were needed and so he invited the young man into his inner circle, despite the misgivings of some of his closest advisers.

The war, which had been expected, never materialised. Now receiving the respect he had for so long ached, Carmine Benini's career soared. At the age of thirty-two he was bestowed the honour of being 'made' and accepted by the Craxxi family as one of their own. Once a family member has been 'made' he becomes effectively untouchable. No one can kill him without the permission of the family heads. It is license, effectively, to do as you please without fear of consequence. Three years later, his godfather and mentor, Don Amadeo Craxxi, was shot dead by FBI agents at what should have been a routine questioning. And so it was, at the age of thirty-five, Carmine Benini became Don Carmine Craxxi and took charge of the 'family'.

He used his new power and political influence to settle grudges he had harboured for decades. It was a time as short as it was bitter. Fifteen years later, on the day of his fiftieth birthday, he was murdered while leaving a restaurant with his oldest friend and accountant Giuseppe Schillaci.

Don Carmine Craxxi never married and left one illegitimate son.

– Cornelius Cuper, asst. biographer.

The rest of the report went into great detail of the significant moments of Craxxi's life in chronological order. Flicking through the pages he saw murders, beatings, bribery and just about any other crime you can imagine. Where did he find the time for it all? There were also significant moments which made it in that were not crime-related: the passing of his parents, the death by leukaemia of his best friend when he was only six-years-old, the time he saw a girl he liked leave a party with someone else (what he did to that someone else), and the fact that the film he had seen more than any other was Citizen Kane. Eric felt sick. As he read, the colour in his cheeks vanished and the top of his head began to burn. He closed the file, sat back and covered his mouth with his hand. It all made sense now: the room, the gifts, the barman, the bomb. How had he managed to get himself into such a mess? In life, Eric had not risen higher than an I.T. assistant manager for an Internet-based firm that never made any money anyway.

Now he was the Godfather.

TEN

Eric paid the cab driver by charging the fare to his account. He had enjoyed the power of giving his name as Carmine Craxxi, but now he knew where they power came from, he felt churlish bandying it about. However, since he had no money of his own, it was either that or walk, go hungry, thirsty and without a place to stay. Until he worked out what to do, he would have to continue using fear as his main form of currency. He hurried into the hotel reception, keeping his head down. A cool blast of conditioned air ruffled his fringe and dried the sweat on his forehead. The reception was busy with new arrivals again and security was tight after the recent attack: neckless men stood against the walls and patrolled the vast marble floor with eagle eyes without really knowing what they were looking for. Occasionally, one would stop bewildered new arrivals, ask to see their membership cards, then send them on their way. Sometimes, a confused or lost arrival would ask one of these guards for information: "Where do I go?" "Is there a lost and found?" "What time do they serve food till?" Each time, the guard would stare back, hoping in vain to hide his stupidity behind a mask of menace, and say nothing.

Eric — with the disdain held by the very weak for the very strong — wondered how such men could be given batons when he, frankly, would not trust any one of them to borrow his fountain pen.

Just then, Eric became aware of a man standing at his shoulder. He was of West Indian origin, and was dressed casually in a tan leather jacket, blue jeans and white trainers.

"My mission," announced the man in a rich Caribbean accent, "is to 'elp you understand."

Eric froze. On Earth, he had lived in the Islington area of north London and would often find himself pestered by men or women suffering from varying degrees of wild-eyed hysteria. This would usually happen when standing on the platform while waiting for a tube train. It is difficult to avoid someone in a tunnel: you cannot, after all, cross the road or sidestep into a shop. The other commuters would watch, relieved they had been spared, as he was harangued on some topic or other, or as attempts were made to indoctrinate him into their church. It seemed they saw something in Eric that led them to latch onto him so eagerly. He preferred to believe they sensed in him an open mind that was capable of ingesting any well-thought-out argument. It was more likely, however, that they knew a man with low sales resistance when they saw one.

Eric made the mistake of turning to look at the man and he took this as an open invitation to continue with his rhetoric.

"I know what you are t'inking. You are t'inking I am a religious freak who want you to "open your 'eart to de Lord.

Halleluiah!"

He rose his voice and spread his arms. A young couple standing just a few feet away with suitcases at their feet pretended not to have heard.

"I am an angel. No one else 'ere can see me 'part from you. Look at me!" he shouted at the top of his voice, but no one did. "Look around you, my friend. Where are you? You are in 'eaven. Your search is over!" The man laughed triumphantly then looked about him with misty eyes at the sheer beauty of it all. "Paradise!" he proclaimed.

"It doesn't look much like paradise to me," said Eric.

The man looked at Eric and smiled as if he had been waiting for just that remark.

"And what does paradise look like to you?"

"Well, I don't know," shrugged Eric. "White beaches, palm trees, flowing streams . . . stuff."

The man nodded in appreciation of the picture Eric painted.

"White beaches, palm trees, flowing streams and stuff!" He seemed to chew the words, savour their flavour, then swallow them down. "Everyt'ing, in fact, dat you would find on de Earth?"

Eric formed a word and then another then closed his lips firmly. The man said nothing. The silence he formed created a vacuum which Eric was being invited to fill.

"Are you saying Heaven is on Earth?"

"It was once, but not anymore. I believe dey place a supermarket dere now."

Eric, still reeling from the shock of discovering whose identity he had so rashly procured, was in no fit cerebral state to add anything further to the duologue.

"If 'eaven exist anywhere now it exist in dere," said the man and he tapped Eric on the side of his head.

"Let yourself go, my friend. Let go of de 'andrail. Let yourself float away. A snowflake never fall in de wrong place."

Eric was still receiving this last phrase when two security guards loomed behind the man and slapped their heavy hands upon his shoulders.

"Come on, Clarence, let's go. We've told you before."

As he was led away, Clarence never took his eyes from Eric.

"Remember," he shouted through a white-toothed smile. "A snowflake never fall in de wrong place!"

Eric made his way to the elevator, which was waiting open, and asked for the seventh floor.

"A snowflake never falls in the wrong place," he repeated to himself, meditatively. There was something in the simplicity of that sentence that made it beautiful. It was as true a statement as he had ever heard, but he could not see the point of it.

Next to Eric's door, a guard reclined in a chair reading a newspaper. When he noticed Eric approaching, he leapt to his feet among a flurry of paper and stood to attention. Eric was embarrassed by such reverence, and he wondered what Carmine Craxxi would have done in his place. With that in mind, Eric wrapped his arms around the startled man and planted a kiss on both cheeks. He entered his room and closed the door behind him, and the guard, now alone, wiped his cheeks dry with the back of his sleeve and wondered if he should tell his wife.

Now inside his room, Eric made straight for the drinks

cabinet and poured a glass of whisky. The harsh liquor stung his mouth and made him grimace. He had always been irritated at the way, in films, actors would swallow whisky as if it were apple juice, which, of course, it probably was. The second mouthful was easier to take down, but still he could not stop his lip from curling. His trousers were still damp from his cross-country excursion that morning and he felt generally grubby. He moved to the bathroom, opened the taps in the bath to full and strolled into his bedroom, still with the glass of whisky in his hand. On his bed lay an extravagant bouquet of flowers. He froze in mid-step and held his breath. He considered asking the guard if he knew anything about them but decided to inspect them himself first. Gingerly, he walked softly to his bed and placed the glass quietly on the bedside table. The flowers did not appear to be ticking. Nor were there any wires visible. Tucked in between the petals was a card. Eric reached in and slipped it out — half expecting the bouquet to explode as he did so. It was from the hotel manager:

Mr Craxxi. We apologise once more for the accident in your room that so nearly led to tragedy. Please, accept this invitation to a gala evening in your honour, next Saturday night at 8:30. I and everyone at the Heaven Hilton look forward to your attendance – Pierre Jabouille, manager.

Eric's plans to maintain a low profile had lasted less than half an hour. He sat on the edge of the bed and covered his face with his hands. Life had been easy. He always thought dying would be the hardest part of death and that everything after that would be a joy. How wrong he had been.

A snowflake never falls in the wrong place.

Well of course it doesn't he thought. It was obviously a true statement, but why did it feel particularly true in that moment? And what was all that about Heaven being in his own head? Was he dreaming, after all? He opened the double-doors and stepped onto the balcony for the first time. Before him, Heaven sprawled. From up there, it did look sort of Heavenly. The sky had looked blue from ground level, but from high up at penthouse level it burnt a brilliant white. There were mountains in the distance. It's always difficult to tell how far mountains are from you, but Eric guessed they were at least a hundred miles from the hotel. Between them and Heaven were green parks and forests, which surrounded what now looked to Eric like a city, built on a flat plane in a grid pattern. Most of the buildings were one or two storeys high, but others curved inwards into the mist and light. They were so tall, even from his elevated position, Eric had to look up. He wondered what they were. To his left, nearer the city, were hills with little, white buildings stuck to them like mountain goats, linked by roads which were carved into the rock, repeatedly jagging back on themselves. At the top of the tallest hill was what Eric could have described as a palace. Its colour matched the white sky behind it so that it almost disappeared into it. More broad than tall, with rows of square windows along its facade, it was clear that something very important happened there. It was the first time since arriving in Heaven that he thought about God. Was that where he lived? The question of the existence of God was one which humanity had grappled with – shed blood over – for thousands of years, but it had remained ultimately unsettled. And there he was, possibly looking at his house.

Let go of de 'andrail. Let yourself float away.

Eric looked down at his hands which gripped the rail. What if he let go of it and jumped? Would he float away? If he didn't, would he fall and die again? If so, where would he wake up? In the hospital, or in another place, stranger than this one? He looked over the edge. This would normally causes his stomach to turn over, but he felt nothing now.

If I can't fall in the wrong place, why not?

He was too high to make out individual people, but he could see moving smudges as groups of people made their way along the pavement. Nothing felt real to Eric in that moment. It was as if he could reach out and touch the mountains that were so far away or step off the balcony and walk away. He had worn virtual reality goggles before: everything looked real. He reacted, psychologically, to the things he saw. Even though he knew they were not really there, they felt real. It was too easy to trick the brain into becoming confused between a simulation and reality. Perhaps that was the point; maybe it was easy to confuse the brain because that was the way nature intended it to be. Surely death should be more obvious than this. There ought not to be any question. All that had really happened was that he used to be absolutely certain that he was alive and that everything around him was real, and now he wasn't so sure. Had he pursued this line of thought, he may have arrived at the idea that that might be all that death was: the end of certainty. But he had gone as far as he was willing to. At least for now. Certainty was a sturdy handrail; letting go of it would take time. All he had done was make himself miserable.

However, he did cheer himself with the thought that he was in the pleasant position, for the first time in his life, of being able to afford room service and he decided to take full advantage of that fact. He lifted the phone to his ear, waited a few moments, then ordered chicken chow mein with fried rice, a dozen poppadoms and a bottle of red wine. However, despite the fact he was now operating under a false identity, he still could not bring himself to order the adult channel. Instead, he spent the evening dipping tortilla chips into a bowl of salsa sauce that was balanced on his stomach, watching Cannonball Run II, which was his all-time favourite film. He was, however, unable to stay awake for what he considered to be the film's best part – the out-takes at the end – as his internal clock was beginning to settle down into some sort of sociable rhythm and by eleven o' clock his eyes blinked heavily a couple of times, before staying closed for several hours.

Eleven

Eric woke in the early hours of the morning amid greasy plates and empty bottles of whisky, brandy and vodka from the mini bar rising and falling on his chest like life rafts being tossed about on a giant swell. He rolled onto his side and draped his arm over the absent shoulders of Amber. His hand fell into a bowl of sweet-and-sour sauce that squelched between his fingers. After a trip to the bathroom to relieve himself, by way of a brief but disorientating detour via the walk-in wardrobe, Eric undressed, slipped between the cool, silk sheets and took comfort from the fact he did not have to get up early for anyone.

Eric had to get up early for the cleaning team. He closed the door to the bedroom while they started on the living area and hurriedly gathered up the dirty plates, piling them pointlessly on the dresser and tossing the empty bottles into the waste basket. He attempted to remove the crumbs from the bedspread and opened the window to remove the smell of Chinese food and alcohol. Then one of the cleaners knocked politely on the door and Eric, still dressed in a bathrobe, let him in. He was not sure of the etiquette required for such a moment. Like so many of his class, he did not feel completely comfortable having someone clean around him. Should he act as if he were invisible? Perhaps he might engage him in conversation for a few minutes; but where would he start? Sensing his discomfort, the cleaner plugged headphones into his ears and turned the volume on his personal stereo up full. Thus, relieved of responsibility Eric sat on the sofa, making sure to cross his legs modestly, and picked a leaflet from the coffee table. It was entitled *Better Off Dead*. Inside, listed by category, were jobs and opportunities for acquiring new skills. If he had not been labouring under a heavy hangover, he may have been excited at the prospect of being able to make his choices all over again. At school, he had shown a flair for art and design, but rather than pursue a career in something creative he had applied for a job in I.T. at the age of twenty-one and never had an original thought ever again.

He did, however, have other things on his mind. He doubted the real Carmine Craxxi would have accepted the invitation from the hotel manager. From what he had read in Craxxi's personal file it seemed he was an intensely private man who rarely appeared in public during the last years of his life. He had no intention of attending the party, but living as a mafia boss was not going to make life easy whether he went or not. He needed to put the record straight and tell the relevant authorities there had been an innocent mix up. But he was frightened what would happen to him if he did. He was not a member. He had never been to church as an adult, except for weddings, funerals and christenings (the big three).

The first thing he needed to do, feeling his head, was stop drinking. And the next thing he needed to do was find out how he had died, which he had no memory of at all. He had not been ill. He knew that much. But he couldn't remember being hit by a car either. He dressed in the most casual clothes Carmine Craxxi had and decided to go out to clear his head with some fresh air.

He had heard of people laying low before, but he had no idea of how they actually went about it. He stood in front of a full-length mirror and wondered how to make himself look less conspicuous. His trouble was that he had always been such an inconspicuous man it was difficult to know where to begin. He settled for spitting on his hands and flattening the hair at the back of his head and departed.

Once outside in the sunshine, Eric scanned the street for mafia hoods – a scheme hampered by the fact he did not know what a mafia hood looked like, or, really, what one was. The Italian gentleman he had spotted before was nowhere to be seen, but everyone looks like a suspicious figure when you know someone is trying to kill you. However, no one looked more suspicious than Eric himself who was looking over his shoulder and dashing from doorway to doorway, like a man with an allergy to the sun. On jumping at the site of a shady character on the opposite side of the street, which turned out to be his reflection in the mirrored glass of a building, he managed to laugh at himself and relax, thus melting into the crowd.

A few hours later, having strolled through flowery parks and handsome squares, he sat down at an outdoor café and ordered tea. The café was busy, so he had to ask to take an empty seat at a table already occupied by a young woman with long, black hair and a honeyed complexion. She was curled up in her chair and reading a book: *The Tao Te Ching*, by Lao Tzu. Eric had never heard of it. She appeared totally engrossed by its content.

Eric's tea arrived in a white cup. A drop had rolled down the side leaving behind a brown streak. He tutted, wet his finger and wiped it clean. The woman looked up from her book at this, smiled, then returned to her reading. He sipped his tea, stretched his legs out under the table and had a closer look at his companion without, he hoped, her noticing. She was beautiful – Turkish, perhaps – with delicate features and eyes that were dark and far older than the rest of her. Her neck was long and stem-like, and he thought, she's beautiful.

The woman's eyes widened and she tried, unsuccessfully, to suppress a grin. She glanced at Eric, caught his stare and looked away again just as quickly. If Eric had not known better, he could have sworn she knew what he had been thinking. Perhaps she would let me buy her a drink, he wondered.

"I'm okay, thanks," she said.

"Sorry?"

"I don't want another drink."

Eric looked around him uncomfortably and then back at the woman who was starting a new page. He finished the tea in his cup and poured himself another from the pot.

"I'm twenty-three," she said, unprompted.

Eric made a face that seemed to say, "?"

"My age. It's twenty-three."

"How did you know I was wondering how old you are?"

She shrugged and grinned, still looking down at her book.

"What am I thinking now?" he asked after what was to him, at least, an uncomfortable silence, but this was only met with another shrug. As disconcerting as this strange woman was, he found he could not take his eyes from her. She drew her legs up to her chest and rested her chin on her knees. Her hair tumbled forward revealing a single daisy tucked between its strands.

"It's not black," she said with a note of irritation.

"What isn't?"

"My hair."

"Yes, it is."

"No, it isn't."

"Well, it looks black."

"But it's not."

"What colour is it then?"

"Dark brown."

"Brown/black."

"Brown!"

Eric dismounted from the debate. He wasn't going to win it, and what did it matter anyway? It was black, though, he thought. She let that one go.

"How did you know I was thinking that anyway?"

"Your head's pretty loud." Then, turning to him: "Do you get shushed in cinemas?"

"What do you mean my head's loud?"

"It sounds like pots and pans in a tumble dryer."

"And you can hear it?"

"You even scared the birds away."

"What birds? There aren't any birds."

"That's what I just said, isn't it?" she replied, proving anyone who doubted it wrong that you can, actually, spit words.

This was all new to Eric. Amber was confident and strong-willed. He liked that about her. They had enjoyed similar back and forths, but at least on those occasions Eric was able to gather his thoughts and choose his words. It rarely made a difference, as Amber always won, but at least he was starting with a chance, however slim. Having someone replying to something you hadn't yet decided to say or how you would say it, left him at too much of a disadvantage.

"What's your name?" he asked, hoping this would put him on surer ground. And for a moment, it did.

"Suzan," she replied, "with a zed."

"Mine's Eric," said Eric, "though you probably already knew that."

"How could I have done? I haven't asked to see your driving license, have I?"

"But you . . ." stammered Eric.

"But I what?"

"Nothing," puffed Eric. "Nothing at all."

"And don't sulk, either!"

"I'm not sulking!"

"Yes, you are."

Eric's frustration mounted, much to Suzan's perverse pleasure. He looked around the café at the other customers, sipping coffees, licking ice creams and chatting away. They were having perfectly normal conversations. Although it did occur to him, that he wouldn't know. To them, if they had been watching, he and Suzan would have appeared to be having a perfectly normal conversation too.

"Do you work at this place, Suzan with a zed?" asked Eric testily.

"Why do you ask?"

"It's just that I'm wondering if this abuse comes free or if I can expect it added to my bill."

"No, it's a hobby of mine."

Eric downgraded his mood from sulking to merely pouting.

"I used to collect stamps."

"I bet you were beating the girls off with a stick, weren't you."

"Philately will get you nowhere."

Suzan closed her book, set it down in front of her and sat as if in anticipation.

"So how did you die?" he asked, abruptly.

"You haven't been dead long have you."

"Is it that obvious?"

"Asking someone how they died is just bad etiquette."

"I'm sorry. No one told me."

"They didn't mention it at your induction?"

"I didn't have one of those."

"Figures."

Suzan reached across the table, slipped her finger into Eric's tea and allowed a drop to trickle down the side, leaving behind a stain.

"What did you do that for?" asked Eric.

"It annoys you."

"And that's a reason, is it?"

"You should be honoured. I don't make the effort to annoy just anybody, you know. There are those who'd have gasped at what I just did and backed away reverently to leave us alone."

Eric stared at the tea stain on the side of the cup and resolved to not give her the satisfaction of wiping it clean. He had to fight against a voice in his head that sounded suspiciously like Suzan's which told him to go on because he knew he wanted to. He tried changing the subject, but the matter of the stain would simply not go away. Very much like the stain. It shone to him like a beacon and there was no way he was going to put his lips to that cup till it was gone. Eventually, as casually as he could, and provoking sniggers from Suzan, he wet his finger on his tongue and wiped it clean. It was not mentioned again.

"So, we are actually dead then, are we?" asked Eric.

"We died, if that is what you mean," she replied, but her emphasis on the word 'died' suggested she was making a subtle point. Too subtle, however, for Eric.

"So what do you do here? In Heaven, I mean," asked Eric in an effort to move things on.

"You know this is Heaven?"

"Isn't it?"

"You tell me."

"What else could it be?"

"I must be then."

There was something in Suzan's final comment that hung heavy in the air.

"But you don't think it is?"

"Oh, I think it is."

"Then why ask?" demanded Eric, exasperated.

"What I think and what you think might be two different things entirely."

"And that makes a difference as to whether this is Heaven or not?"

"More than you realise."

"There's a lot I don't realise these days," he said, after a brief pause, and lapsed into contemplative silence.

"I live at a commune," said Suzan at last.

"What?"

"You asked what I do here. I'm telling you. I live at a commune."

"Really? That's interesting. How does that work?" asked Eric, glad to be off the previous topic, though it still ran around in his head along with everything else.

"We just sort of all muck in. We've all got things we're good at, but so long as everything gets done and you do your fair share, it doesn't really matter."

Eric tried to imagine himself living in that sort of environment and although it appealed, he just could not see himself fitting in. It would be all tie-dyed clothes, dreadlocks and white people drumming by the fire.

"It's not what you think," said Suzan, reading his mind.

"No, it's not really me. I'm no good at anything for a start."

"If you don't mind getting your hands dirty someone will find you something to do."

"I like to cook," offered Eric after a moment's reflection.

"Well, there you are then. We can always do with good cooks."

"No," said Eric again after a short pause. "I've got things here to take care of."

"What things?"

Eric shook his head.

"Just things."

"Important things?"

"I'll let you know as soon as I do."

A curl of hair, dark brown or black, depending on who you asked, came unhooked from behind Suzan's ear. She replaced it with a finger and said, not looking at Eric: "You know the really important things in life? I mean the really important things?"

"No, but go on."

"There's always enough time for them. No matter what else you busy yourself with, there is always just enough time left."

"I'll bear that in mind."

"That's your whole problem."

"What is? My mind?"

"I think it is about time you made it up."

"Make up my mind? Is that what you mean?"

"Stop asking what I mean."

"Then be a little clearer, and I won't have to!"

"It isn't me who isn't clear."

"There you go again!"

"There I go again what?"

"I'll need a boy scout to untie my brain from the knots you've left it in!" said Eric, after first having to unscramble his words, which were all trying to get out at the same time, like Italians alighting a train.

Suzan cackled delightedly.

"That's quite a laugh you've got there," said Eric, bitterly.

"Isn't it just!"

The bell went for Round Two, or was it Round three?

Eric was too punch drunk to count. He sat in his corner, unwrapped a biscuit that had come with his tea, bit into it, brushed away the crumbs from his shirt, and contemplated the other customers once more. They seemed to be coping well enough with being dead, if that is what they were (he still wasn't ready to completely concede that point). Then again, most people seemed to be coping well enough with life, and he knew that was definitely not true for most of them. Even those who seemed the most together, you'd often find out, were struggling as much as, if not more than, anyone else. Being human was difficult, and the effort required to make it look easy must be exhausting. Those who refused to pretend otherwise were often labelled as troubled, but refusing to adjust to a society that had it all wrong was surely the most sensible thing you could do. It was, at the very least, authentic. For a start, humans generally had to work more hours than they slept and would often be too tired to enjoy what little free time they had. And yet everyone seemed to just go along with that, even though they knew it was absurd. Added to that, despite all the hours they worked, almost everyone struggled to get by, to live in a decent house, to eat and go out once in a while. Not without getting into debt. Their solution? Work harder; work for longer. Again, people just went along with it, as if it were a force of nature they just had to accept and not just an idea that someone had and can't believe they're getting away with. Pretending it's all okay must cause a dissonance that's unsustainable. No wonder there was so much stress and anxiety about. The point Eric was getting to was that if people could smile through that and say 'I'm good' every time they're asked, then making out you're fine with being dead shouldn't be too difficult.

Seconds out, Round Four.

"Good book?" asked Eric, hoping this change of subject would be more successful than the last.

"Yes, thank you."

"What's it about?"

"I could tell you, but you wouldn't understand."

"Too complicated for me?" asked a wounded Eric.

"No. Too simple."

"How can anything be too simple?"

"It's the simple things that are so easily overlooked by people like you."

"People like me?"

"People who don't see the simple answers *because* they're simple."

"I don't do that," protested Eric, though it was not something he had given much thought to. Perhaps he did.

"Really?" replied Suzan, doubtfully. "I suppose that explains why you're so on top of everything right now."

"How do you know I'm not?"

"Because you're too easy to send round in circles. It's almost no fun at all."

"Then don't do it!"

She leant forward and ruffled Eric's hair.

"Oh, you love it really!"

She regarded his crown, critically.

"You look better with messy hair. Almost passable."

"Really?" replied Eric, rashly. "You should see me first thing in the morning."

"I wouldn't count on it."

His face may not have actually turned red, but it certainly felt hotter when he realised what he had walked into.

"Oh, no, I didn't mean . . ."

Suzan slurped the remaining milkshake from the bottom of her glass, popped the book she had been reading into her bag and stood up. She wrote down an address on a napkin.

"That's the commune if you change your mind. I think you'd like it there."

She kissed Eric on a thinning patch of hair on the top of his head, which he didn't yet know was there, and bounded off with long, reaching strides for such a short woman.

"Bye!" shouted Eric.

"Bye, Mr Craxxi!" yelled Suzan over her shoulder.

Eric inhaled a mouthful of tea down the wrong hole and sprayed it out of his nose and back into the cup without spilling a drop, a feat he would not be able to repeat if he tried.

"What did she call me?" he spluttered, wiping salty tea from his chin.

TWELVE

Sun Yu sat cross-legged, grinding dried herbs into a fine powder with a mortar and pestle. His clear, green eyes never blinked as the steady rhythm of the motion caused a strand of white hair to become unhooked from behind his left ear and settle against his cheek.

He was an old man but sustained by a spirit which kept him youthful. Even trees which are many centuries old are renewed every year with fresh vegetation as nature exhales gently after the winter months and its warming breath returns life and colour to all things. And that was Sun Yu's secret. When nature sighed, his own lungs filled with life. He had lost nothing with the passing of the years except his youthful fierceness. The universe had been to him back then a horse to be tamed and ridden. And before he learnt that answers would come to him, he went for them like a gold prospector, willing to give up his life for the sake of discovering a rich seam to mine.

He had given up everything he would later come to miss for the sake of knowing. His pursuit was not, however, for knowledge. That was what scientists with microscopes and test tubes sought: a myopic understanding of reality that was far too limited for the boundless nature of his mind. He had, as a young man, committed himself to the life of a monk, but it did not take long for him to clash with his peers and leave them behind too in his search for truth.

He wandered for months through the forests and mountains of his country in an ever-desperate attempt to be alone and to find a space broad enough for him to feel accommodated. But no landscape satisfied him.

All that remained for him to be free of was his own body. He made a home in the hollow bough of a tree, bound his knees to his chest, closed his eyes, and waited to die.

He woke up days, perhaps weeks, later in a monastery being administered small pieces of bread that had been soaked in goat's milk. The young monk who had been given the job of looking after him did not look especially wise to Sun Yu. He certainly wasn't kind. Caring for this stranger was an inconvenience for him that stood between him and his spiritual practice. Had he thought that caring for another human was spiritual practice as was, for that matter, sweeping the floors, tending to the garden, chopping vegetables, washing and even breathing in and out, he might have gained something. He too was young, however, and was still learning.

Sun Yu slowly regained his strength and took up duties of his own. At first, it was he who had to wake before everyone else and restart the fires by adding wood and gently blowing on the still orange cinders, before suspending a cauldron of water over the flames and laying out the bowls for breakfast. It wasn't a particularly challenging task. You had to make sure the water didn't boil over and put the flames out. If you took too much wood out, the water wouldn't boil at all. But once you got used to that, there was nothing to it really. This went on a year, without any talk of being promoted to the one who mopped the floors. Allowing impatience to get the better of him, in a very un-monk-like way, he stopped by the head monk's room, making sure he wasn't meditating.

"While I am pleased to be performing such an essential service," Sun Yu said, "I was hoping you might see fit to moving me on to another duty."

The head monk didn't smile, but his eyes sparkled as if he were. Sun Yu couldn't tell how old he was, but there was no one at the monastery who started there before him.

"What lessons have you learnt from your morning chores?"

"None," he admitted.

The head monk returned Sun Yu to his morning routine. He felt like he had been sent back to square one while playing a game of Snakes and Ladders. He considered leaving the monastery. He had paid off his debt to them for looking after him long ago, and he really didn't owe them anything anymore. But go where? He wasn't ready to return home, so he stayed.

Lack of challenge led him to become complacent though. He'd set the fire and started on his next job before making sure it was not too fierce or too weak. Often, the cook would arrive and there would either be luke-warm water over a weak fire, or no fire at all as it had been put out by the boiling water above it. Eventually, a complaint was made, and Sun Yu was summoned to the head monk.

"What lessons have you learned?"

Sun Yu was embarrassed to even be there. He had one simple job, and he couldn't manage it. He shrugged.

"Take better care of the fire."

The head monk seemed satisfied with the answer and sent him away. The next morning, he woke earlier than usual, determined to not mess up again. He hadn't slept well. The shame of not being able to progress from the bottom-rung of all chores after so long ate at him. If he couldn't even do that right, what chance did he have of becoming enlightened? Still berating himself, Sun Yu went down to the kitchen and, admonishing himself under his breath, he set about starting the fire and filling the cauldron. Instead of starting on laying the bowls out, he crouched by the fire, while keeping one eye on the water. The fire raged as he added thicker pieces of wood. Slowly, the water began to boil. At first, tiny bubbles popped at the edges of the cauldron. Then, later, larger bubbles erupted at the surface near the middle. That was Sun Yu's cue to remove the largest of the pieces of wood. By removing and adding variously sized pieces of wood, Sun Yu kept the water boiling nicely. When the cook turned up, he looked at the fire, noted the water and nodded his approval at Sun Yu. Every morning after that, he woke early and performed the same meticulous ritual, and the cook never failed to give him an affirming nod. After several months of this, Sun Yu became an expert at knowing how much wood to place onto the fire and when. And far from being frustrated with his lack of progress, he found himself more relaxed than he had been for a long time. Perhaps ever. Every time he became worked up by thoughts of impatience he would think of the fire and, as if they were burning logs, remove those thoughts from his mind. Likewise, when he worried he was getting too comfortable where he was, both literally and spiritually, he focused on a thought and let that burn inside him.

Two years after their first meeting, the head monk asked to see Sun Yu again.

"What have you learned?"

Sun Yu still didn't know. And then the head monk did something that took him by surprise: he removed a long stick from inside his gown and hit Sun Yu across the head with it. It was not a gentle tap either. He brought his hand down and saw blood smeared across it. Sun Yu was more confused than angry. However, three more blows to his head cleared up that confusion. Now he was just angry. The head monk was now standing over him as he cowered. Sun Yu waited for the stick to come down again and caught it. He tore it from the old man's hands and held it with both hands, over his right shoulder, ready to strike back boiling over, as he was, with hurt and rage. But the head monk made no move to defend himself. In fact, he appeared to be waiting happily for the attack that was coming to him. He stood perfectly still and smiled.

Sun Yu felt some of the heat leave his mind and, though still breathing erratically, he calmed down. He lowered the stick and sat back down heavily. The head monk knew better than to speak in that moment. He simply waited. Sun Yu saw an image of the cauldron boiling over. He could hear the flames hissing beneath as they began to go out. He saw himself removing the largest log. The water settled into a steady boil and the fire continued burning: a beautiful balance now achieved. He closed his eyes and his breathing settled into a slow, steady rhythm. He allowed his angry thoughts and emotions to arise one by one from wherever thoughts do, and just as they appeared, they unravelled and vanished back to nowhere. After an hour of sitting like that, only observing as thoughts and feelings came and went, he opened his eyes: a beautiful balance now achieved.

The head monk had not moved at all.

"What have you learnt?"

"Observed, our thoughts neither send our minds raging out of control, nor do they allow us to sleep through our days."

"Balance," said the head monk.

He continued in his role of starting the fire every morning. The only progression he really needed had already happened. In the years that followed, he never allowed the water to boil over. Nor did he let the fire go out, always keeping a perfect equilibrium between the two elements.

He left the monastery ten years after being rescued and walked back to his family, following the course of the river through steep valleys, sleeping by the water's edge at night and living off berries and edible leaves. It took him three months to reach the outskirts of the city he had left a decade prior. He descended the horseshoe shaped hills against which the sprawling buildings and roads nestled like a baby in the nook of its mother's elbow. As he got closer, he could hear the bustle of the people below him and smell their cooking, their animals and their sewage.

He made his way straight to the busy central market and entered the frantic throng. He had not noticed before, but it was so clear to him now, that people in crowds follow patterns. What seemed to him before nothing but chaos emerged in his vision now as a flow. One which he could step into and ride without being bumped, elbowed or shouted at.

From there he followed the quieter side streets to his home where his wife and three children would doubtless still be. He had no speech rehearsed for his reappearance. Nor any explanation for his sudden absence. He was comforted by the confidence of knowing that the person he was now could cope with anything that came his way.

But one thing he had not known was that his wife was dead. She had passed away four months previously from a tiny cut that had become infected. In his home now his wife's sister looked after his children who had been so young when he left that only the eldest recognised who he was; but barely.

The sister was angry, he could tell that, but she bit her tongue and prepared a meal for him, which he ate mindfully. Despite his prior confidence, his sister-in-law was less forgiving than he had expected, and his children found it difficult to reconcile the reality of him with the space he had left behind and which they had filled with their imaginations built on fragments of memories and stories of him.

But he was enlightened now. They couldn't see it perhaps – how could they, any more than a beginner at chess can recognise a good move made by a master from a bad one? However wise he was though, he found that keeping a pot of water from boiling over was a lot easier than keeping his sister-in-law from finding it increasingly impossible to hide her anger towards him. What was the point of gaining spiritual knowledge, he asked himself, if he couldn't apply it to a routine family dynamic? Disconcerted by this he spent as much time away from his home as he could. News about his spiritual journey had become widely known and he had gained some small measure of fame and respect from the community. What right he thought he had dishing out wisdom when his own personal life was in a mess, even he couldn't have told you, except maybe that he saw it as his duty.

The life of a busy city turned out to be far too complex to be captured by what he had learnt in the solitude of the mountains. Too often, those he had imparted advice to came back disappointed, demanding more. And sometimes, the fruits of his wisdom caused matters to become worse. He was at a loss to understand what was going wrong and about a year after his return from the wilderness no one went to him for advice anymore. His own life, too, had not yielded to his superior knowledge. The words sprinkled from his mouth like seeds, but the ground they fell upon was sterile and they never grew into flowers.

He had married his sister-in-law, who was herself a widow, but that was only for propriety's sake. She still despised him. His greatest efforts to second guess the situations he found himself in inevitably failed. He retreated into his garden more and more, where he found solace in growing vegetables. He took comfort in being able, there at least, to sow seeds and make them grow. There, if nowhere else, he could control the way things turned out. But even there, he was to learn he was wrong. One spring, to attract pollinators, he sowed two sunflower seeds and watered them regularly. They both germinated at about the same time and grew, at the beginning at least, at the same rate. After a month, however, one plant grew more rapidly than the other and was soon at least twice his height, with a flower the size (he exaggerated) of a wagon wheel. The other was a little shorter than he was, but instead of growing just one flower, it grew as many as fourteen much smaller ones, up and down its rigid, prickly stem.

Two seeds, apparently identical and grown the same way, yet growing in an utterly unpredictable fashion. He could know, he realised gloomily, that a sunflower would grow from a sunflower seed, but beyond that there was nothing else he could predict. Every seed he had ever sown had grown just as unpredictably. Every word he spoke, every action he took, were causes which had effects he could no more foresee than he could control. It was, he understood suddenly, just chaos. Out of that chaos an order would emerge, but the appearance of order should not fool him into being so arrogant as to think he could shape it to his will. The crowd in the market he had walked among on his first day back had order but underpinning it all was disorder.

Being involved in change makes us all, he knew, agents of change; but only unwittingly so. What intrigued him now was why had he been so certain of himself before? How could he have been so arrogant as to assume himself to be some sort of barometer of reality, not least of all because at the time he had thought himself humble. Perhaps it had all been nothing more than a conceit. The idea that he could truly know by not knowing. That by emptying his mind there would be room for the universe and everything it knew too. Was it all just an elaborate ruse laid by his ego to allow him to think he was wise while, all along, pretending to be too humble to ever really think so; a giant edifice built by his pride to let him convince himself he was better than the ignorant masses?

When you know, you know, he had told people who wanted to be able to recognise the truth when they saw it. He winced at the memory of telling an earnest young man who doubted him that some things were beyond words; that he could not explain to a fish what it was like to live on dry land.

Had he really said that?

Thinking that you know the secrets of the universe or have access to some sort of universal truth is powerfully seductive. It goes to the heart of our humanity. We have always wanted to know. So desperate can we get that we are willing to rush to it. Science begins with the premise that we do not know and are not arbiters of truth. It requires us to form hypotheses and to test them, to conduct experiments, to repeat the results, and for other people to be able to repeat them too. It was the most humble position before the universe humans had ever taken. And he had once thought the scientists arrogant.

Science, he still knew, was limited. There would be some things, perhaps, that it would never discover. But in acknowledging those limits, scientists were not so very different from the true sages he had met. The men and women who had appeared so wise that they never made mistakes. The truth of that was that they knew what they did know and fully accepted what they did not. They did not stumble, not because they were omniscient, but because they were not so foolhardy as to tread blindly on a path they assumed, incorrectly, had no obstacles. They trod carefully, not boldly. Since his return, Sun Yu had been consistently making the mistakes of a blind man who thought he could see.

He finished watering his garden and walked back inside where his sister-in-law and three children were. He wanted to say sorry to them. But all men say sorry. What they deserved was for him to know that he did not know anything and to remember that. He would stop trying to be wise, begin embracing his ignorance and give up on the need for certainty in a chaotic universe. He would no longer take it upon himself to attempt to shape events but to watch them flower instead. That was the very best way he could make it up to his family and to honour the memory of his late wife. At the thought of her, tears dampened his eyes for the first time since he had learnt about her death. He had thought himself too wise to cry. Now he wept.

~

Now, grinding herbs in his hut, he smiled warmly. Carmine Craxxi had come for answers to a man who had long ago given up hope of finding them. If he could make his student give up too, he might just find the Heaven he was looking for.

Carmine Craxxi kicked the door to the hut open and dropped a bundle of logs by the fire. Wind and rain swept into the hut and Craxxi slammed the door shut. Wiping wet hair from his forehead where it was sticking to his skin, he let out an exclamation.

"It's hell out there," he said.

"No," replied Sun Yu, tapping the side of Craxxi's head. "It's hell in there."

Craxxi peeled his wet jacket off and removed his trousers before drying himself roughly with a towel.

"You were gone a long time," observed Sun Yu.

"I had to go a long way to find a halfway decent tree."

"There is a tree just a few yards from the door."

Craxxi finished towelling himself down, flattened his hair and moved onto the floor closer the fire.

"That twisted thing? It's useless."

Sun Yu continued to grind though by now probably unnecessarily.

"Why useless?"

"It's gnarled. You can't get an axe through that."

Sun Yu raised his eyebrows and dropped them again in a gesture that let his student know he found this interesting.

"What?" asked Craxxi after a moment spent trying to work out for himself what the old man had meant.

"That tree is very old."

"Because no one wants to cut it down."

Sun Yu did not reply. Carmine Craxxi was already beginning to find the old man's silences more significant than the things he said and wondered what he was trying to say.

"So, what am I doing here?" asked Craxxi after a minute's silence.

Sun Yu shrugged.

"Come on, old man. You're holding out on me. I know it."

"You are assuming too much."

"Well, I am not going to rot away out here."

Sun Yu said he was glad to hear it, but in a disinterested tone of voice.

"So, what is this place, anyway?" asked Craxxi. "You've never actually said."

"We are," said Sun Yu, resuming his grinding, "neither here nor there."

"Why can't you give straight answers?" asked Craxxi, frustration tugging at his voice.

"That was a straight answer," insisted Sun Yu.

Craxxi arched his back and rubbed his face roughly with the palm of his hands.

"Tell me what question I should ask, and I'll ask it."

Sun Yu rose from his cross-legged position without having to push himself off the floor with his hands.

"Come with me."

"Where are we going?" asked Craxxi who looked as if any movement was an effort too far.

"Fishing."

The rain had abated but tiny droplets were being swirled around by the wind and attacked Carmine Craxxi like ice cold pin pricks. He was woefully dressed for the weather in his now tattered suit, and he wrapped his arms around his torso for warmth. The two men were standing beside a stream that had broadened at that point and was moving slowly.

"Are you out of your mind?" he yelled at Sun Yu, who seemed unbothered by the chill wind.

"You have to catch our supper. We have nothing left to eat."

"We don't have any rods," protested Craxxi, not unreasonably. "What do you want to use? Our hands?"

Sun Yu smiled.

"Not our hands. Yours."

"Why me?"

"Because it is you, not I, who wants to find Heaven."

"And I'll find it in there?" he asked pointing to the shallow water.

Craxxi stared at Sun Yu thinking, then shook his head in a gesture that made it clear that what he was about to do ran contrary to his better judgement. He hopped on one leg, taking his shoes and socks off. He rolled his trousers up and waded into the cold stream, up to just below his knees, treading carefully on the sharp stones.

"My toes are going to freeze off," he said and started to move about in a stoop looking for fish as Sun Yu watched on, faintly amused.

"And you can stop smiling," he bellowed.

Craxxi stepped heavily, staring hard at the water, trying to ignore the cold. After several minutes he stood up straight and protested.

"This is ridiculous, and I am going to die from hypothermia here."

"Then give up."

Carmine Craxxi was a proud and stubborn man and had no intention of failing quite so easily. A few minutes later he spotted his first fish. It was about six inches long and shimmering ripples moved down its sleek body as it held itself steady against the flow of the stream. Craxxi's eyes widened with anticipation. He held himself still for as long as he could bear before lunging clumsily forward and toppling headfirst into the freezing water.

Sun Yu laughed wildly while Craxxi's rage burnt so hot it might have caused his wet clothes to dry in an instant. Undeterred, he righted himself and resumed his hunched over stance. A minute later another fish caught his eye. This time he kept as still as he could, though he was betrayed by now uncontrollable paroxysms of shivering. The fish darted forward, then held its position, allowed the flow of the water to push it back, before darting forward again. Craxxi coiled his legs and leaped forward in a froth of displaced water and plunged his hands into the water, but they came out empty.

Craxxi cursed vividly, turning the air as blue as his extremities were becoming. He could no longer feel his feet and his hands were numb, so it was doubtful he would have been able to grip the fish if he did manage to get that close to one.

That evening, Craxxi sat on the floor of the hut, wrapped in a blanket, and his feet as close to the fire as he could get them without burning the skin. In his hands he cupped a bowl of rice, which he ate hungrily with his fingers.

"I am getting bored with rice all the time."

"Catch a fish and we'll eat that."

"Get me a rod and I'll catch a fish," replied Craxxi, his voice louder than it needed to be. "I must have been out of my mind to go along with that."

"Try again tomorrow."

"Are you crazy? You can't catch fish like that. I'm not going back in there."

"I told you. When you want Heaven more than you want air to breathe, then you can have it."

"I won't find paradise in a fish."

"You'd be surprised," was Sun Yu's enigmatic reply, and that was the last thing he said all night.

After eating they made themselves comfortable and talked long into the night. Sun Yu was unusually talkative, telling Craxxi of the myths and legends of the culture he had grown up in. As the fire was dying down, he started on the story of the two monks who were walking along a riverbank when they came across a beautiful woman who wanted to get across to the other side but didn't want to make her clothes wet. The first monk blushed and turned his eyes to the ground, but the second monk, in a direct contravention of the rules of the order they belonged to, which forbade any physical contact at all with the opposite sex, gathered the woman up in his arms and carried her across. He then waded back, and the two monks carried on their way. About a mile on the first monk, clearly troubled, admonished his companion for his previous actions. To this, the monk who had carried the woman across the river said: "I put her down a mile away, but I can see you are still carrying her."

Sun Yu allowed silence to get to work and ceased speaking. Craxxi pondered this story for a about thirty seconds then delivered his verdict.

"He would say that, wouldn't he."

"Why?"

"It's like a politician who is caught doing something he shouldn't have been doing. He stands up in front of the media, says he's sorry and now it's time to move on. But he just wants the story to go away so it won't damage his career anymore."

"The moral of the story is that the first monk was holding onto the past whereas the second monk was living only in the present."

"I should have tried that," said Craxxi, grinning. "Your honour, so I used threats of violence to extort money from my victims, but that was in the past: you wanna try living in the present a little more."

Sun Yu laughed and admitted he had not thought of the story like that before.

"Or maybe I'm just missing the point."

"No," said Sun Yu, happily. "You just discovered another."

Craxxi gathered his bedding around him and settled down beside the fire. Smiling still, he slipped his hands under his head for a pillow, closed his eyes and went to sleep.

The following morning, Sun Yu woke early and Craxxi was already nowhere to be seen. He arranged himself into a meditation position and closed his eyes. He was unable to get his mind to settle, however. While unusual, this was still not a thing of the past for Sun Yu. But he had learnt to persist. There was no such thing as a bad meditation. It was not something you did to quieten the mind; the human mind just doesn't work that way. Thoughts come and thoughts go. There was nothing you could do to stop that. You could either live a life where you became lost in those thoughts for several minutes, days, or even years, or you could learn to notice them. That was usually all it took to make them go away. But you needed to remember to notice. That was what meditation was for: to get you used to it, so that when you were washing pots, cooking or taking a walk, you didn't forget to notice.

By mid-morning he had finished meditating and had begun preparing rice for lunch. The rain of the previous day had moved away, but while sunny, it was still cold. He had just poured the rinsed rice into the boiling pot when the door was kicked open and a soaking wet and frustrated Carmine Craxxi barged in, slamming it behind him.

Sun Yu said nothing. Craxxi dried himself and sat staring at his crossed feet, bare and blue, for several minutes. It had been many years since he had felt so helpless, and he did not like it. When life did not go the way, he wanted it to, he was used to having something — or someone — to rage against. And for that rage to make things happen. But there was nothing for him to direct his anger at now. He was a wind in search of a sail, and the effort to stay angry when no one else noticed was becoming difficult to maintain.

The only person left to be angry at was himself, and in that regard, he had formidable opposition.

Once the rice was boiled and served, the two men ate in silence. Or at least, there were no words exchanged between them. The space between Craxxi's ears was a noisy place, with several voices straining to be heard over each other. He finished his food and, without a word, strode purposefully out of the hut into the fresh and heavily scented woodland air.

A thick branch of a tree had snapped off at some point in the winter during a storm and now a shaft of warming sunlight shone through the broken canopy and onto the damp, soft ground. Already, seeds which had lain dormant for years were sensing the warmth beneath the surface of decomposing leaves and a chemical reaction was being triggered within them. Within a couple of weeks green shoots would emerge, uncurling into the light, racing to be the quickest to grow so as to make the most of the favourable conditions for life, while shading those beneath so that their own growth is checked.

If they could think and could look out beyond themselves into the dense, wooded area, they would see no evidence of life that they could recognise as such, anywhere else. They may then be forgiven for thinking that they were somehow special: singled out for the gift of life. For as far as they could see, nowhere else were the conditions for life so perfect as they were right where they existed. The coincidence would be too mind-boggling for them to calculate or to not imagine that they were blessed. By what, or by whom? They would look above them to the source of their life: the warm, golden rays that broke through the gap in the ceiling of the world so well placed that it had to have been wrenched open by an unseen hand. But one day the canopy of leaves would fill in, slowly cutting off the sun, shutting down the Heavenly beam and rendering the patch below lifeless once more.

Carmine Craxxi stepped by, unaware that he was witness to the birth of a civilisation, did not stop until he reached the stream. He rolled up his trousers and waded into the cold water. Standing perfectly still he enjoyed the feeling of the water rushing through the hairs on his legs. The sun was now at its highest point, and it warmed the area between his shoulders pleasantly.

What Craxxi did not appreciate was that direct sunlight was something fish shied away from. Instinctively though he began searching the shaded areas beneath the overhanging bushes, which grew from the rocky sides. It took a minute or two for his eyes to become adjusted. Once they were he saw the reproachful eyes of a fish, itself hunting for food. He slowed his breathing and leaned in closer. As he did, he blocked the sun and cast a shadow over the fish, which there one moment, was gone the next. He cursed quietly to himself but kept his temper in check.

Thirteen

On Earth, Eric had always kept himself busy. Now he knew why. Three days alone in a hotel room, living off room service and occasional infusions of whisky, were enough to make even him sick of his own company. He was appalled at how boring he really was. Deprived of human contact and intellectual stimulation he was left to rely on himself for original ideas only to discover he had none.

He had tried avoiding thinking any more about those he had left behind. But in the absence of anything else he was finding them increasingly difficult to ignore. He fell into thinking about Amber and wondering how she had coped with his death and how quickly she would move on. He wanted her to meet someone else and be happy—of course he did—it was just the thought of her with someone else, no longer sad for him, that he was having trouble with. The memory of her stirred in him a feeling he had dreamt about the night before. He closed his eyes and tried to remember it, but whatever it was, it remained just beyond his vision.

He thought back to the last thing he could remember.

He had left work a few minutes before one o'clock to meet Amber for lunch. This was something they tried to do once a week, as their places of work were close to each other. He thought about taking the newspaper he had bought on the way to work with him, but decided not to and dropped it on his desk. What was the article he had been reading?

Cameras. He was thinking about buying a digital camera. There was a shop that sold some next to the pet shop. He remembered a sign which amused him. It said something like: a camera takes pictures like a phone, only better! Clearly aimed at the younger person who probably had no idea that cameras and phones used to be two different things.

Perhaps if he could remember what he had to eat that day? He thought hard, until he realised they had never made it to lunch. But why not? What had happened?

They were walking. Amber was replying to a text on her phone. Eric was thinking about glasses. He had been working at a computer for ten years now, and he was sure he was beginning to notice a deterioration in his sight. Amber wore glasses, and he liked them on her. He just wasn't sure any would suit him. He had tried growing out a beard once, but he had to admit that he just wasn't the beard-wearing type. Perhaps glasses would make his face more interesting.

Then nothing.

He closed his eyes and attempted to force the memory from his mind. He rolled out of bed, in which he had practically set up camp and picked up a newspaper which had been delivered that morning. He sat on the sofa and thumbed through to the information section hoping there would be some sort of department that could answer his question but there appeared to be no such service. He threw the paper down and buried his head in his hands. Between his fingers, however, he caught a glimpse of the word 'obituary'. He picked the paper up and, running his finger down the page, looked for the correct date and his name.

Panish, P; Paolo de, M; Peel, K; Peel, S; Pickles, A; Pickles E: Born 12 June, 1984. Died January 23, 2014. Cause of death: Murder.

Eric let the paper sag between his knees.

"Murder?"

He had been assuming that whoever had planted the bomb in his room had wanted to kill Carmine Craxxi. It never occurred to him to think that he, Eric, could have been the intended target all along. But who would want to kill him, and why? He had pretty much accepted that he was dead and not dreaming. However, coming to terms with that he had been the victim of a murder was going to prove much more difficult. Everyone died eventually, but how many were actually murdered? Had his life ended, not by some indifferent illness, freak accident or old age, but by some conscious, deliberate action that decided he would not get to live the rest of his life while others did? He stood up and paced the room, which for a hotel, was a good size for pacing. He clenched his fists and tried to make sense of it all. How dare they? What right did someone have to make that decision? And why were they, not satisfied with killing him once, trying to kill him again now he was in Heaven? How many times can you actually kill someone? He needed answers, and he headed out to the one place he knew of that might have them.

Eric took a cab directly to the Public Records Office this time. Laying low was all very good, but it took a huge chunk out of your day, and Eric wasn't in the mood to wait. He knew where to go now, so swept past the guard and made his way straight to the correct floor, took a number and sat, his right knee bouncing with nerves. When that number was called, he dried his palms on his trousers and attempted to look and sound calm when he arrived at the desk. Presenting his card, he asked to see not Carmine Craxxi's, but his own record. As he spoke, he was suddenly dubious that Carmine Craxxi would have permission to access someone else's file, but apparently, in Heaven they don't mind that sort of thing. He waited for the officer to return with the folder containing his life and went straight for the reading room, leaving the directions the officer gave him hanging in the air.

The first thing he noticed was that his file was thinner and lighter than Craxxi's. He didn't mind that. It was to be expected. He skipped the summary, went to year one, and scanned the pages for anything interesting. His early years had about a paragraph each, but as he got older, the paragraphs turned into pages. Much of it was already known to him, of course, but some of it was new. For instance, he didn't know his father had left him and his mother for two weeks when he was five years old. He did have a memory of him not being there and being told he was away working, but now he discovered it was more serious than that. His father had returned, and everything was apparently forgotten, but he thought about his mother and how she must have felt. He scanned his teenage years, not really wanting to go over all that again, and stopped at the point he met Amber. It was his first week of university. He had never been away from home before. He was anxious and excited in equal measure. He felt that everyone else was so much more confident about it all than he was, and that they were better prepared for life as an undergraduate. Of course, everyone felt the same. They just hid it well; as did Eric. He heard about a block party going on where he lived. He didn't like parties, really. He was not good at starting conversations, and he was even worse at keeping them going. He sat on the thin mattress on his narrow bed, pushed up against the edge of his cell-like room and realised he had to make up his mind about what sort of university experience he wanted. He wasn't sure, but he knew what was expected of him, so he doused himself in a cheap cologne he'd received for Christmas, gelled his hair rigid, and joined the party. He planned on the way up the stairs that he would stay for half an hour then go back to his room. At least he could say then that he had been. He let himself in. The nervous energy among the eighteen-year-olds, away from home for the first time and not used to drinking alcohol, could have caused electrical equipment to spark and die. He had brought a can of beer, which he opened and sipped from. He didn't like the taste, but it was too late to admit that now. He found a space against a wall and stood, his head nodding to the music, and trying to give the impression he was happy to remain aloof.

"You don't want to stand there on your own. I'm Amber."

And that was it. He didn't know now if he fell in love

in that exact moment or if he was just overwhelmed that a beautiful, well-dressed woman had made the effort to talk to him. He did know though that he had never quite got over it.

He skipped forward to graduation, then forward a few more years to his late twenties, depressed that in some years, the text didn't even reach to the bottom of the page. Then he came to the last page. He placed his finger under each word as he read:

On his way to lunch with Amber Eric was shot by a sniper. It was a crime that made national news. The police investigation was closed after six months for lack of evidence. The coroner concluded that his death was most probably the result of mistaken identity.

Six months? He had only been in Heaven three days. So, time flowed differently where he was. What was he to make of the mistaken identity verdict? If someone had killed him when he was alive, and wanted him dead again now he was already dead, there had to be a link, surely?

After a minute thinking about it, he went to close the file, but noticed a 'Profile' page at the back that he hadn't spotted in Craxxi's.

Eric lived his life as a frightened man, but he had no idea what he was frightened of. He held himself back from pursuing the life he wanted and had drifted into a pattern of behaviour that was safe.

Well, that's just not true, he thought.

If life were a swimming pool, Eric would never have swum out of the shallow end, even though he could swim. He fantasised about a life that was more interesting than his own, but he took no steps toward it. However, his ambitions were modest and not by any means unreachable. The tragedy of Eric's life is that he only ever had to let go of the handrail of life.

'Let go of the handrail.' That's what the strange man claiming to be an angel had said to him. But it was nonsense. He did have the life he wanted. Or at least he did, while it had lasted. He was with Amber; that was all he had really wanted. But was he all she had ever wanted? He hadn't thought of that before. She was smart, confident, ambitious, great with new people, inspiring to those around her and successful. If he looked up to her then did she look down on him? She would never have thought of it that way, but really, what did she see in him? The person he was or the person he could be? It was an awful thought to consider that Amber had been disappointed in him but loved him too much to say so. That she had hoped for more but settled for less. But what could he have done differently? He had no interests, really. Could that be true? Why be so sorry that he was almost definitely dead when he had done so little with his life while he had it? He had left nothing behind. Amber had tried in the months before his supposed death to bring up the subject of having children, but he had always tensed up inwardly and claimed to be too tired to have such a heavy conversation.

If he ever had the chance to do it all again, he promised himself, he would try harder to be, not the person Amber wanted him to be–she would never have wanted that–but the person *he* had always wanted to be. That's what would make her happy: to see him happy. As for what sort of person he wanted to be . . . well, finding that out could be fun. Did Heaven do second chances, though?

He returned the file and walked out of the climate-controlled building and into the warm, scented air of Heaven thinking about himself and about life. One question bothered him still, however: how can a person be killed in Heaven? Perhaps it was the same as being killed in a cartoon, he wondered, where anvils are not as heavy as they look and being shot makes your face spin around your head with a whizzing sound.

He considered going to the police, if there was such a thing in Heaven, and seeking their protection. However, as he soon realised, that would mean admitting to entering Heaven under a false identity and he was certain that would take a dim view. Suddenly, he felt very unsafe standing, as he was, beside a park, surrounded by tall buildings, from out of the windows of any of which might be poking, at that very moment, a sniper's rifle. He set off back to his hotel, walking in unpredictable zigzags all the way to foil the would-be assassin. This may have solicited odd looks from passersby, but they, Eric told himself, were not being lined up in someone's cross hairs.

By the time he reached his hotel he was cramping with nerves, and it was not until he had got back to his room that he started to relax. He poured himself another whisky, in defiance of his previously held plan to drink less and sat down. The party for Carmine Craxxi was the next day and he had no intention of attending it. It had been advertised all over the city and was far too much of a risk. He would not even have to offer an excuse, which Eric had always been terrible at doing; he even had the knack of making genuine reasons sound terribly contrived and implausible. No. He would simply not attend. He looked again at Suzan's address and decided that a life where each gave according to his means and took according to his needs sounded just about right at that moment, even though his needs, right then, outstripped his means several times over.

FOURTEEN

Carmine Craxxi was still hungry. He stared down at his empty bowl that had once held steaming rice and vegetables and groaned. There was more if he wanted it, but he couldn't live on that alone. The fishing expedition hadn't gone well. Using only his bare hands, he had been unable to catch his and Sun Yu's dinner. Even being as stubborn as he was, he had not been able to stand the cold water for long. Only now, having warmed his hands and feet by the fire for an hour were they somewhere near to their healthy colour. But he was still cold and wondered if he'd ever be warm again. Sun Yu, by contrast, had eaten lightly and gratefully, manipulating the chopsticks as if they were extensions of his own fingers. Craxxi's fingers had been too numb to hold them, so he used his hands, much to his dining companion's disgust.

"What was your life like?" asked Sun Yu, once they had settled with a cup of tea each.

"My life was good," said Craxxi, without hesitating.

"All good?"

"It came with its problems."

Sun Yu was curious what sort of problems such a powerful man might encounter in his life. He had known powerful men and women himself, and he had noticed just how vulnerable they really were. Not that they would have thought of it that way. If a person has to surround themselves with an army, how strong were they? He had never needed the protection of a fortified palace guarded by armed men, and he had always been perfectly safe. This had led him to meditate on the notion of power. Not many kings and queens lived to old age. The ones who did were lauded for the achievement. He had known a beggar who had lived well into his nineties, possibly more. He had nothing but had seen the rise and fall of ruling elites.

"Well, you know," continued Craxxi, "the higher up you go, the more there are guys who want to knock you off your perch and take over."

"I see."

"There's always a challenger. Even among your friends and family."

This sparked a memory in Sun Yu. When he was just a boy of about ten, his village had become excited by an older boy. He was particularly talented at martial arts. This meant something to the other villagers, because having someone like him as one of their own conferred status. Sun Yu would see him training every day, for hours, among a group of onlookers. One day, he heard his father and uncles talking about a challenge. From what he could tell, the older boy was going to travel to a village about a day away to challenge someone there to a fight. His father told him when he asked that that village had boasted the best fighter in the region for years and now they had a chance to take that distinction as their own. That's what the boy had been training so hard for.

Sun Yu had seen the boy training one morning on his way to school, but when he walked back that afternoon, he had gone. He found out that he had left to challenge this great fighter. Village life carried on, but not quite as normal. Sun Yu sensed that the adults were distracted. Then the older boy returned. Even Sun Yu could tell straight away there was something wrong. He didn't look like he had been defeated in a fight. He was not bruised or cut. He didn't exactly have the demeanour of a triumphant warrior either. A crowd soon gathered around him. Sun Yu continued on his way home, knowing he'd hear all about it from his father when they ate. And when they sat down with their food, his father just kept shaking his head. He didn't understand it. The boy had reached the village and made his challenge, but the warrior had taken a quick look at him and refused.

"So, we won," said Sun Yu.

"No," said his father, putting down his bowl, "don't you see? He didn't think our challenge was worth his trouble. He could have at least given him a thrashing. But to not even bother to get up from under his tree... it's too much."

"At least our challenger isn't hurt," Sun Yu replied.

"Not hurt?" His father was incredulous. "He's humiliated! He can never show his face. He was to be married when he returned, but the bride's father has called it off now. It's all over for him."

Sun Yu thought his father was being dramatic, but a week later, the boy was dead. He couldn't take the loss of face so took his own life. What shocked Sun Yu was that his father and uncles, and pretty much the whole village, agreed that he had done the right thing and soon the whole thing was forgotten. But Sun Yu didn't forget. He kept thinking about the man in the other village. He must have been a great warrior indeed if he could kill a challenger without having to even stand up.

Sun Yu asked, "Is that what happened to you? Someone knocked you off your perch?"

Craxxi looked off to one side, toward a memory. He didn't like it, so changed the subject.

"I'm going to catch a damn fish tomorrow."

The next day, Sun Yu woke and was surprised to see that Craxxi was already up and out of the house. His pupil was ankle deep in a freezing stream, hunting for his breakfast. His feet were beginning to turn blue, but he forced the pain from his mind. Stooping with his hands cradled above the surface of the water, he moved between the rocks, but when he saw a fish, it was only because it was darting away, startled by his motion.

By the time Sun Yu made it to the river and crouched unseen behind a shrub, Craxxi was keeping perfectly still, his hands inside the water. Sun Yu watched motionless as Craxxi stood without moving for several minutes. Craxxi was waiting where he knew the fish liked to feed, in the shade and protection of vegetation. Although cold, he enjoyed the feeling of the fast-moving water rushing around his legs. Confronted by someone like himself he would have stopped and tried to move him out of the way. But water, in its ego-less way, just went around him as if he were not there. How much further, he wondered, could he have made it in life had spent less time trying to move obstacles to his progress and instead, like water, just carried on going. He paused his breathing as a fish swam elegantly from behind a smooth rock toward him. He waited till it swam into his interlocked hands before snatching it from the water and holding it above his head and laughing crazily as it thrashed in his grip.

Sun Yu was already back in the hut when a triumphant Craxxi strode in and placed the still twitching fish on the table. He was shaking from the cold, but he didn't care.

"There, old man!" he said. "We're gonna eat well today."

Later that day, picking the last of the fish from its bones with chopsticks, Craxxi was feeling better than he had since the day he died.

"You know," he said, "I've eaten at the best restaurants, but I'll swear I never tasted anything better than that."

Sun Yu smiled.

"I never asked you how you managed to catch it."

Craxxi licked his fingers.

"I just kept still. I was spooking them with all my stomping. I kept still and it came to me."

"Just like answers."

"What do you mean?"

"When you first came here, your questions were scaring the answers away."

Craxxi placed his now empty bowl down. He could see now how he had been making a lot of noise. Most of it in his head.

"You're saying the answers will come to me if I stop asking questions?"

Sun Yu had come to like Carmine Craxxi. He even enjoyed his company, but now it was time to say goodbye to his guest. He picked up Craxxi's bowl in his bony hands and washed it lovingly. It wouldn't be needed any more.

"Come with me."

Craxxi followed Sun Yu into the second room. The old man pointed at the cauldron gathering water from a leak in the roof and asked him what he saw. Craxxi had been there before.

"Only a fool stares at the finger that points," said Sun Yu.

Craxxi stepped to the cauldron and bent at the waist and placed his nose to the surface, knowing what was about to happen. For the sake of form he asked, "What am I looking at?"

He felt Sun Yu's grip on the back of his neck and took a sharp last breath before being forced into the water. Instinctively, he gripped the sides of the cauldron and tried to force himself up.

When, even at the point of death, you desire the truth more than even air to breathe, then you may leave this place.

So powerful is the survival instinct that even though Craxxi had resolved to not fight for his life, the natural urge to breathe proved too powerful. He regretted giving in. He couldn't believe he could have been so stupid. What had happened to him that he would so easily surrender to this torture? But just as before, Sun Yu's grip was iron-like. He threw his fists and kicked out, but he never managed to land on anything solid, except the cauldron itself. His head began to throb, then pound. Sheer terror took him over. He had only seconds to live and he knew it. Terror gave way to peace. Peace to acceptance. He thought of the fish he had caught, and how he had caught it. He stopped thrashing and let death come to him. He let go of the sides and relaxed his body, his eyes open and staring at the black bottom of the cauldron. Then in the blackness, a smear of blue and green emerged. The coldness of the water was replaced by warmth on his back. Instead of the dull thump of sound travelling through water he could hear children playing.

He was standing in a park, under a blue sky and the late afternoon sun beating down on him. He spun around, but Sun Yu was gone. So was the hut and the forest. A cyclist's bell chimed, and he stepped out of the way onto the grass, his clothes now dry. He took a deep breath and found a bench to sit and orientate himself. Was this Heaven? He looked at his hands. They were no longer cracked from the hours spent fishing in the freezing stream. The park was surrounded by tall, white buildings that gleamed in the light. People strolled by, never in any hurry. A young couple walked past, holding hands and eating ice creams. He wondered if they had died together or had met here in Heaven. He didn't know what he needed to do next, but at that moment, none of that mattered to him. He'd made it. He heard the rattle of a tram pass by behind him. He looked round. On the side of the tram as it glided away on its rails was a poster:

Heaven welcomes Carmine Craxxi
Join him today from noon at the Trinity Hotel for an afternoon of
celebration.

Under the words was a picture of a smiling Eric.

The spiritual calm that had helped him into Heaven slipped like a tectonic plate. From beneath it, rage–hot and red–bubbled to the surface.

"Son of a bitch!"

FIFTEEN

Eric woke late. It was another beautiful day in Heaven. He stood on the balcony, wrapped in a thick, white robe, sipping tea and wondered if it ever rained there. People liked the rain. Perhaps not all the time, but after a long period of hot, dry weather, it felt good to stand outside in a storm. He'd never done it, of course, but he'd heard of others claiming they had. He scanned the city below and looked for where Suzan's commune might be. It was probably nestled somewhere in the ribbon of green that surrounded it.

After showering and packing some clothes and a wash bag into a holdall, he shut the door to his suite, perhaps for the last time, and made for the elevator. It was a long way down to the ground floor. When the doors swept open, the hotel manager spotted him and bounded over, arms apart. Eric had a flashback of vomiting all over him and cringed inwardly. The manager had appeared to have forgotten–or at least forgiven–the incident.

"Mr Craxxi! he enthused. "I am so glad to see you. Your guests are eager to see you."

Eric looked at his watch. It was one o'clock. Of course, the party in his honour. The manager took him by the arm and led him through to a ballroom where at least a hundred people were mingling, snatching at canapés as they passed by on trays and sipping free wine.

"Look," protested Eric, "I have somewhere I need to be."

"Nonsense!" said the manager, with a dismissive sweep of his free arm. "This is your party. You can't miss it!"

Eric still hoped to be able to slip out unnoticed, but that was dashed when a band started playing and everyone in the room turned to applaud him. Okay, thought Eric. I'll stay an hour, speak to a few people, then sneak out.

Like most people, Eric was not great at parties. He was especially not looking forward to being the centre of attention. He had always wanted to be that kind of person, but he just wasn't built that way. Amber was. She didn't crave the spotlight, but when it fell on her, as it usually did, she handled it with grace. Eric could be standing at her elbow, but he may as well have been invisible. Not to Amber, though. She would squeeze his hand to let him know that he was at the centre of her attention at least. He had been missing her, but he felt her absence keenly now. He took on the guests and it occurred to him that they must all believe he was a notorious New York gangster, and yet there they all were anyway.

The first of the guests approached: an elegant woman in her forties, dressed in a lime-green dress that followed her figure down to her ankles. Her bare shoulders were broad and slender, and large jewellery slid up and down her arms, swung from her neck or dangled from her ears.

She was beautiful. She held out a gloved hand, which Eric took in his, but then didn't know what to do with. He shook it, but in the way you would shake a dog's paw.

"Mr Craxxi," she said, in a European accent Eric couldn't place, "Ms Beatrice Kozlov. So pleased to meet you."

It was perhaps too late for him to worry about now, but Eric realised he would be expected to put on a New York accent. He could not do accents, and he had little more than a second to make a decision. The smile on Ms Koslov's face began to solidify.

"Ma'am," said Eric, gruffly and approximating a New York accent not rooted in any actual place.

"And how are you settling in?"

Eric smiled and nodded, suggesting that he was settling in well enough. He knew from films that mafia bosses tended to not speak very much. They'd whisper orders to those second in command, but generally their very manner seemed enough to convey what they wanted to say.

Ms Beatrice Koslov let him know that she was always at his disposal should he need a guide, as she had been dead for several decades herself. She was eager, she said, to hear news of what life was like on Earth. Eric made a show of pondering this and nodded again. Ms Koslov gracefully stood to one side to allow Eric to move through the room. Between nods, monosyllabic replies while biting into a canapé or sipping wine, he was pretty much getting away with no one noticing that he had never been to New York, let alone once ruled it through fear. It was especially useful that silent menace seemed to fit his stolen persona.

About an hour and several glasses of wine into the event, Eric was beginning to relax. It would be too much to say he was enjoying himself, but he did allow himself to attempt more complex sentences with an accent. He bluffed his way through questions and even made up some tales from his murky past. He was still not drunk enough, however, to realise he was beginning to place too much faith in his improvisation skills and decided to leave. The party was beginning to thin out anyway. On his way out, a man saw him approaching, excused himself from the conversation he was having with a lady, and held his hand out to Eric, smiling.

"Hi," said Eric, taking the man's hand, which gripped his tightly.

"Carmine Craxxi. How do you do?"

"Eric Pickles," said Eric.

Oh.

The man, who had not yet let go of Eric's hand, pulled him closer. He was broad and strong and, speaking through his teeth, said, "Let's take a walk."

The two men left together. No one who watched on would have thought they were anything other than old friends.

"You're staying here?" asked Craxxi, when they had reached the lobby.

Eric nodded.

"Let's go," ordered Craxxi, nudging Eric to the elevator.

If the ride down was long, the ride up was longer. At least now he was sharing the confined space with a man who had once killed for a living and whose identity he had stolen. They didn't speak until they were in the suite, which Eric hadn't been expecting to see again so soon, or ideally, at all. Craxxi poured them both a whisky. He handed Eric his and told him to sit down, gesturing to a dining chair. Eric sat silently, watching Craxxi as he paced and gulped the whisky back in a single mouthful without it registering on his face. He stopped pacing and regarded Eric.

"Talk."

"This has all been a terrible misunderstanding," began Eric. This was a mistake. Craxxi had heard those words out of so many mouths, usually before he pointed a gun at their heads and pulled the trigger. He shook his head and suggested Eric start again.

"Okay," said Eric, trying to conceal a tremor in his voice. "I'm sorry."

"How did you get hold of my golden ticket."

"A man."

"What man?"

"I don't know who he was. I was stuck. I didn't have a membership of my own and this man offered to sell me one. I didn't have any money. Anyway, he punched me-"

"Why?"

"Well, he walked away, and I chased after him. He didn't like that."

Eric paused and studied Craxxi's face, from which he got very little information. But Craxxi remained silent, so Eric continued.

"When I got up the man had gone, but he must have dropped the ticket. I didn't think. I just took it and ran."

Craxxi was thinking that that was exactly what he would have done, but that alone was not going to count in Eric's favour.

"I thought I could just keep myself to myself for a few days then, I don't know, hope everything sorted itself out."

"That downstairs was your idea of keeping yourself to yourself?"

"I didn't want to go. I was on my way somewhere else when that little hotel manager, that Frenchman, saw me. I was about to disappear and not come back. That was the plan anyway."

Craxxi pulled out a chair and sat opposite Eric. Eric didn't know if he were better off keeping eye contact or looking away. He settled for alternating between the two.

"You expect me to believe you were going to just walk away from all this?" he asked, gesturing with his large head to the rest of the room.

"Well, after the bomb, it seemed sensible."

That was the first Craxxi had heard of any bomb.

"Just, a bomb. I don't know" he said when urged to explain what he meant. "I was in the bar downstairs when it went off. Then they gave me this room. I think that's what the party was for."

Craxxi sat back in his chair, visibly relaxing, although he appeared to Eric to be coming to some sort of conclusion.

"I wouldn't have gone to the party."

"I didn't think you would."

Eric wanted to know what Craxxi was going to do with him. He didn't have to ask. The man opposite him had been in similar situations many times before and it was at about that point in the conversation they tended to ask, but he had a question of his own.

"You can be killed here?"

"Well, that's what I'd like to know. You can get hangovers. You bleed if you nick yourself shaving."

Craxxi's thoughts turned to just how much of a changed man he really was. In his last moments with Sun Yu, he had experienced a peace that he had not previously thought possible. All his rage and fight had left him as he gave himself up completely to something he could only sense but not understand. But then he had seen the poster with his name and Eric's face and there they were again. He couldn't deny, though, that he was not the same man he had been. What would Sun Yu say if he were there? Probably nothing. He had not been much for talking, but he had taught him a lot. He had caught the fish by keeping still; by doing nothing. He had made it into Heaven by surrendering completely. His former self would not have hesitated. He'd not have killed Eric, but he would have hurt him. He didn't know what to do, so he chose to do nothing. Just as he had when standing in the freezing stream waiting for a fish to swim into his hands.

"Go on, go."

Eric hesitated. He wondered if it were a trick. Craxxi sympathised. Usually, it was. It usually meant he just wanted the other person to be beaten or killed somewhere else.

"Don't come back. If I ever see you again, you'll regret it."

That last threat wasn't true, but it felt like the best thing to say. It was best for both men if Eric disappeared for good.

Eric stood, thanked Craxxi, said sorry again, and left.

Craxxi continued sitting, the taste of whisky lingering. He chuckled to himself.

"I hope you're proud, old man," he said out loud to Sun

Yu.

He stood and walked out onto the balcony. He was in Heaven. He thought that would have been the end of it, but now he knew that someone wanted him dead, as improbable as that sounded. But who? When he was alive, the list of names would have needed a ticker tape. But in Heaven? He hadn't been the only one who had bought his place in Heaven. He had planned to look up his parents, and some of his old friends. But perhaps first he needed to track down his enemies. Where to start, though? He looked down to the road below. He saw Eric leaving the building. A black car that had been parked about thirty feet away moved off and stopped next to him. Two men got out of it, grabbed Eric, and forced him into the back. The doors slammed and the car pulled away quickly.

Inside the car, Eric was pressed up against the back seat with the acceleration. Either side of him were men poking handguns into his ribs. Facing him opposite a tanned man in a shiny suit lifted his dark glasses and looked him up and down.

"Who's this guy?"

"Boss?" asked one of the men beside Eric.

"This ain't Carmine Craxxi."

The two men exchanged nervous looks. One of them rummaged in Eric's pockets and produced his membership, which fortunately for Eric, Craxxi had not thought to ask him to return. He handed it to the shiny man, who lifted his dark glasses again and examined the name on it.

"This don't mean nothin'."

"This is the guy we've been tailing. He's staying in the suite under the name of Craxxi. That French hotel manager was yelling his name."

"Yeah," joined in the other man. "And he's just been at a party for him for the last three hours."

He produced a poster for the party with Eric's face on it beneath Carmine Craxxi's name. The man in the dark glasses was not convinced, but he was thinking.

"You're Carmine Craxxi?"

Eric didn't have the presence of mind to keep up the fake accent and answered in his own.

"That's right."

The two men either side of him exchanged another look.

"What's Hugh Grant doing in my car?"

The two men didn't know what to say. However, thinking more quickly than he had ever done before, Eric spoke up.

"They've given me the wrong body."

The man in the dark glasses squinted. Not that anyone could have known, of course.

"What the hell are you talkin' about?"

"There's been a mix-up. My soul ended up in the body of some Englishman. It happens, apparently. They've said I'll get mine back. They just have to find the Englishman who has it."

The man in the dark glasses wasn't at all sure, but he considered the evidence.

"Okay, let's say I believe you. For now."

Eric was relieved, but guessed correctly that the real Carmine Craxxi wouldn't have let it show, so he simply stared back.

"Who are you and what do you want with me?" he asked,

hoping that the real Craxxi and this man didn't already know each other.

"My name is Primo. Primo Fortunato. And you're going to do me a favour."

Sixteen

Primo—the first—had been dead a long time. On Earth he had not been involved in organised crime. He had carved out a career as a corporate lawyer, based in Chicago, and became a partner in the firm he joined as a sixteen-year-old by the time he was in his mid-forties. But he had not had the chance to toast his success for very long because a heart attack struck him unexpectedly and killed him.

The resentment of having led a blameless life that was cut short so suddenly festered in him in the months and years after his death. The reward of paradise was not enough for him to be placated. What made him more bitter still was that Heaven seemed to be letting anybody in: petty criminals, corrupt politicians, drug dealers, murderers, rapists, suicides and even atheists, though for the latter, any sort of afterlife left a nasty taste in the mouth. They also allowed admission to gangsters, some of whom, he had heard, had bought their places with bribes.

He had no intention of spending eternity in Heaven pursuing the same lie, as he now thought of it, as he had in a handful of decades on Earth. If the rules of the game he was being made to play were so lax then he would take full advantage of them. He set about building a business empire of hotels, restaurants, gambling (technically not allowed but no one seemed to care), construction, publishing and property letting. These were all legitimate businesses, but he had acquired them and built them by means of a ruthless pursuit of personal gain that was inexhaustible. However, whereas on Earth a finite existence put a natural break on otherwise unlimited ambition, where eternity is concerned, the failure to progress beyond a glass ceiling of what is possible to accomplish can lead to frustration. And that was where Primo Fortunato found himself now; and that was what he wanted with Carmine Craxxi.

Eric sat in the basement of a building he suspected was a restaurant—at least judging from the contents of the many bags of waste piled up by the rear entrance he had been led through. A single shaded light bulb cast its triangular beam over him but did not illuminate the corners of the cold, damp room, in which he sensed characters lurked. He was seated on a hard-back chair with his hands, untied, resting gauchely on his thighs. His mouth was dry from nerves.

Fortunato had not followed him down the wooden steps when they entered, but he came now, a few minutes later, self-consciously making an entrance. The gloom forced him, against his wishes, to remove his glasses and slide them into the top pocket of his grey suit. He ran a hand through his white and grey hair, dragged a stool a few feet from Eric, and sat. He lit a cigar and offered it to Eric, but Eric declined, politely. Fortunato shrugged and puffed lavishly, enjoying the poetry of smoke swirling in the yellow light. He considered the glowing end of the cigar for a moment and spoke.

"You will forgive me, I hope," he said slowly, "for bringing you here like this. I am sure you understand the necessity."

Eric did not, but he said he did anyway—guessing correctly that Carmine Craxxi would have known.

"In truth, I need you only for something very little."

It was important to Fortunato that he made that clear. It was not to soothe Eric, for he knew he knew he had no choice but to comply. It mattered to him that Craxxi knew that he, Primo Fortunato, was not desperate for his help. Just as the nouveau riche often felt the need to make it plainly understood that they had dragged themselves up on their own, with no silver spoon to remove from their mouths to sell for start-up capital and with no help from anyone else, so the new organised crime leaders, like him, bristled at being referred to as mafia, or gangsters. He was not like them. He was a businessman, first and last. Somewhere in between he had occasions to bend the rules, and other people's wills, but that did not make him one of them. In his eyes, the man seated before him was nothing more than a thug, though he looked nothing like he had imagined.

"My empire, vast as it is, has reached a point where if it is to grow any more it needs to do so upwards."

He gestured toward the light on the ceiling with his cigar but, again, Eric was not on the same lap as the lead runners in this conversation.

"Some very old families have enjoyed for countless centuries the fruits of partnerships with God. They consider themselves," he said, with a curl of the lip to register his disgust, "aristocracy. But in reality, they are nothing more than businessmen who built connections on Earth that others did not."

Eric was under the unmistakable impression that this latest fact was supposed to bring him fully up to speed, and he nodded knowingly to hide his distress at still not knowing what it was he was supposed to be in on.

"Connections," Fortunato went on after exhaling more smoke, "that I as an honest man had no cause to even consider worth my while. How little," he said, smiling, "did I know."

"But you, Don Carmine, you knew, didn't you," he went on with a grin, jabbing a finger toward Eric.

"I did?"

"You donated heavily to the Vatican, you won contracts to administer land they owned, you even washed a little dirty money for them once or twice."

The fact he knew so much about Craxxi was supposed to impress him.

"Okay."

"And in return for your money you secured this place here in Heaven."

Fortunato stood at this clearly well-rehearsed moment in his speech and paced slowly in front of Eric.

"But for that money, Don Carmine," he said, suddenly stopping and facing Eric, "you bought more than just that, didn't you."

Eric did not answer, and Fortunato took this as encouragement he had his man on the run.

"You bought access to a higher authority."

"Did you plant that bomb in my room?" asked Eric.

"Why would I," asked Fortunato, spreading his arms in a gesture of innocence, "want to harm you? I need you. After that, you can go your own way."

"So, who did? Any ideas?"

"Well let me see," said Fortunato, sarcastically, "who could possibly want to take revenge on you?"

He paused for a moment before continuing.

"How many men did you send to the afterlife in the course of your career, Don Carmine? It could be any one of those poor unfortunates who have been waiting a long time for you to join them. But," he said, after a brief pause during which a thought occurred to him, "if you do me this little favour, I can make all that go away."

"What little favour?"

"Your name can open doors. Big doors."

Eric, though now fully up to speed, was still no closer to knowing what the man standing grandly opposite him wanted. Apparently, it was his name. But even that wasn't his. And with the real Carmine Craxxi now in Heaven, how long would it be before Primo realised he had the wrong person? The speech over, Primo clicked his fingers. Eric had been right about the shadows. Figures stepped forward from them. Primo told them to make his 'guest' comfortable. Somehow, he managed to enunciate the quotes, so that Eric knew not to feel too comfortable.

A few minutes later and Eric had been made to sit on a red leather sofa where he accepted a whisky from a tray held steady by a waitress. He was sure by then that he really didn't like whisky, and he wondered why he didn't seem able to get away from the stuff. He was still very much in the dark. His interview with Primo Fortunato had ended on that enigmatic note. He had been shown upstairs into a nightclub which was becoming busy, but he had a roped-off section to himself. A band of musicians were scattered about a low stage and were tinkering with their instruments, tuning them, and tapping at microphones. Groups of people sat down on vacant tables, lit by candles, and clicked their fingers to attract the attention of passing waitresses.

Beside him slid, as if poured onto the sofa, a dark, long-haired woman moulded into a red dress.

"Hello," she said with a Latin flourish, "I am Margaretha."

"Pleased to meet you," said Eric, and he offered a limp, sweaty hand in friendship, which Margaretha took in hers and squeezed gently.

"So, you are the famous Carmine Craxxi?"

"So they say."

"An Englishman?"

"Only temporarily," replied Eric, winking and tapping his nose.

"You are going to introduce Primo to God?"

Eric stared at Margaretha.

"I'm sorry, what?"

"He didn't tell you?"

"Tell me what?"

"He has been after an audience with God for years. You're the one who will finally get it for him."

"I am?" asked Eric, a shrill note entering his voice. "How?"

Margaretha shrugged.

"I don't know. But he has it all worked out."

Eric injudiciously swallowed the contents of his glass

in one gulp and made a sound like a llama clearing its throat of a blade of grass.

"Are you nervous?" asked Margaretha once Eric had regained his composure.

"Nervous? Me? No. Why should I be?"

"It is not for me to say," she replied in a probing manner. "The very thought of meeting God would be enough to drive most men to question the lives they had led."

Eric stared into his lap, then at a non-existent object to the side of him. Margaretha smiled.

"Don't worry," she said, squeezing his knee. "He is much nicer in real life."

"You've met him?"

She nodded.

"What's he like?"

Margaretha reflected for a moment.

"He was very nice to me."

"How did you meet?"

"I was in a relationship with his son, and he took me to meet his parents."

Eric was incredulous.

"You dated Jesus? What was he like?"

"He has more than one son, but yes, Jesus," said Margaretha, replacing the 'J' with an 'H' and leaving out the 'S' all together, "and I were very close at one time."

"What happened?"

"It's personal."

"Oh, yes, of course," said Eric, admonishing himself for his directness.

"He was a lot of fun, but I wanted more. He is not the type to want to settle down."

"You're kidding me, right?"

Margaretha smiled again.

"He's a good boy. He just needs to grow up a little."

"And I am definitely not dreaming?"

Margaretha leaned back as if to get a broader view of Eric.

"You're not like any mafioso I have met."

"In what way?" asked Eric, concerned.

"You're easy to be around."

"You don't think my head's too loud?"

"Who told you that?"

"No one, it doesn't matter." then, hastily trying to get back into character, added, "I have another side to me. You know, when I'm . . . working."

"You have another side to you? Now I *know* you're not a mafioso."

"We're not all the same."

"Apparently not," replied Margaretha, settling a lingering look of doubt on him.

The band members took their positions on stage. They were joined a moment later by a suited man of middle years, holding a glass of whisky loosely by his hip. He removed his hat, hooked it on the back of a chair, rested one hand on the microphone and smiled. Eric had a feeling he recognised the singer. He had a nondescript face but a pair of the bluest eyes he had ever seen.

"Hit it," he said over his shoulder and the band struck up into Mack the Knife, and as soon as the singer made a sound, Eric knew who he was.

"He's a very good impersonator," said Eric into Margaretha's ear.

He had to repeat himself because Margaretha had not heard him over the music.

"You think," she asked, shouting, "he's an impersonator?"

Eric thought for a moment.

"Oh, look, here come the rest of the Rat Pack."

He listened for a while, tapping his foot and singing along to the words he knew.

"I'll tell you what, though," said Eric after a few songs, "that little fella who's suppose to be Sammy Davis Jr. can really dance."

Margaretha nodded her agreement and started clapping as the song had finished.

"The Dean Martin one is even singing with a drink in one hand," added Eric, impressed. Very authentic."

Margaretha stared at Eric, quizzically. She didn't know who the man before her was, but she most definitely knew who he was not. Being the only woman in such a male environment, however, meant that Eric's secret was safe with her; at least for the time being. For Margaretha, being the girlfriend of Primo Fortunato meant that any little advantage she had over him was worth keeping until she knew what to do with it.

"Don Carmine!" laughed Fortunato as he loomed behind Eric and Margaretha. "I see you've met my girl. She's quite something, isn't she?"

"Yes," said Eric, "she's very nice."

"Nice?*Nice*? She's a knockout! Just don't try to get anything in the way of conversation out of her. Her mouth's no good for speaking, just other things! Am I right, baby?"

He grabbed her cheek between finger and thumb and

shook it.

"Beautiful!"

A slight-looking man in an over-sized suit placed his hand on Fortunato's shoulder and whispered something in his ear.

"Don Carmine, I've got to leave you again. But you'll be okay in such beautiful hands, huh?"

He roared with laughter and left Eric with an embarrassed looking Margaretha.

"He's very fond of you, isn't he." was all Eric could think to say.

"Yes, he's very fond of me," she responded, flatly.

There followed a long and uncomfortable silence that was not penetrated even by Frank, Dean, Sammy and now Peter Lawford and Joey Bishop, singing *Summer Wind.*

Eric spoke first.

"You know, tell me it's none of my business if you like, but you really don't have to put up with that."

Margaretha turned from the stage and looked at Eric but said nothing.

"I mean, you're a very beautiful girl. Someone like you could do better than being treated like that. I think he knows it, too. That's why he puts you down."

Margaretha placed her drink on the table firmly.

"Who are you?" she demanded.

"Sorry?"

She repeated her demand.

Eric swallowed.

"I'm Carmine Craxxi."

"No. Who are you?"

"I don't know what you mean."

"I think you do."

Eric felt nausea rising from his stomach.

"What makes you think I am not who I say I am?"

"Because I knew Carmine when we were both alive. That's why Primo keeps me around."

"But they gave me the wrong body," said Eric, weakly. "You don't even recognise me."

Eric was considering whether or not he could claim memory loss when Margaretha pressed on.

"And you have never killed anyone."

"How do you know? I might have?"

"Men who have killed show it in their eyes. And it's okay. You can tell me. If you don't, I'll tell Primo you're an impostor. He'll believe me. It's why he wanted me to talk to you."

"And then what will he do?"

Margaretha shrugged. Either she did not know, or she knew and simply did not care. Eric stared at his glass and thought fiercely about what his next move should be. He so wanted to tell Margaretha who he really was. At the very least, he did not want her to think he was anything like Primo Fortunato. It mattered for reasons he could not fathom that she knew the truth. More than anything else, he just needed someone to tell.

"My name's Eric Pickles," he said, allowing it all to pour out. "I'm not the godfather. I'm in computers, and I am in way over my head."

He looked up and stared at Margaretha, desperately.

"You mustn't tell anyone. Please! I have a plan. It's going to be okay. Promise me you won't tell a soul."

Margaretha nodded.

"Promise me!"

"I promise."

Eric told Margaretha the rest of his story and the relief was enormous. He explained everything, right up to the moment he had met Carmine Craxxi at the party. That was when she stopped him.

"Wait," she said, sitting forward. "You met Carmine? You know where he is?"

Eric finished the story.

"He let you go?"

Margaretha clearly found this difficult to believe. The Carmine she knew would have thrown Eric from the balcony.

"Where is he now?"

Eric wrote the address on the back of a napkin and Margaretha slipped it into her shoe when she was sure no one was watching.

"Don Carmine," spoke a waiter. "If you'll forgive the intrusion, Mr Fortunato has instructed me to escort you to your room for the night."

Margaretha stood with him and kissed both his cheeks. With her lips close to his ear she whispered, "Tell God I said hello."

Eric followed the waiter out of the room. Margaretha, sat back and finished her drink, trying to decide what to make of Eric and whether or not she wanted to see Craxxi again. Fortunato sat down beside her heavily.

"So?" he growled.

"So, what?"

"Is he really Don Carmine?"

She stared, blankly, at him. He squeezed her arm.

"Is he Don Carmine?" he asked again, with added menace. She nodded.

"He's Don Carmine."

"Are you sure?"

"Men tell me everything, Primo."

He stared at Margaretha for any sign that she was keeping something from him.

"Good girl. Now, freshen up. I'll be along in a half hour," he said lustily. "You know what I'm like when I'm about to close a big deal."

She knew.

SEVENTEEN

Eric was woken by a knock at the door.

"It's your big day!" came Primo Fortunato's voice from outside.

Eric turned over in bed and spread himself across the cool half of the sheet he had not slept on.

"Come on, Don Carmine, rise and shine."

Eric groaned a verb as part of an unintelligible instruction to Primo to leave him alone.

"We leave in an hour."

Eric sat up and rubbed his eyes and noticed the empty pillow beside him. He missed Amber and wondered how she had coped in the days after his death. She was a strong and well put-together woman, but that did not always lend itself to managing stress. Standing firm under such things was her first reaction, but it is the way of sturdy structures to collapse quite spectacularly and without a moment's notice when the strain becomes too much to bear. In comparison, his parents were much more likely to break early on, before too much damage could be done. They would be able, he felt, to pick up their pieces long before Amber, who would be lost under the rubble of her own defences.

He sat opposite Margaretha at the breakfast table. She was wearing one of Fortunato's shirts. Her hair was tangled and stuck to her neck and cheek. She was wearing no makeup, but that, if anything thought Eric, made her even more beautiful than she had looked the night before. Their eyes met for the briefest of moments but neither gave away any sign of recognition or of the secret they shared. Eric buttered his toast, silently, and sipped strong coffee from a tiny cup.

"When we arrive at our meeting with God, let me do the talking," instructed Fortunato.

This pleased Eric.

"This calls for the utmost sensitivity, Don Carmine and, with respect, that was never your strongest point."

Margaretha poured some coffee for herself. Eric struggled to finish his toast, which was too dry for him to swallow.

"What's the matter, not hungry?" asked Primo. "You're just nervous. It's understandable."

Fortunato was clearly excited. He was having his moment and he intended to make the most of it.

"Just think, Don Carmine, with God on our payroll what we could achieve."

"You're going to employ *God*?" asked Margaretha, moodily.

"Why not?"

Margaretha placed her coffee cup on the table.

"The Alpha and the Omega? The creator of Heaven and Earth?"

"Look at the royal houses on Earth. Once, they were war lords, wielding terrifying power. Now they work for the tourist industry for handouts. Things change and power shifts."

"What do you want him to do for you?"

"I'm sure we could find a floor for him to sweep."

Margaretha ignored the laughter and excused herself from the table contemptuously.

"Women!" winked Fortunato, conspiratorially, in Eric's direction.

Eric managed to force a weak smile and pushed his half-eaten toast away from him. Fortunato and his men dived into their breakfasts while Eric watched on. When Fortunato was finished, he decided that everyone else was finished too and announced their departure.

"Okay, guys, let's roll."

Eric was guided out of the front of the building and into a waiting car. He stroked his rough, stubbled cheek and felt grubby, particularly seated opposite the immaculately groomed Fortunato. He was on his way to meet God, after all. He should really have shaved.

They headed out of town and joined a five-lane road that cut through the city like an hour hand. They were glowered over by tall hotels and colourful billboards. One building, which he took to contain a swimming pool, had a tangle of red, yellow and blue tubes spilling from the side inside which could be seen, at intervals, silhouettes of people sluicing down at tremendous speed.

The tall buildings were eventually replaced by squat, concrete ones, mostly containing small businesses. Grubby-looking filling stations slid past. Wire fences sealed in dogs on chains. Hand-painted signs warned drivers to not park in front of gates as they were in constant use, which, thought Eric, looked like a lie. When that particular scenery ran out it was replaced by a more pleasing one of broad stores selling flowers and garden equipment. Once past them, there was nothing but soft verges and trees on both sides of the road and the occasional diner, and ahead of them sharp, snow-capped mountains rising from the horizon like shark fins.

The trees thinned out and Eric's ears popped as the car climbed the hill upon which God's official residence was built. They turned a corner and a panorama of Heaven spread out below them. For the first time, he could see a vast ocean sparkling in the early morning sun, and shrouded in haze, an island could be just made out several miles from shore. Between them and the water, broad thoroughfares swept across the flat plain and formed, from so far above them, the sort of patterns that reminded him of those carved into South American plateaus. And scattered about, tall buildings with their blinking red beacons to ward off low-flying aircraft soared into the crisp, blue sky.

The car's automatic gearbox shifted down as the incline increased and the passengers were gently jerked in their seats. After about an hour, the road levelled out and they approached a set of iron gates. A guard in a booth slid the window open, poked his head out and had a brief conversation with the driver. Eric could not hear what was being said, but the exchange appeared to end to everyone's satisfaction because the gates swung silently open, and the car drove through.

The residence was a further two hundred yards along

a gravel drive. It was large but modest and gave the impression that there were many more floors below ground, burrowed into the hillside, than there were above it. It was a hefty, white building with lofted windows and a grand entrance guarded on either side by marble pillars that appeared older than their surroundings by several thousand years.

Built onto the side of what looked to Eric like the original architecture, a more modern extension reached out. The net curtains in the windows were too large for their spaces and crumpled up at their hems. Eric remembered that government buildings in the middle of London had the same thing. He had learnt that there the curtains were weighted at the bottom and were intended to catch shards of glass if a bomb went off in the street outside, thus protecting the occupants. He wondered if the same consideration had been made in this case.

They were pointed to a space beside two other cars outside the main entrance and directed to the reception area where Primo Fortunato announced their arrival.

"If you'll take a seat," said the lady behind the desk, "God's office will call down for you, presently."

Eric and Fortunato sat down on a sofa. One of Fortunato's men, Enzo, filled a plastic cup with water from a cooler and paced about while he sipped. The other, Bruno, eyed the lady behind the desk.

"Don't worry about a thing," said Fortunato, betraying, as he did, the first signs of nerves.

Eric noticed a sign on the wall that pointed down a flight of steps. It read: *Customer Service Call Centre*. Retirement age for those who work in Heaven's call centre, as with air-traffic controllers, is low. However, it is rare that anybody can tolerate the job for long enough to receive a golden handshake from the management. The emotional stress of listening to hundreds of prayers for seven-and-a-half hours a day, four days a week (workers in Heaven enjoy three-day weekends) is enormous. It is said that if, as a new recruit, you return to your desk after lunch on your first day, you are tougher than most. For the majority, the first prayer from, say, a young child asking that mummy, who has cancer, does not die is far too heart-breaking to manage.

Then there is the sheer workload. One-hundred-and-fifty million telephones, constantly ringing, and never more than two hundred operators at any one time to answer them, which makes Heaven's customer service call centre, as a ratio of phones to people to answer them, the most manned anywhere in Heaven or on Earth (figures for Hell are not available and would not be considered reliable even if they were).

Waiting times for held calls average twenty-two years. This has led millions of Christians on Earth to believe that their prayers are going unanswered. However, although it can often feel that way, due to 'higher than average call volumes', all operators are busy, but someone will answer your call as 'soon as possible'. Your call *is* important to them.

Although extra staff are hired on a temporary basis at peak times (Christmas, Easter, major sporting events), support for the permanent staff is woeful. Of course, any non-Christian who is thinking of becoming one, calling what is affectionately known by staff as the *Road to Damas-*

cus line, gets through first time.

Eric leaned forward and picked up a magazine from the coffee table. It was faded and dog-eared, but an article caught his eye: New Heaven, which, according to the author, was founded in nineteen fifty-seven. It seemed that 'Old Heaven' had grown apart from the people who felt they had become disenfranchised. Heaven's ruling body convened and, despite fierce internal opposition, agreed that radical changes had to be made. The difficult part was not improving on Paradise but reconciling the differences that existed between the many factions that made up the governing body.

The hard-liners, who represented the majority, were incensed that the liberal minority among them were beginning to exercise a disproportionate influence on God and, in their view, pollute his thinking with 'woolly minded, lily-livered, sandal-wearing' policies.

The fact was that the liberal minority had a point. Christianity had become too right-wing for most people to swallow, who then turned their tactical worship to minority religions like Buddhism and Wicca, or else had taken Pascal's Wager and spent their lives with their fingers crossed. Most people, however, simply did not turn out to worship at all. For decades, this growing section of society had been dismissed as apathetic and it was said that such people relinquished all right to complain at the way God was running humankind. Heaven's policy makers realised, however, that these people were not necessarily apathetic but should, more correctly, be thought of as abstainers. An abstention, according to an internal report, was equally valid to a declared belief and that the sooner Heaven's policy

organisers understood this, the better. It was also understood that since abstainers made up the majority, any religion that could win even half of them over to its side could
rightly call itself the religion for the new millennium.

So, it was then that the biggest upheaval in the history
of Heaven was undertaken. Resolutions were fought for
and passed—often only narrowly—and New Heaven was
launched amongst much pomp and ceremony.

After the initial euphoria, disillusionment quickly began to set in. The cry from Haven's leaders that change
was slow fell on cynical ears that had heard it all before.
It was not as if all the right noises were not being made.
Necessary changes to Heaven had taken place—vast sums
of money were being spent—but something about it all
just did not feel right. Many of the old sins were, if not
actually abolished, certainly allowed to slide. For instance,
working on the Sabbath, eating shellfish and wearing two
different kinds of thread were, it was agreed, okay in the
modern world. However, a number of so-called 'stealth
sins' were brought in, as it were, through the back door
such as stem-cell research; so, it was felt that, really, no
one was any better off than they were before. The lack of a
credible alternative (the only alternative available being a
return to the bad old days of the burning of witches) meant
that the people were forced to put their hope, if not their
trust, in the incumbents.

"God will see you now."

The corridor that led to God's office was lined either
side by vaulted, marble pillars. Between each one, secretaries in open-plan offices worked at computer terminals
and fielded telephone calls. There were other secretaries

who seemed to be in perpetual motion, holding folders of documents close to their chests as they criss-crossed the corridor from one side to the other with the precision of formation-flying acrobatic pilots. One got the distinct impression that if just a single secretary mistimed her journey across the corridor, then the resulting pile up would be catastrophic. Careful not to cause any deviation in the secretaries' paths, the men negotiated the fifty yards to God's office and presented themselves to his P.A.

"You can go in," she said, replacing the telephone receiver.

The men looked at each other, each waiting for someone else to step forward. Bruno and Enzo took half-steps back. Even Fortunato seemed suddenly uncertain. None of them had led good lives. They had each done terrible things. Would he know just by looking at them? At least they had believed in him. Eric couldn't even say that for himself. He hadn't murdered anyone, though. It depended, he supposed, on what sort of things God himself valued most. It was Fortunato who decided it should be he who went in first. The room they found themselves in was the kind that Eric always associated with university professors at Oxford or Cambridge. It was dark and cluttered with dusty books and piles of paper. Giant bookshelves, which required a ladder on runners to reach the upper-most shelves, lined the room. It smelt of old, yellowing paper too, polished wood and strong coffee.

Fortunato cleared his throat.

A chair rolled backwards from behind a stack of books. Seated upon it was a man who appeared to be in his sixties. He had white hair, but the beard, contrary to the popular image was missing. He wore terracotta coloured hessian trousers, a tie-dyed Tee-shirt and nothing at all on his feet.

"Please excuse the clutter," he said with an English accent that was rich with age and learning.

The men approached, slowly, and stood at what they perceived to be a respectful distance from him. God, for his part, was squinting at a monitor and tapping repeatedly at the escape key.

"Does anyone know anything about these cursed things?" he asked.

"I do, actually," replied Eric, stepping forward, much to the surprise of Fortunato. "What seems to be the problem?"

"It says it can't detect the modem, but it's right there! It's right next to it on the desk—look!"

God picked the modem up and tapped it against the side of the hard drive as if a formal introduction would help. Eric leaned over God's shoulder and took the mouse, which he operated deftly with swift flicks of the wrist and judicious use of the left and right buttons.

"Have you just installed a new modem?" Eric asked.

"Yes."

"That explains it then. The computer is still looking for the old one."

"Why? I thought computers were supposed to be clever?"

"They are, in their ways, but also incredibly stupid."

Eric closed the windows that were open and clicked Connect. The speakers beeped melodiously as the modem dialled out.

"Why don't you go to Wi-Fi? You could set up a network really easily and it's much faster and reliable than what you've got now."

"Oh, they've been arguing for years now about which system to introduce. Personally, I think the I.T. boys are worried that if they install a system that doesn't go wrong all the time then they won't be needed. I can understand their reasoning, I suppose."

Eric, having worked in I.T., understood this but also knew that it was rarely the machines that were the problem but the operators. So long as they existed, people like him would never be out of work. They were distracted by the hard drive whirring with the effort of digitally rendering an egg, which cracked and produced a baby pterodactyl that flew off the screen before the routine was repeated.

"I've got mail!" said God, who excitedly opened his In-box. "Pawn to queen six?" He consulted a chess board on the desk beside him. "What's he playing at?"

"You're playing E-mail chess?" asked Eric.

"Yes."

"Who with?"

"Lucifer."

Eric exchanged looks with Fortunato, who was, for the moment, struck by a rare inability to speak.

"The devil?"

"Well," smiled God, wryly. "He can be when he loses."

Eric took a moment to process this.

"There's an attachment," said Eric, pointing at the scr-een.

"Not bloody likely!" exclaimed God. "I am not falling for that one again. Last time I opened an attachment from that little sh . . . shyster it contained a virus that shut us down for weeks. By the time we got it all up and running again the twentieth century had been and gone. He had a ball. Two world wars, pandemics, sodding computers and that dreadful social media. Not to mention his sidekick whom he managed to manoeuvre into a top job while I wasn't looking."

"Who?"

"You know who," God replied. "I am not going to say his name. He has libel lawyers on his permanent staff. I'm not being dragged through the courts—again."

This was not how Fortunato had rehearsed the meeting and he was growing impatient, but he dithered over how best to address his host.

"Sir, I appreciate you must be a very busy man and I am grateful that you spared the time to see us."

"Not at all. What can I do for you?"

Fortunato stepped forward, opened his mouth but utterly forgot his prepared speech.

"It's like this," he said, improvising. "I'm a businessman. I started with nothing and worked hard and now I employ approximately two thousand people."

"Congratulations."

Primo was not yet into his stride and hoped God wasn't going to keep interrupting.

"Thank you. But my expansion plans have come up against a brick wall."

"I am sorry to hear that."

"You are in a position to help me."

"Always glad to do what I can."

"Heaven is ruled by an oligarchy. Old families that go back centuries, some further, and they have divided politics and business between them. What they don't want they throw as scraps for the rest of us."

"Is that right?" asked God, then, shaking his head and speaking to himself, "no one tells me anything."

"All I ask for, sir, is a seat at that top table."

"I am not sure what you mean."

"I just want," said Primo, trying to keep calm, "to be included in the process. The decision making."

God thought for a moment. At one point, Eric thought he might have fallen asleep. But with a sudden movement he stood and paced evenly to the back of the room and back to stand directly in front of Fortunato.

"I didn't catch your name."

"Fortunato, sir. Primo Fortunato."

"Mr Fortunato, as you know, we do not operate a democracy here in Heaven. I prefer to call it a benevolent dictatorship—with a light touch."

"Extremely benevolent, if I may add, sir," interrupted Fortunato with a servile bow of the head.

"You may. But over the centuries my role has somewhat diminished. I am less an ultimate authority than a figurehead. To be wheeled out at ceremonial occasions but otherwise kept where I cannot cause any trouble."

"You are too modest, sir," said Fortunato.

"Not at all. They do their best to keep me in the dark. In fact," he said, pursuing a new point, "perhaps you can tell me what's going on."

"How do you mean?" asked Eric.

"Earth," he said, speculatively. "All right, is it?"

Eric wasn't sure where to begin.

"Well, there are still wars going on, but on the whole . . . yeah."

And there it had been. Eric had been given the chance to present the case for humanity; to demand an end to poverty, cancer, war and suffering. But what had he said? 'On the whole . . . yeah.' And the chance was gone. It had fallen to him to represent the many billions of humans living, dead and yet to be born and he had summed it all up as fine really.

God seemed satisfied with this. It matched what he had been told, at least. He had been hoping for more detail, but perhaps there wasn't any.

"How's Norway?"

"Norway?"

"Yes, I was always particularly pleased with Norway. Still there?"

"Um, yes, it's still there. The fjords are very nice."

God retreated into a private memory, which seemed to be making him happy.

"Good. I am pleased," he said, eventually.

"Sir," said Fortunato, hoping to bring the subject back to himself. "Heaven is like a river. It moves so slowly the water has become stagnant. It needs new voices to get it moving. To bring in fresh ideas."

"There is something in what you say," said God after a moment's reflection. "But, to borrow your river analogy if I may, a river will always re-take its natural course, no matter how much effort you make to redirect it. One day, on Earth, every dam will crumble, every concrete bank will corrode. And long after the last human breathes for the last time, ancient riverbeds will flow once more. It is the way of things."

Fortunato was becoming frustrated but didn't let it

show.

"But there will always be a Heaven. It will never crumble the way man's greatest attempts to tame nature will."

"True enough," admitted God. "But I fail to see why you are still so ambitious. You seem to have done very well for yourself."

"But it's not enough," replied Fortunato, loudly, passion galvanising his words. "It's not the money or the power. It's about what's fair. I should be allowed to grow as far as I can. The old men at the top are atrophying. I'm what you need."

"Change," said God, after a minute of silence, "lasting, meaningful change, cannot happen suddenly. It begins with an idea that gets forgotten. An old seed buried deep. Then one day, quite by accident, an event causes it to come to the surface again. It is bathed in light and germinates. No one knows where it came from, but there it is, growing quite naturally, and at the right time."

"So what are you saying?"

"I am saying you need to be patient. As patient as a buried seed, waiting to be germinated. When the time is right."

"I *have* waited," pleaded Fortunato.

"Besides, I am not," smiled God, "an agent of change. I am subject to it. Just like anyone else."

"Not like anyone else, surely," said Eric.

"Where I may have an advantage, Mr Fortunato, is that with the benefit of my many years of experience, I have learned how to harness change, the way a sailor might the wind, or a farmer the altering seasons."

"You won't help."

"I am helping, sir. But you are in too much of a hurry to realise it."

"But can't you see, it's not working anymore! Heaven is broken."

"I do realise that this is difficult for you to-"

"Oh, I understand, all right." Fortunato was now openly angry. "I know all too well how it is."

"I'm afraid-"

"What do you have to be afraid of? Almighty God!"

Bruno took half a step forward.

"Boss."

But Fortunato was not to be restrained.

"So this Heaven, is it? This is what we were promised?"

"Heaven is-"

"Heaven is, what? Are you about to say what we make it?"

"I was about to say, if you had let me finish, that-"

"I don't want to hear it," said Fortunato with disgust.

"Then all I can do is say I am sorry."

"You will be."

Bruno took Fortunato's elbow gently while Enzo made the sign of the cross.

"Do you know who this man is?" he asked, pointing at Eric.

"I don't believe I have had the pleasure."

"He is not a man you want as an enemy."

Enzo took a step back to distance himself, not just physically, but morally from his boss.

"Are you threatening me?"

"Mr Craxxi would be very grateful for your assistance," said Fortunato, flatly, "and to have the gratitude of such a man can be useful."

"And how might I benefit from the gratitude of a man like Mr Craxxi?"

"You benefit from Don Carmine's gratitude by not incurring his ingratitude."

"Primo!" shouted Bruno and Eric was about to proclaim his innocence in the whole matter even if it meant coming clean about his entire story.

"Now, look here," said God before Eric could speak. "I don't know who you think you are, but threats do not carry any sway with me. I don't think we have anything more to say to each other. Good day to you."

Fortunato broke away and paced angrily to the door, kicking over a pile of books, and left, with Bruno and Enzo right behind him, the latter genuflecting in God's direction. Eric paused at the door, mouthed, "I'm sorry," and followed.

"Jesus Christ!" Fortunato boomed as he strode down the corridor, sending secretaries scattering. Perched at the edge of a desk, flirting with one of the office girls who stared up at him with spellbound eyes, a man with shaggy hair and a beard looked up.

"Did somebody just call my name?"

The girl shrugged, utterly oblivious.

"So," he said, dismissing the interruption, "you type at eighty words a minute? That's very impressive. How quickly can you write your name? Wow! How about your address? That's fast! Your phone number? Not bad!"

He ripped the paper from the typewriter with the skilfully gleaned information on it, made a telephone shape with his hand by curling it into a fist except for the thumb

and little finger, shook it by the side of his face and winked.
"I'll call."

Eighteen

Primo Fortunato and his men swept into his restaurant. It was clear to Margaretha that all had not gone well. She took hold of Eric's arm and pulled him to one side.

"What happened?"

"He refused."

Margaretha bit her bottom lip gently.

"Go to him. And be careful."

Eric rejoined Fortunato, who was pacing in his office, bellowing vituperation at the air.

"Who the hell does he think he is?"

"He thinks he's God!" said Bruno.

"He's yesterday's man!"

He sat down behind his desk and composed himself.

"He needs to be taught a lesson he won't forget. What do you say, Don Carmine?"

Eric had poked his finger through a buttonhole in his jacket and was struggling to release it.

"Hmm? What do I think about what?"

"About the situation. About God's refusal."

"Ah, well, we tried."

"I don't try; I do."

He placed his hands together and rested his index fingers against his lips.

"We can't be seen to be weak."

"Yes, but in the face of the Almighty, I don't think it reflects as poorly on us as you are making out. Not if you put it in its correct perspective."

"But don't you see?" pleaded Fortunato, leaning forward out of his seat. "If we win this battle, we win the war!"

Eric had the cautious man's reluctance to take on challenges that were unlikely to succeed, and he gave voice to his concerns in the form of advice regarding choosing one's battles wisely. But Fortunato felt that decision had been already made—not by him, but by God—the moment he had refused him.

"He's someone we have to work with," was all Eric could think to say.

"You know," said Fortunato's accountant, who had a head for figures, but, apparently, no stomach for Holy War, "I think maybe Don Carmine is right."

Fortunato lashed out at a reading light and sent it shattering against the wall.

"God damn it! What's wrong with you all?"

The accountant pushed his glasses back up his nose, swallowed hard and brought his briefcase up in front of him as a shield.

"Why don't we take a break? Have time to calm down, relax. We don't want to act rashly, do we."

Fortunato took a deep breath and repressed his rage for another day.

"All right. We'll talk about this tomorrow."

The men, who had been holding their breath since they entered the room, exhaled as the tension drained away and they filed out into the restaurant leaving Eric and Fortunato alone.

"What do you say, Don Carmine, you and I take a walk?"

"A walk?" Eric chewed on his bottom lip. "Oh, I don't know. You know? I think I'll just take a shower and have a bit of a nap. It's been a big day."

Fortunato clapped his hands together and got up.

"What do you say, Don Carmine," he repeated, "you and I take a walk?"

Eric squinted as if having second thoughts.

"You know what? I don't really see the point in having a shower in the middle of the day. I'll only get sweaty again and need another one. A walk sounds great."

The two men left under the concerned gaze of Margaretha who had had her ear pressed up against the door during the meeting. They walked in silence for a few blocks with Fortunato deep in thought and Eric grateful for the peace while it lasted. They crossed a busy intersection and entered a park.

"Don Carmine," said Fortunato, "what do you think of the line from the Lord's prayer that goes: Thy will be done on Earth as it is in Heaven?"

Eric knew the line very well. Indeed, he had spent most of his childhood reciting it by rote. Strange then that he had no opinion to offer.

"I haven't really given it much thought."

"I have, Don Carmine. I have given it a great deal of thought, in fact. It is God's will that is imposed on Earth from Heaven. From Heaven, all beneath are subservient."

"Yes, I suppose so."

"I do not have to illustrate to a man such as yourself the possibilities that affords. Ultimate power over the lives of men."

Eric had not thought about it that way before and admitted so.

"Why should you have done?" asked Fortunato. "Men like us have never before been so close to such a thing. Could not have conceived of it even. But, Don Carmine, it is now within our grasp. He who rules in Heaven rules the Earth and the destinies of all those who walk it. Think about it!"

Eric was thinking and it seemed like rather more responsibility than he was prepared to take on.

"You kidded yourself," continued Fortunato, "that you were respected, but you were never respected. You were feared. Fear is what gave you your power. Imagine how much more you and I could achieve with the fear of God."

Fortunato's creeping megalomania was beginning to worry Eric but not unduly. For all his ambition, Primo Fortunato was not God, nor was he likely to ever be.

The two men strolled on. They bought an ice cream from a stall and found a bench beside a lido, where they watched couples and families peddling little plastic boats with numbers painted boldly on their sides.

"I must say," said Fortunato, departing from the previous line of discussion, "that you are not what I expected."

"No?"

"But you don't fool me. I can see right through you."

Eric's stomach turned.

"This act of buffoonery you put on. It's all a clever deception."

"It is?"

"A deception designed to make men underestimate you. I am not about to make that mistake. Not when it has cost so many so dear. You may fool the others, but you don't fool me. You're a cunning man, Don Carmine, but I am more cunning, and I for one, do not plan to take my eye from you. Not for a single second."

Fortunato dropped the remainder of his ice cream in a waste basket and stood up to walk again. When they exited the park on the other side a tram rattled towards them.

"I haven't ridden a box car since I was a kid," said Fortunato, smiling. "We'll jump on this one."

The tram shuddered to a halt at the roadside and its pneumatic doors hissed open. As Eric stepped forward, Fortunato dropped his change on the pavement and, cursing to himself, crouched down to pick it up.

"Hold the car!" he barked at Eric.

"Just a moment," called Eric to the controller. "My friend's just coming."

The controller shook his head.

"Sorry, buddy. We've got a schedule to keep."

He pulled down on a lever. The doors shut and the tram pulled away. Fortunato, who had now gathered up his change, ran along the road behind it shaking his fist. Eric shrugged his shoulders uselessly at him and watched his pursuer give up the chase and double up, sweating and breathless in the middle of the road.

The significance of this unexpected turn of events was momentarily lost on Eric. It dawned on him, eventually, however, that he was now free. No longer surrounded by thugs whose lips moved when they were thinking, Eric was finally at liberty. He had been on his way to Suzan when Fortunato and his men had snatched him, and that's where he was going to go now.

Nineteen

It was ironic for Suzan that, having seen ghosts her whole life, she was now surrounded by dead people, and even counted some of them among her best friends. She had been in Heaven for several years and had lived in the commune for almost all of that time. She was invited to live there by Lola, a young girl who heard her playing her guitar for money on a street corner one day.

While many people came and went, a hardcore of four or five never left the commune. As one of them, Suzan was given her own bedroom, which she did not have to share with anyone and that was just the way she liked it. While a social person, she appreciated more than most being able to escape and simply be alone. For Suzan, although not quite unique, was unusual in that other people's internal processes of thoughts and feelings came through loud and clear to her and the din in a crowded room could sometimes be unbearable. No one knew about her rare gift—if a gift it always was—and that was the way she intended to keep it. Bitter experience had cautioned her to keep her secret to herself. Many a time had good friends drifted from her, driven away by the discomfort of feeling naked before her.

Worse still was being considered an object of scientific interest. A child psychologist at her school, to whom she had been sent when a rather cynical poem about suburban life had been anonymously pinned to a notice board but quickly attributed to her had alerted the well-meaning concern of her teachers, quickly spotted her ability. Not that it took much spotting. Made petulant by boredom she poked around inside the psychologist's head and revealed a few choice items that had dwelt within. Excited by this and quite forgetting why she had been referred to her in the first place, she encouraged Suzan to submit herself to closer examination, which, out of boredom and curiosity, she agreed to. The rather nondescript facility she arrived at early the following Saturday morning turned out to be run by a research group funded directly by the British government. They did not admit as much, of course, but Suzan knew where she was and why within two minutes of meeting the researcher, who lied about her name and about what they were both doing there.

Suzan realised, wisely, that that was the moment to play down her talent by the giving of deliberately incorrect answers, but she could not resist doing so in such a way as to leave no doubt in the researcher's mind that she could have got all the answers right if she had wanted to. From then on, she decided to keep her thoughts, and those of others, to herself.

She was in the back yard tilling sun-dried soil. The morning air was fresh, but already warming up to what was going to be another hot day and a fine sheen of sweat made her dark hair stick to her neck, and to the side of her face. She may have been only short, but Suzan was a determined figure and most certainly not afraid of hard work. In the years she had been a resident at the commune, the back yard had been almost completely transformed from weeds and stones into a farm, so that they were now entirely self-sufficient. All the food they ever ate was either grown or reared in the yard now. Even the wine they drank came from grapes grown there.

She stuck her gardening fork into the dirt, stretched her back and took a drink of water from a bottle. There was not much more to do, but when one job was finished there was always another that needed taking care of. Sebastian, who had started the commune and was its unofficial leader, was on the roof fixing loose tiles. She could help him with that after. She and Sebastian had been more than just friends at one time. She had liked him, and it had all started with so much promise, but he soon became too emotionally needy for her liking. As someone who was hypersensitive to those around her, Sebastian made it difficult for her to breathe. That was two years ago now, and their relationship had settled down into a good friendship that she would not want to be without.

Around the yard, about a dozen residents were earning their keep: digging holes, and filling them in; uprooting vegetables, picking fruit, mending broken fences, feeding and cleaning out the animals and generally contributing whatever they could to the running of the commune. No one was expected to do more than they could manage, which meant that some did more than others. While that occasionally created resentment, so long as each resident was a reasonable, fair-minded individual who understood that everyone brought his or her own skills to the environment, the system worked very well. Everyone, no matter for how long they stayed, felt a great sense of pride at what they had achieved together. The commune had grown from a ramshackle death trap to a warm and welcoming home that provided all anyone who lived there could ever need or, indeed, want.

"Suzan," called Lola from the kitchen door. "There's someone here to see you."

Suzan went into the cool shade of the house, kicking her dirty shoes off outside the door.

"If it isn't Mr Craxxi!" she said once inside.

"It isn't. It's Eric."

"You've sorted that out now, have you?"

"Yes. I hope you don't mind. You did say to look you up."

"I did! What changed your mind, because you weren't too keen as I remember."

"It's a long story and, anyway, I've got nowhere else to go."

"Charmed!"

"No! I didn't mean it like that!"

"That's all right even if you did," smiled Suzan. "Everyone here has nowhere else to go."

"And long stories," said Lola, who was so intrigued that Suzan should have taken an interest in someone like Eric she had decided to hang around and be nosey.

"Like I said," continued Eric, "I'm not very good at a lot of things, but I'll do my best to help out."

"You can help me dig," suggested Suzan. "You *can* dig,

I take it?"

Eric followed Suzan outside. She gave him her fork and retrieved another for herself from the tool shed.

"We just need to turn the earth over. It's hard because it hasn't rained for a couple of weeks, so don't go mad. And don't go skewering your toes."

Eric wasn't aware it ever rained in Heaven.

They dug in silence. Eric removed his jacket and rolled up his sleeves. It was a good exercise for him to be able to disengage his brain and concentrate on a simple manual task for a change. As Carmine Craxxi there was always something to think about. As he tilled, however, all those old worries faded away. With the sun on his back and the soil beneath his feet, he left Carmine Craxxi behind and went back to being Eric. Simple, boring, slow-witted Eric. But it occurred to him, after some more of this, that simple, boring, slow-witted Eric was someone else he could leave behind. The old Eric was, quite literally, dead. He may still have been himself, but he had been reborn no more than a week ago, and if that was not a chance to start anew, he didn't know what was. In fact, he realised for the first time, death was a profoundly liberating experience and not the spanner in the works he had always assumed it to be. On Earth he had been desperately unsatisfied with his job but had lacked the courage to make a change. Now, though, he was starting out again with all his choices yet to be made. Many a time he had wished that he had known as a young man what he had learned as an adult. Now he was effectively a young man again, with everything still ahead of him. He was faced with the endless opportunities and possibilities of youth with the hindsight of a fully grown man. By the time he and Suzan had finished and taken the time to admire their work, he was quite happy again.

"There," said Suzan, swigging water and handing the bottle to Eric, "you feel better already, don't you."

"I always felt I should be doing something with my hands," he replied, breathing hard.

"Well, there's plenty of opportunity for that round here," she said with a salacious intonation that went over Eric's head. Apparently, whatever traits of the old Eric he had resolved to dump, slow-wittedness was probably with him to stay.

"So do you eat everything you grow?"

"Not everything."

"What do you do with the rest; sell it?"

Suzan smiled.

"We smoke it."

Eric nodded, knowingly, though he wasn't sure what she was referring to.

"What are you like at painting?" asked Suzan.

"I got a D in art at school."

"Not that sort of painting, idiot! There's a wall that needs whitewashing. Fancy helping me?"

Eric, like most people, was not greatly pleased at being called an idiot, but there was something in the way Suzan said it that made him feel somehow special. They took their forks to the tool shed. Suzan went into the gloom to look for paint and brushes, but Eric stood outside. Spiders lived inside tool sheds; lots of them. His aversion to arachnids did not go quite so far as a full-blown phobia, but the very thought of one dropping down his neck or crawling up his leg was enough for him to stay where he was. He recalled a time from his youth when he woke up in a tent while on a camping trip to find that one of his peers had placed a crab the size of a Frisbee on his chest. A crab doesn't have eight legs, but Eric, at that precise moment, was in no mood to count. As far as he was concerned, something with a great many moving parts—which included among their number a couple of giant pincers—was making progress up his body, albeit sideways. To make matters worse, his friends had removed the outer layer of his tent, turned it round, and pinned it back down so that when he unzipped the door and made an attempt to exit sharply, he merely bounced back off the canvas. The incident was by no means the trauma that triggered off his dislike of spiders, but it was never going to be the event that helped him get over it.

Suzan emerged with a pot of paint and a couple of brushes—and an unbidden companion, which was dangling from her hair.

"Spider!" pointed Eric as the colour flushed from his face.

Suzan let the spider crawl onto the back of her hand, and she watched in fascination as it climbed underneath and clung upside down to her palm.

"I love spiders," she said.

"What's there to love?"

"They're beautiful things, don't you think?"

"No. Not really!"

"Look at him," said Suzan, reaching out with her hand.

"No, I won't, if you don't mind," he said, recoiling.

"You get set up over there," she said, gesturing with a nod. "I'll put this little one back and fetch a bowl of soapy water to give the wall a quick once over with."

Eric made his way to the side of the house, his skin creeping, down a narrow path that was bordered on one side by a fence. He lifted the lid on the tin of paint and placed it carefully on the ground.

Suzan appeared a few moments later, holding a washing bowl full of water, trying not to let too much slop over the side. They scrubbed the outside wall clean with wire brushes and stood back to let it dry. The side of the house they were working on was still shaded from the sun, so they had a few minutes to pass. Eric was desperate to break the silence but was uncertain as to how. Suzan, for her part, sensed Eric's discomfort and chose to maintain the hush, because his squirming amused her. This was not as cruel of her as it may at first seem. Suzan liked Eric's inane innocence and after having had to bear the darkest thoughts of even the most ordinary people, she found his dumb simplicity refreshing.

"How did you know about Carmine Craxxi?" he asked, cracking under the strain at last.

"Why do you find silence so uncomfortable?"

"I don't," he protested, then folded his arms. "You didn't answer my question," he added after a about half a minute had ticked by.

"I know."

Suzan picked up a brush and pushed the pot of paint between her and Eric.

"I think it's dry now."

Eric, determined to prove that silence held no misgivings for him, resolved to not utter a sound while they painted. He didn't have to, however, as there were more voices in his head than there were buzzing through a telephone exchange. The voices were mostly arguing with each other, and they all belonged to him. Had that simple truth occurred to him, he might have smiled and stopped quarrelling with himself at once, but it didn't.

When the first coat was finished, they stood back to admire their work and to rest their arms, which were beginning to ache.

"So how did you get out of it?" asked Suzan.

"Get out of what?"

"Being Carmine Craxxi."

"The same way I got in. I sort of stumbled."

"That's not a bad way to live."

"I don't know about that. It's what got me into the mess in the first place."

"And what got you out of it, don't forget."

Eric thrust his hands into his pockets, self-consciously, and hummed tunelessly. He wondered how his escape was being taken back at Primo Fortunato's club and if Margaretha had told him the truth about his identity. He didn't imagine, either way, that a man like Fortunato was a 'win some, lose some' type, but he felt he was safe enough where he was. The commune was many miles out of town and not the sort of place where he was likely to be bumping into him accidentally.

"Is this how you imagined it?" he asked.

"Imagined what?"

"Heaven. Paradise."

"You're disappointed?"

"Aren't you?"

Suzan shrugged.

"My life now is everything I always wanted it to be, so I suppose it's close enough to Heaven for me."

"I wish I had your attitude."

"You'll be fine. It takes time."

"But do you think it's worth dying for?"

"No. I think it's worth living for. It's just that most people need to die first before they start."

Eric snorted and nodded.

He resumed painting. The white surface reminded him of waking up as a child during the winter and seeing the back garden and the farmer's field beyond it blanketed in snow. What was it in humans, he wondered, which meant that when confronted by an unblemished landscape like that their first thought was to run across it, destroying its virgin beauty? Perhaps it was not its beauty that they wanted to ruin but its blankness, he thought as he painted. Except the thought, while in his own voice, was not his but Suzan's, who had been listening. Did vast plains of nothing disturb people so much that they had to break it up with some sort of mark of themselves? Was the urge to yell out too powerful to resist when surrounded by silence? Is that why people spread their arms and shouted at the tops of their voices from mountain tops? It made him think of people who were comfortable in their own company and wondered if he had ever really met one. The fact that he had not himself shut up for the last few minutes was now no longer lost on him. Suzan had made sure of that.

He glanced at her, surreptitiously. Or at least as surreptitiously as men can be when trying to steal a glance at a beautiful woman. The tips of her hair had flecks of white paint on them, and somehow, they made her look even more attractive. He noticed her long neck again and how her jaw line disappeared delicately just below her ear, as if the line had been drawn in with a pencil and then smudged with the artist's thumb. When she reached up to the top of the wall, her Tee-shirt rode up revealing her stomach and pelvic bone above her brown, corduroy jeans. He became aware that he was staring and refocused his attention on the wall before he was caught and accused of leering. He just wanted to know what she was thinking, since she seemed to know so much about what was going through his head.

"It all changed for me when my grandfather died," Suzan said, distantly. It was the first time she had spoken to Eric about her past. It was the first time she'd spoken to anyone.

Eric Looked up, for a moment disorientated.

"You wanted to know what I was thinking. The moment he stopped breathing I knew he was gone. I don't mean dead, either. I mean he was absent. No longer there. They asked me if I wanted to spend some time with him, but I told them that the body lying in the bed was not my grandfather. I walked out and just kept walking. I went to the beach. I walked right across the sand and stopped at the water." She paused for a full minute, her body still there but her mind back among her memory. "I sat down and watched the waves rolling toward the shore: one after the other on their relentless course towards death.

"But as I watched the waves crashing against the beach, I realised they were not dying at all. They were simply ending their journeys and then flowing back into the sea: the sea that they were never really apart from anyway.

"Then I thought about my grandfather, and I knew that the same thing had happened to him. He had returned. His so-called life and death were only illusions and that for him it was the end of the illusion. The end to the lie that we are somehow separate from everything else. Nothing had actually changed.

"And the ironic thing was that when he was alive, I felt he was separate from me. If I were not with him, I was apart from him. But when he died that illusion died too and I had never felt more close to him than I did at that moment. And ever since. After his death I felt him everywhere. But it wasn't just him. Nothing was the same ever again. From then on, I was never alone. I had the four corners of the universe at the tips of my fingers, and I couldn't hate or fear anything anymore."

Eric let Suzan find her own way back into the present moment before speaking in a hoarse whisper.

"That's beautiful. Thank you."

"The air is full of music," she said more brightly. "All you need to do is turn the dial on the radio and you can hear it."

"Is that supposed to mean something to me?" asked Eric after a moment's reflection.

She smiled.

"It means whatever you make of it, Eric. There," she said, taking a step back when they had finished. "I couldn't have done it without you."

"Oh, I am sure you could."

"Yes, but it wouldn't have been as much fun."

"Are you being sarcastic?" "

No," said Suzan who was aware that Eric was in the

kind of mood where he wanted to be wounded and decided to be nice to him.

"I like you."

"You like me?" said Eric, incredulously.

"Why wouldn't I?"

"Well, I hardly seem your type."

"I said I like you, Eric. I didn't say I wanted to jump into bed with you."

Eric flushed red.

"Oh, no, I didn't mean-"

"Don't worry about it, Fungus," said Suzan, playfully. "We'll clean these brushes and go grab a drink. We've earned it."

"I'm fungus now, am I?"

"Yep!"

"Any special reason?"

"Because I have this feeling I won't be able to get rid of you."

"Well, if you want me to leave I'll-"

"Oh, shut up!" she replied, impatiently. "Now, come on, I'm thirsty."

Eric and Suzan cleaned the paint brushes and put them away. When that was done, they washed their hands and went into the kitchen, which was busy with residents who had the same idea.

"Everybody, Eric; Eric, everybody," said Suzan.

'Everybody' nodded and mumbled greetings collectively and returned to what they were doing. It was not uncommon for new people to arrive and leave on the same day, so no one was going to go to any special effort to get to know Eric until they felt sure he was going to stick around a while. Only Sebastian paid Eric closer attention.

"So how do you know Suzan?" he asked him when Suzan left the kitchen to answer the door.

"We met a few days ago at a café. She said I should pop along. Seemed to think I might like it."

"Did she now?"

Even Eric was able to detect an edge to Sebastian's voice, and he didn't appreciate the suspicious eye of his which settled on him now. Suzan shambled back in and rescued him from further interrogation.

"Let's sit outside."

"Who was that?" asked Eric once they had made themselves comfortable, cross-legged on the lawn.

"Sebastian? Oh, he's okay. A bit protective of me."

"I think he likes you."

"He's sweet. Harmless. Don't worry about him."

They sat drinking fruit juice, shaded by a tree.

"Do you think you like it enough to hang around a bit?" asked Suzan.

"Sure. If I'm welcome."

"You can be my guest."

"I get the impression I annoy you, though."

"You do!"

"And you still want me around?"

"Yeah, but don't get too comfortable."

Eric was not sure what to make of Suzan. It didn't seem to matter how harshly she spoke to him, there was always something affectionate in her words he appreciated.

"This afternoon you can help me fix the tiles on the roof. Seb was going to finish it, but he's got to go into town for something."

"I'm not very good with heights," said Eric, who didn't like the affectionate shortening of Sebastian's name by Suzan, which would have been interesting had he noticed.

"You'll be fine; so long as you don't fall off."

"That's what I'm worried about."

"Always worried. That's you."

"Sometimes I wonder who knows my mind the most: you or me," replied Eric, with unconvincing petulance.

"Oh," said Suzan, enigmatically, "I hope there is not going to be any doubt about that."

"Quite," said Eric, uncertainly and fondled his glass.

Eric decided that Suzan was not like anyone he had met before. He knew that everyone was different, in their ways, but to him they were only superficially so. Everyone was basically the same as far as he could tell. But not Suzan. She was like something that exists only fleetingly at the corner of his vision that when looked at directly would disappear. There she was sitting beside him; yet there she was not. If he had possessed the poetic ability to say so himself, he would have been able to express this shapeless feeling by saying she was more like a movement than a thing: a verb, not a noun. She was as indistinct from her surroundings as a whirlpool is from water, or a sound wave is from the air it travels through. While on Earth he had developed a layman's interest in quantum physics. He enjoyed watching documentaries about its counter-intuitive properties; he bought and read books that the presenters of those documentaries brought out just in time for Christmas; and he had watched on the Internet live coverage of the Large Hadron Collider in Switzerland being cranked up to full power. One of the many facts about physics which staggered his mind was the quantum leap, where a single electron would move from orbit around the nucleus of the atom and into another orbit. Except it wouldn't move in a conventional sense. It would not pass from one point to another via all points in between. One moment it would be in one place, then it would be another. Just like that. Not that anyone had seen an electron, though. Like everything else in the strange quantum world, it didn't take well to being looked at. Just as with Suzan, which is what made him think of them in the first place. Physically she stayed in one place as much as anyone else. But when it came to understanding her–of getting some sense at all of what she was thinking or feeling, he felt as if he had slipped into the world of quantum weirdness.

"What did you mean," he asked, "back at the café when you said my head was loud?"

Suzan thought of the soughing of a tree. The audible rustling of its leaves comes not from the tree but from the wind. The clutter in Eric's head caused the universe to howl as it passed through it. But she knew that if she said as much to Eric, he would think so hard about it he would be even further from where he so obviously yearned to be. So, at the risk of appearing deliberately maddening to Eric she smiled, finished her drink with a single gulp and left her cup on the picnic table. Eric emitted a protest and followed Suzan to their next job. Uncertain on the wobbly ladder, he climbed toward the roof.

"Are you sure this ladder's safe?" he called up, keeping his eyes fixed solidly on the wall in front. "It's very bendy."

He climbed the final few steps and scrambled over the gutter and onto the tiles, mumbled words leaving his mouth urgently as he scalded his palms on the sun-baked surface.

"Yeah, be careful," warned Suzan, too late. "The tiles are hot."

"Hot?" said Eric, gingerly standing tall. "There's someone frying an egg over there!"

The house did not seem so tall from the ground, but from up by the chimney it felt as if he were looking down from the top of a skyscraper.

"Are you okay?" asked Suzan.

"I'm fine."

The afternoon heat was oppressive up on the roof, so they worked slowly and made sure they kept drinking lots of water, which Suzan was sensitive enough to fetch from the kitchen herself when they had run out, rather then send Eric to negotiate the ladder. About an hour into the task, Eric again became fascinated by Suzan. Her gaze was so intense when she concentrated on the job in hand that he would not have been surprised to see the tiles float telekinetically from their pile and slot themselves into the gaps left by the missing ones all by themselves. His own concentration was made more difficult by the way her hair kept tumbling down over her face, and the way she would then hook it behind her ear absentmindedly, which he had first seen her do at the café.

As Eric became more comfortable, he started to rationalise his fear of heights. Heights alone, could not hurt him he realised. It was the falling that was the major concern. But the thought of falling never crossed his mind. The fear of jumping was what really gripped him. Eric had no death wish by any means, whatever that meant in his position, but all his life he had not been able to peer down from a great height without feeling a compulsion from deep inside him to throw himself over. It was not something he would ever give in to, but he would receive brief flashes of vaulting over the railing and accelerating toward the ground, and that would be enough for him to stand well away from the edge. A trip to Africa with Amber several years previously had taken him to Victoria Falls bridge, which arched more than a hundred metres above the lordly Zambezi river. He had walked along the full kilometre length of the falls from the opposite side of the fissure, close enough for it to rain down on him and soak him through. He stopped periodically and looked through the rainbows and thick mist at the sight of Mother Nature flexing her muscles to the full. Even then, as the ground rumbled beneath his feet, the thought of dropping through the rising steam to a certain death invaded his thoughts, and he would back away, not trusting the impulse. It was with overpowering emotion, then, that he found himself back on the bridge the following day, pigeon-stepping out onto a metal platform with an elasticated rope around his ankles.

"Jump up and away from the platform," the man had said.

Jump up and away from the platform, he repeated to himself as Amber watched on and the countdown began.

"Five! Four! Three! Two! One!" they shouted together. "Bungy!"

He jumped up and away from the platform without hesitating. For a moment he hung in the air, motionless, and all he could see was hazy sky. Then the tree-lined tops of the ravine on either side came into view, followed by the sliver of green water below and then the roar of wind that threatened to tear the clothes from his body as the river approached rapidly. He felt the rope around his ankles tighten and he began to slow down. Pressure built up behind his eyes and he closed them, tight, genuinely fearing they would pop from his head.

Now, utterly disorientated, he accelerated once more, this time in the opposite direction. He had turned in mid-flight and was staring up at the iron girders of the bridge from underneath, before becoming weightless for a brief moment then dropping again. With surprising presence of mind, he remembered to give a thumbs up to the photographer on the bridge at the top of the next bounce.

Eventually, he stopped springing and found himself hanging, upside down, some fifty metres or so above the Zambezi, and the crocodiles that lived there. He was not in the least bit perturbed by this. It was the thought of what to do with his hands that bothered him at that precise moment. He reasoned that he could not very well let them hang down for fear of appearing dead. He could hardly fold them, either, or put them in his pockets. In the end, he swung gently from side to side, punching the air, ecstatically and whooping like an American until someone was sent down on a winch to take him back up. He was gathered in by outstretched arms from a walkway beneath the bridge and the rope was detached.

"You can step out of the rope now," said the man. "I said," he repeated, a few moments later, "you can step out now."

But Eric was frozen to the spot. Apparently, hanging

upside down from the end of a glorified elastic band suspended beneath what was then the highest bungy-jump platform anywhere in the world did not phase him. But stand him on a narrow walkway with no harness and nothing to stop him jumping except his own resolve, and suddenly his knuckles went white with the force with which he was gripping the handrails.

He remembered Clarence in the lobby of the hotel. *Let go of the handrail*, he had said. *Let yourself float away. A snowflake never falls in the wrong place.*

"A snowflake never falls in the wrong place," he said out loud.

"What?" asked Suzan.

"Nothing. Sorry, I was just talking to myself."

"Nothing new there then."

His eyes were drawn again to Suzan. He was in his thirties, and she was barely into her mid-twenties, if that, but somehow, he did not feel very much older than her. In fact, if anything, the opposite was true. There was a knowledge in her eyes that stretched back centuries and it made the little more than five years between them laughable. In every single way except the most obvious, she was older than he was. The afternoon wore on and the sun started casting long shadows across the landscape. An hour later they were finished. Eric started to pack the tools away, but Suzan stopped him.

"Look," she said, pointing to the horizon.

The sun was just touching the tips of the distant hills and the sky was ablaze as if someone had tossed a match into the air to ignite and burn away the thick, stale evening air. They made themselves comfortable beside each other and watched. Eric had been taught at school that sunsets were red and orange, but now that he looked, he could see greens and purples and blues and even browns. It was as if he were seeing a sunset for the very first time. He wondered what else he had been wrong about because he had just not looked properly.

"It's beautiful."

They watched in silence as the sun finally disappeared leaving a belt of lime green behind the silhouetted mountains. As the sky above their heads darkened, Eric felt as if they had been joined by a third person.

"There's someone out there," he whispered.

Suzan smiled, privately.

"Who?"

"It's more a feeling."

"Describe it."

Eric struggled for words at first, but a rare eloquence took him over.

"It feels . . . maternal. Safe. As if everything were alive and conscious and . . . in love." He turned to Suzan. "You know?"

Suzan squeezed her knees to her chest and breathed in deeply.

"I know."

"Do you feel it, too?" asked Eric.

"All the time."

"Is this why you brought me up here?"

"I brought you up here to fix the tiles."

Eric looked at Suzan and saw, for the very first time, not a young girl but the depth and breadth of the universe in the *shape* of young girl who did not know what to do with it all. Had he not already met God, he would have wondered if, perhaps, Suzan were him in disguise. He reached out and stroked the hair away from her face so that her lips were revealed. He slid his fingers gently across her mouth. Suzan closed her eyes, lost for a moment. She became aware of her heart thumping in her chest and a hesitation take her over. Eric leant in to kiss her.

"Dinner will be ready soon," she said, abruptly and scrambled to her feet.

The spell was broken, and Eric attempted to gather his scattered thoughts and emotions. He was not embarrassed that he had been so bold and rejected. He knew Suzan had been just as much a part of what had happened and that neither of them had acted consciously. It was as powerful a moment as he had ever experienced, and he did not feel ashamed for having given in to it. They gathered the tools and descended the ladder without speaking. Once the tool shed was locked up, Eric followed Suzan inside and up the stairs to her bedroom.

The room was small. In one corner, an unmade mattress lay flat on the floor. Beside it was a small set of drawers upon which stood a reading lamp. On the floor beside it, stacked neatly, were books, including, Eric noticed, the one she had been reading at the café when he first met her. In the opposite corner, a guitar was propped up against the wall beside a stereo player and a pile of compact discs that had toppled over and scattered across the floor. Although a little dishevelled, the room was clean and smelt nice.

She handed Eric some men's clothes that she just so happened to have—though from whom she would not tell the harmlessly jealous Eric—and they changed together.

He was glad to get out of the formal trousers and shirt but felt awkward removing his clothes in front of Suzan. He looked over to her to see if she was looking at him. She wasn't. At that moment she had just removed her corduroys and was slipping her slim, dark legs into a pair of clean jeans. She then lifted her top above her head and rummaged about, wearing just a white bra, for a clean replacement. Her shoulders, though feminine, were strong looking. Her back, with its flawless skin, tapered gently into a narrow waist and disappeared into the waistband of her trousers that hung loosely on her hips. Though not a classic beauty, she was certainly captivating to him. He suddenly became aware of his own semi-nakedness and hurried into his second-hand clothes. He looked down at his scruffy jeans and hessian top and had to admit he did at least look less like a refugee from a wedding. Suzan stood on tiptoes in front of him and ruffled his hair.

"There. You look slightly less embarrassing for me to be seen with you."

"I'll take that as a compliment."

"You're learning at last," the tension from their moment on the roof had almost dissipated. "Now, come on, I don't know about you, but I'm starving."

Downstairs, residents sat on sofas and beanbags and cross-legged on the floor with plates of food on their laps. A few sat around a heavy, wooden table while more sat out on the patch of lawn they had kept back from being cultivated. Suzan led Eric into the kitchen and grabbed a couple of plates—passing one to him. They stood in line and made their way along, scooping food from bowls and slopping it onto their plates. Eric was famished. Physical labour, fresh air and a worry-free mind fuelled his appetite, but he was too polite to take too much.

"Get stuck in!" said one of the cooks—a young girl with an Irish accent—sensing Eric's display of etiquette. "There's plenty more where that came from."

Eric and Suzan took their plates outside and sat on the grass. The sky was mottled with stars—constellations that Eric had not seen before. With no clouds to trap the heat of the day, the temperature outside had dropped to a comfortable level. The food was delicious, fresh and well-prepared, and Eric ate quickly, against the advice of Suzan who had told him to slow down and chew thoroughly. Soon, Eric had cleaned his plate and did not require very much encouragement to go back for a second helping. When they had finished eating and handed their plates back to be washed, they lay beside each other on the cool, damp grass with the very special type of contentment that comes only from being well-fed at the end of a day of hard work.

"Still think Heaven isn't so great?" asked Suzan.

"This is much more like it."

"Such a man! All you needed was a full belly."

"Well," protested Eric, laughing, "they do say it's the way to a man's heart."

Suzan rolled onto her side and propped herself up on her elbow.

"Oh, I don't know," she said, placing a hand flat on his stomach. "There are more fun ways."

Eric looked up at Suzan whose hair had tumbled down and encircled his face. For a moment, he was reminded of sitting inside the weeping branches of a willow tree.

"If I thought for a moment it would get me anywhere,

I'd rise to that comment."

"What makes you think it won't get you anywhere?"

Eric squinted at Suzan, trying to second guess her, but found it impossible.

"I'm not your type."

"I don't do types."

"But I am growing on you."

"Like fungus."

"You mean," said Eric, making a stab at corny humour, "I am a *fun-guy*?"

Suzan rolled her eyes and laughed. Eric joined her.

"You know," he said, "I haven't laughed . . . at all since I died. Not until today."

"Carmine Craxxi wasn't the sort of man who had a lot to laugh about I suppose."

"No, he wasn't."

Eric frowned and was momentarily serious.

"Thank you," he said.

"For what?"

"For being nice to me."

"Yeah, well, don't get too used to it."

Eric laughed again.

"I don't think I could get used to anything with you around."

There was a brief pause when Eric wondered if their aborted kiss from earlier was going to be back on, but if it ever was, Suzan changed her mind. She rolled onto her back again. Had Eric chosen this moment to prop himself up on his elbow and pursue the matter it would most likely have concluded the way he wanted it to. But, endearingly to Suzan's mind, he failed to spot this subtle move on her part and quietly gave up.

"So," he asked once the tension had evaporated again, "what's your story?"

Suzan hesitated. Eric sensed there was something she wanted to tell him—something she had told no one—but that she had reined it in.

"Nothing really," was all she offered.

"I'm an open book. You're so closed. You say I'm frightened, but you're terrified."

"Oi, leave the deep, personal probing to me. You just . . ."

"Look pretty?"

"Or as close as you can manage."

Eric was correct, though. What was more, he knew it.

"And don't think," said Suzan, as Eric was doing just that, "that you're going to lure me into pouring my heart out. I'd see you coming from a mile away."

Eric, protesting that he was thinking no such thing, crossed his hands beneath the back of his head to form a pillow. He could hear drunken laughter coming from inside the house, but it seemed so distant; other-worldly. Outside there was only the sound of crickets and the occasional rustling of leaves in the trees. His arms and legs were heavy from the physical exertion of the day, but it was a nice type of tired; not the heavy headed weariness that overcame him midway through an afternoon at the office, sitting at a computer, staring at the clock and having to drink endless cups of coffee just to prevent his head from coming down hard on the desk.

Suzan was also tired, but not from the work, which she was now used to. What had worn her out was Eric. The chaos in his mind sounded to her like a large orchestra tuning up before a concert, and it required all her emotional strength to not be overwhelmed by it all. Ordinarily, she would have given him a wide berth, but there was something very familiar about Eric that intrigued her, and she wanted to know what it was. She knew things about him she shouldn't. He wanted to know how, but the truth was, she didn't know either. Her instinct was to trust him; to share with him. It had been a long time since she had confided in anyone. Her parents had suspected there was something different about her when, as a young child just learning to speak, she would blurt out what they were thinking—often to embarrassing effect. A few years later, troubled by nightmares and increasingly fretful, she was taken to see her maternal grandmother who, in an effort to cure her, tied a dead crow to her wrists and chanted a mantra in a low, rasping voice. This did not cure Suzan, but from that moment on she had a number of new neuroses to contend with on top of whatever else had been already bothering her. She came to a decision she hoped she would not be made to regret.

"I am going to trust you now, Eric," she said, "and if you abuse that trust, I'll kill you."

Eric flinched at the threat.

"Okay."

"I think you've probably guessed by now," said Suzan after a long pause to gather her thoughts, "that I can hear what other people are thinking."

"That much is obvious."

"To you it is, but only because I wanted you to know. No one else has a clue. No one."

"Why me then?" asked Eric.

"I don't know, but that's what I want to find out."

"I don't understand."

"I have known you before. That's what I am sure of."

"Before?"

"I don't believe in past lives the way others do, but I do believe in a connection between people."

"A connection?"

"Look, I'm not very good at explaining things. That's half the reason I've never told anyone this before. You'll have to bear with me and please stop just repeating what I say."

Eric made the decision to simply listen and do his best to follow.

"I just get this sense," said Suzan, "that we've been together before. Many times."

"Eh?" asked Eric, abandoning his attempt to muddle through without asking questions instantly.

"We were together, but something happened."

"What?"

Suzan lowered her head and seemed to be wrestling with something.

"You killed yourself."

Eric sat up.

"I killed myself? Why?"

"We were meant to be together, but we couldn't be. I don't why, before you ask. I begged you to live for me and not die for me, but you were too much the dramatic type."

Suzan fell silent.

"Then what happened?" asked Eric.

"You've been stuck ever since."

"Stuck?"

"In a loop. Making the same mistake over and over again."

"You mean, I keep killing myself?"

"And winding up back at the beginning."

"But I didn't kill myself. I was murdered."

"I don't have all the answers, Eric," she replied after a long pause.

"And what about you? Where do you come into it?"

Suzan thought carefully about the next words out of her mouth.

"It's been a long, long time," she said, suddenly sounding so tired. "Must be why I am so snappy with everyone else; I use all my patience up with you."

"When you say long . . ."

"Thousands of years, if years mean anything."

"And then I sit next to you at a café?" Eric thought for a moment. "Was that a coincidence?"

Suzan shook her head.

"Nothing's a coincidence. We won't get anywhere until you do what you have to do."

"Do what? What do I have to do?"

"I don't know."

This was true; she really didn't know.

"And if I do whatever it is I have to do, then what?"

Suzan turned to stare at Eric.

"Heaven awaits."

TWENTY

It was approaching midnight and most of the residents at the commune had either gone to bed or fallen asleep wherever they happened to be at the time. Eric and Suzan stepped hand in hand over sleeping bodies and made their way upstairs.

"We haven't sorted out where I'm going to sleep," whispered Eric.

"You're sleeping with me."

Eric felt a rush of anxiety.

"Are you sure? You don't mind?"

Suzan didn't mind. In fact, her dreams had been increasingly disturbing the last week and she appreciated the chance of having someone with her through the night. They entered Suzan's bedroom. Eric stood, awkwardly, noticing just how intimately narrow the bed was while Suzan lit candles. She liked candles for what they represented. To most people, passion is waving your arms around, pulling at your hair and, for some reason, using bad language. Anything more quiet and contained is deemed passionless and cold. To Suzan, candle flames made a mockery of that idea. They were an example of focused intensity: burning quietly and in harmony with their environment but burning with no less heat–no less passion–for it.

"The generator's off, so it's candles after twelve."

The room became illuminated by an amber light and long shadows that danced on the wall like witches around a cauldron. Suzan, with no trace of self-consciousness, pulled her clothes off down to her underwear.

"Are you just going to stand there staring at me?" she asked.

Eric sat down on the edge of the mattress, shielding himself with his back and took his top off. The trousers were more awkwardly removed from a seated position, but with a well-timed bounce he whipped them down and kicked them away. He took his socks off but kept his shorts and Tee-shirt on. Suzan was already in bed. Eric assumed she had been discreetly facing the wall, but when he turned round, he saw she had been staring at him, enjoying his bashfulness the whole time. She had had quite enough of narcissistic men who preferred to display themselves in the middle of the bedroom before bed. Nothing impressed her less. Eric manoeuvred himself under the sheets and lay next to Suzan, careful not to touch her with any part of his body—even his elbows.

"Are you okay?" asked Suzan.

"Yes. Fine. You?"

Suzan was fine, too; but then that was never in question.

Eric slid down farther until he was flat on his back. He was not at his most comfortable like that. The trouble was, if he turned to face her it might be received as being forward; but if he turned the other way, he would be showing her his back, which was just rude. Suzan decided to let Eric off the hook by resting her head on his chest, draping an arm across him and slipping her leg between his. Almost straight away Eric relaxed. He even reached up and stroked her hair away from her face.

Without thinking, he started talking.

"I have a girlfriend. I *had* a girlfriend. Back on Earth. We'd been together years. We'd have got married if I hadn't . . . if I hadn't." He was quiet for a long time. "I just wanted you to know that."

Eric suddenly felt unsure of himself, but he decided to carry on regardless.

"I am telling you this because, well, I think I have feelings for you. I can't explain it. I know we've only just met, but if we've known each other for as long as you say we have—if it really is thousands of years, which I still don't get—then it makes sort of sense. It's just like picking up from where we left off. And you're not the only one who gets these intuitions, you know. Since meeting you I've been having them too. I get this sense that . . . I know you don't need looking after. I know you've done well enough at that on your own, but I want you to know that I want to protect you. It feels like . . . I want to make it up to you . . . make amends for something. Something I did to you once. Perhaps it was when I . . ." Eric had trouble saying the words. "When I killed myself. That must have been awful for you. I can't believe I did that to you. That I left you behind like that to deal with it on your own. I just want you to know I'm sorry for that. But we've found each other again and . . . well, I don't know what's going to happen next. But whatever it is, I'll be there with you. I won't let you down again."

Eric was overwhelmed with the feeling of freeing himself from a burden he had not known he had; something that had been inside him, weighing him down, for longer than he could possibly know.

"You probably already know," he went on, more confidently now, "that . . . well you seem to know how I feel before even I do, so really there is no need for me to say it, is there."

Suzan said nothing.

"All right," said Eric. "I suppose some things just have to be said out loud. What I want to say to you is that . . . well . . ."

Eric sighed, heavily, finally on the verge of releasing the last of some very old karma that existed between the two of them. Suzan's breathing was slow and deep. Her body rose and fell rhythmically.

"Suzan?"

Nothing.

"Suzan?"

How long she had been asleep for and how much of Eric's speech she had heard he didn't know, but he decided it was probably for the best anyway. To Amber he had been gone months by then; perhaps years. She would have moved on, but for him, he hadn't been dead more than a week. However powerfully he felt that he had known Suzan before and for a very long time, he couldn't help feeling that he was being unfaithful. Those left behind always struggled with that guilt; it had not occurred to him that the same would be true of the dead. And one day,

Amber would be dead too. Would she join him? He didn't know how that worked. If she remarried, who would she spend her eternity with? He could imagine that getting awkward. He was sure he was overthinking it. Heaven had been around for a long time; surely they'd worked it all out by now.

"Sweet dreams," he whispered and closed his eyes.

Suzan's eyes were still open. She had heard everything. Her eyes were red and wet. A single tear drop gathered at the corner of her eye and rolled down her cheek.

Eric slept soundly and, with someone in bed beside her, for the first time in months, so did Suzan. Eric woke first. Her head was still resting on his chest, though her hair had become tangled in the night. The candles Suzan had lit the night before were all extinguished—pools of hard wax spread out around their bases. He was not sure what time it was. The sun was shining, and the birds were singing, but there was no sign that the house had woken up.

He slid out from underneath Suzan and slipped a pillow under her head. She stirred, looked at Eric through barely open eyes, then went back to sleep. He dressed in the previous day's clothes, crept out onto the landing with its creaking floorboards and went downstairs. The living room was pretty much as he had left it the night before: bodies lay scattered about the floor as if a gunman had showered the house with bullets from the street outside. He tip-toed between them and made it to the kitchen. No one was asleep there, but the counters were cluttered with glasses, empty bottles and discarded bags of snacks. He began opening and shutting drawers and cupboards, looking for clean cups, but in the end had to settle for rummaging through the basin for them and rinsing them out with hot water and wiping them with his fingers. He boiled the water and went on a treasure hunt for the coffee and sugar, which he found behind empty bottles of cola. The fridge was almost empty, having been ransacked hours before, but a lone bottle of milk lay on its side beside a tube of tomato paste and several roles of undeveloped photographic film. He sniffed it cautiously and decided it was fit for human consumption.

Encumbered now by two cups of coffee, Eric retraced his steps across the living room, but this time he spotted a clock on the wall. It was six o' clock.

"You're joking!" said Eric out loud, spilling coffee on someone below.

He shook his head and went upstairs to Suzan, nudging the door open with his foot and wondering whether or not he should wake her. She rolled over and opened her eyes.

"What time is it?"

"Six."

"Six? Are you mad?"

"I didn't know what time it was. I was wide awake and thought it must have been late."

"You made coffee?" Suzan sat up and brushed her hair from her face. "Thank you."

Eric, sitting on the bed beside her and placing the cup to his lips, caught sight of Suzan and smiled.

"What?" she asked.

"Your cheeks are all puffy."

Suzan swore, telling Eric, in her mother tongue something that, in English, might have got her arrested in several countries.

"Not a morning person then?" he said, at great personal risk to himself. "So how long do they take to go down?" he asked, poking her spongy cheek with the tip of his finger. This was a mistake. Suzan snapped at Eric's finger with her teeth, causing him to recoil so suddenly he spilt coffee on his lap. "All right, all right!" he said. "I get the message!"

Suzan sipped her coffee.

"What's it like downstairs?"

"Like a bomb's hit it."

She rolled her eyes.

"I'm not clearing it up."

They finished their coffee in silence.

"So," said Eric, "what's the plan for today? What jobs need doing?"

"It's Sunday. It's the commune's day off."

"Sunday?" said Eric, quizzically. "You know, this is the only time since I died that I know what day it is."

"Well, there you go. I told you you'd settle in."

She slid back under the covers and closed her eyes.

"Are you going back to sleep?"

"Do you have a better idea?"

He didn't. He lay above the sheets next to Suzan and smiled.

"What are you grinning at?" asked Suzan, muffled by the pillow, without opening her eyes.

"How did you know I was smiling?" asked Eric. Although he did not know so at the time, this was destined to be a rhetorical question. "If you must know," he went on when Suzan declined to comment, "because I'm happy."

"That's great," said Suzan, sounding as if she were falling asleep again.

"I just feel like I belong, you know?"

Suzan grunted that she did know, and that at that precise moment she did not care. Eric looked down at her and his heart felt as if it were filling with warm water. He made himself comfortable beside her, closed his eyes and within minutes, despite the recent injection of caffeine, he too was asleep.

Twenty-one

Later that day, Suzan and Eric were sitting beside a river. Suzan had made a picnic and taken him to a place she often went to be alone. The riverbank was crumbling, and Eric could see where large chunks had fallen into the water. They sat in the shade of a tree, its roots reaching out from the clay above the water line.

"It's nice here," said Eric, eating a sandwich. Suzan lay on her back, squinting against the sun.

"Are you going to talk a lot?"

Eric took the hint. They were not in a park but in what he would definitely call the countryside. He had lived in a city all his life, but he always felt that he'd be more at home in a small village. Perhaps by the sea. To him, growing up in London, the countryside was like a theme park: somewhere to visit, enjoy then leave. He'd watch the locals with wonder. He couldn't believe people actually lived somewhere like that. He felt the same way when he went to Paris with his school. He was genuinely surprised that such a busy, exciting place had existed at all. That so much life could be going on somewhere he never thought about was something he struggled with. He knew, of course, that there was a reality beyond that which was in his own experience, but it still felt odd. He saw a fish break the surface of the slow-moving water and disappear again. What did it think existed beyond the river?

"Rivers are weird," he said.

"Why?"

He picked a blade of grass and started dividing it into strips.

"It's this whole other world passing through this one."

"So?"

"Well, the fish don't know we exist. I mean, how can they even begin to imagine?"

"Their brains are too small."

"You know what I mean."

Eric returned to his thoughts. Is it the same way with Earth? Do the living pass through Heaven all the time and have absolutely no idea? Is dying just leaving the water?

"You can learn a lot from a river," said Suzan, as if listening in. "A river will always find the easiest way through. If there is a rock in its way, it doesn't waste time and energy trying to move it; it just goes around it. Eventually, the rock will have been worn away to the size of a pebble."

Eric was leaning back on one of his elbows. He brought it up to inspect it. It was criss-crossed with marks left by the grass. He blew an insect from his forearm and lay on his back with his hands folded beneath his head.

"We all face our problems head on," continued Suzan. "We come up against an obstacle and we try to force it away. Things go wrong and we spend so much time refusing to accept it we forget to go on living. But no matter how difficult life gets, there is always a way through. Always."

"The line of least resistance," said Eric, staring at the blue sky and wondering what the translucent spots dancing about in his vision were. "But isn't that just giving up?"

Suzan rolled onto her elbow. "No!" she said, irritated. "No one says you have to stop or turn back. You keep going, but you find a better way."

Suzan tutted at her own inability to find the correct words for the moment. She did not learn her philosophy from books, which was why she often had trouble expressing what she felt. She would have had you believe she was not very good with words; the truth was, unlike most other amateur philosophers, she simply had no one more clever than her to quote.

"Pride tells us we can move mountains," she went on, looking to nature for her cue, "but we can't, and we die trying. Rivers have no pride. That's how they find the easiest path: the lowest ground where no one else wants to walk. Pride stands on top of mountains having conquered them; rivers are happy just to crawl along at the bottom of the lowest valleys. It's not about triumph for them. That's why they always make it to the other side."

"What about dams?"

"What about them?" asked Suzan, who already knew where Eric was going to go.

"Man builds dams and rivers have to come to a halt. Man diverts rivers and there is nothing they can do about it."

"Eric," explained Suzan, patiently, "nothing made by man lasts forever. When the human race is extinct there'll be no one left to maintain the dams. They'll crumble and the river will carry on. Rivers that have been diverted will find their natural courses. Always," said Suzan, emphasising the word, "nature's balance is restored."

"That's what God said."

Suzan had more to say on the topic of rivers, but this brought her to a halt.

"God?"

"Yeah, we met. Well, I met him. He thought he was meeting Carmine Craxxi."

"And when were you going to tell me this?"

"I thought you knew everything I was thinking."

Eric's attempt at facetiousness didn't go down well with Suzan.

"I don't know everything. Anyway, forget that. What's he like?"

It was perhaps only at that moment that the full enormity of Eric's recent meeting became clear to him. Everything had happened so quickly since then that he hadn't really stopped to think about it. A week ago, he was looking for a holiday; now he was reflecting on having met God himself. A lot can change in a week. He knew that. But he was having a remarkable week by any standards.

It's an odd thing with humans: how the extraordinary can so quickly become commonplace. The world sat up and watched as one of them stepped on the moon for the first time. The world was never going to be the same. But by the time the fourth or fifth man had done it, few were paying any more attention. Life just went on as it always had. As a species, they're unique in being so intent on seeking out novelty yet becoming so bored with it so quickly and looking for the next new thing. Eric had met God. But that was yesterday.

"I mean, he was . . . well, not like a god at all. He was just a normal man. Well, obviously not normal at all, but that's how he came across."

"I've seen him talk on the telly, but I've never been in the same room as him."

"He had this confidence. When Primo threatened him, you could see it just did nothing."

"Who's Primo and what did he threaten him with?"

Eric explained who Primo was and his vision of Heaven with him having more of a say in how things were run. He told her, too, about meeting Carmine Craxxi and about Margaretha.

"Who's Margaretha?" asked Suzan. Eric was sure he could sense some jealousy in her.

"She's Primo's girlfriend. She was good to me."

He thought of Margaretha and hoped she was all right. He guessed, quite correctly, that Fortunato had been furious and taken it out on anyone who happened to be near him.

"Do you think God's a person?" asked Suzan.

Eric had met a man who everyone agreed was God. However, he couldn't help but think about their shared experience on the roof as they watched the sun set together. He had felt something powerful then that he simply had not in the presence of God.

"That's a good question. I don't know."

A silence settled between them. Not a 'pregnant pause' or tension. It was the silence between two pieces of music when the last reverberation of the violins ceases, and the wood wind section raise their instruments and fix their collective gaze on the conductor.

"You're amazing," said Eric. "The way you see things."

"Nature's amazing," said Suzan. "All you have to do is look at it and learn. Nature's wisdom belongs to us as much as it does to the rivers and mountains. But you have to stop thinking of it as something that has to be conquered."

"Rivers and mountains are wise?"

"They're not clever. They're not intelligent. They can't split atoms or build televisions or complete The Times crossword."

"I can't do any of those things."

"But wisdom," said Suzan, ignoring Eric, "is not about what you know, it's about what you don't know. It's not about what you do, it's about what you don't do. It's not about trying, it's about not trying."

"How can you not try?"

"The river's not trying, is it? It's just following its natural path."

"And I have to follow my natural path."

"Yes."

"But how do I know which is my natural path and which isn't?"

"Just be quiet and listen."

"I tried that before and didn't hear anything."

Eric felt suddenly demoralised. There are things that are beyond some people and for him this, he decided, was one of those things. What made him unhappy was that he wanted to be able to go where Suzan went; to understand her, to become closer to her; to fly with her where she was most happy instead of forcing her to the ground to which he seemed so firmly rooted.

"I'm sorry," he said, sighing.

"Never say sorry to me," said Suzan softly.

She had brought her guitar with her. She unzipped the case and removed an old, faded-looking guitar. She crossed her legs, perched the instrument on her thigh and started to tune it.

"I didn't know you were left-handed," said Eric.

"All geniuses are."

She started to play. Eric brimmed full of admiration for anyone who could play a musical instrument. He had been blessed with long, pianist's fingers, but if his ears had feet, they would have both been left. The richness of music being played outdoors, right beside him, went straight to Eric's heart.

It was only through music that Suzan was able to communicate that which she struggled so much with through words. Instead of her soul passing on messages to her head that then had to find a way to express them simply, it was now talking directly to his in a language common to them both. Unlike his intellect, Eric's heart understood immediately what was being said to it. Suzan played for several minutes, gently, utterly composed. Her attention never wavered; the music never faltered. She let the final note cling to the space between them then dissipate into the trees and plants and water until there was only silence, which Eric was loath to interrupt.

"That was," he whispered, a frog in his throat betraying the emotion roused in him, "beautiful. It was really . . . beautiful."

Suzan laid the guitar in its case, took a deep breath and looked around her. With the music still wrapping its ethereal arms around her, everything seemed brighter, more colourful. There was so much harmony in the universe, and she was happy to have contributed, in her small way, to it.

"What was it?" asked Eric.

"Hmm?" she asked, dreamily.

"The song, what was it called?"

"It doesn't have a name."

"Who wrote it?"

"No one. I just made it up."

Eric was incredulous.

"On the spot? You just made it up as you went along?"

"Sure," shrugged Suzan.

"But . . . you're a genius!"

"I told you I was!"

"You weren't kidding!"

Eric puffed his cheeks out.

"But how?" he asked. "How do you do it? It just, what, comes to you?"

"You just let go."

"You stop trying?"

Suzan smiled.

"And you forget you're a little drop of water in an ocean and you become the ocean."

Suzan stood on her knees, suddenly impassioned.

"Have you ever had a moment of inspiration, Eric? Or intuition?"

"Not really."

"They came to you in flashes, didn't they. Sudden realisations. You go 'Oh! Of course!' and you wonder why you hadn't worked it out before."

"That's me forgetting I'm a drop of water?"

"Forget the drop of water!" snapped Suzan. "It's when you let go. It's like . . ." said Suzan, struggling again to find the words, "you're continually aware that you're Eric. You're aware of your so-called limits and you can't go any further than them."

"Because I'm aware of them?"

"Shut up! And then something causes you to forget, and you become unaware of who you are and what your limits are."

"Like that bloke who couldn't solve a problem until he got into a bath, and it suddenly came to him, and he shouted 'Eureka!'?"

"Yes, just like that bloke in the bath."

"And that's where your song came from?"

"Your mind can go places your flesh and bone can't. Think about it. If you want to make a sculpture, you need to find some clay or marble. But creativity itself . . . ideas, music, art, stories, they exist nowhere in the universe until you bring them into it. You can't go looking for something that isn't there until you think it."

"And all that from just letting go?"

"Yes."

"And you came back with that song?"

"Yes."

"Is that what genius is, then? Being able to let go?"

"And then being able to express the universe within the limits of the world."

"That can't be easy."

"Ever wonder why so many geniuses go mad?" asked Suzan. Another rhetorical question.

Eric puffed his cheeks out again. He had heard someone say once that great music was in the silence between
the notes and that great art was not about what the artist
painted but what he or she left out. He had not understood
what they meant—until that moment. Eric pondered this
for a few minutes, then his face lit up.

"That's how you know what other people are thinking!"

Suzan smiled and walked towards him on her knees
and draped her arms around his neck. She pushed him
onto his back and came down on top of him. She kissed
his lips slowly, then smiled some more.

"What, here?" asked Eric, looking around them.

Suzan nodded.

"And now."

TWENTY-TWO

Bruno and Enzo stood outside Primo Fortunato's office. They were there to stop anyone from going in, but it was also as far as they were willing to go themselves. The office was silent. Or at least, now it was. It hadn't been a few minutes before. Fortunato had been turning over furniture, throwing the smaller pieces, and kicking at those which looked fragile enough to break under the assault. He'd also been shouting a lot. Bruno and Enzo had had trouble understanding all of it, but the version suitable for day-time audiences was that he had not had a very good day: first, God had not agreed to his proposal; second, he had lost Carmine Craxxi. He was still under the impression that Eric was Craxxi. If he knew the truth about that he might have needed emergency medical attention.

"Not right now," said Bruno, holding out his palm.

Margaretha had heard what had happened and wanted to know what state he was in. That had not been her first instinct. That had been to go home and stay there a few days until he had started to calm down. But she was worried about what he might do to Eric if he found him, which he almost definitely would, and to her, when he learnt that she had lied to him about Eric being who he claimed.

"Primo," she called through the door.

"Let her in," said a tired-sounding Primo.

She stepped in cautiously, having to push the door against a broken chair, which scraped on the tiled floor. Closing the door behind her, she searched the room with her eyes for him.

"Primo?"

She found him sitting in a ball in the corner hidden behind what remained of his desk—his head in his hands. She sat down beside him and rested her head on his shoulder.

"This place," he said, "it's no different from Earth. They've got it all sewn up."

"On Earth as it is in Heaven," she whispered.

"I'm going to kill him," he said, finally.

Margaretha took three breaths and said, not wanting to betray her concern for Eric, "Why bother? He's a nobody here. He's beneath you."

Primo took his head out of his hands.

"Not Carmine. God!"

Margaretha recoiled from him.

"What are you saying?"

"Something needs to be done; and I am going to do it. Then things will change."

It was difficult for Margaretha to know which thought she wanted to attend to first with so many scrambling to be heard. The sheer audacity of it made her sick. But more than that, what would the consequences be? For them, and for the universe. Even if you could kill God, was he not so intrinsically a part of reality that without him nothing could exist at all? But that wasn't it either. Humans crave certainty. Especially the ones who say they don't. Yes, it's nice to be surprised every now and then, and nobody wants to keep treading the same path, but there is a freedom that comes with knowing that some things can be depended on; that they will never change. It may be liberating to pack a bag and set off on an adventure, but that's only really possible if you know that in the event of it all going wrong, your home, your family and your friends will still be where you left them. There could be no greater source of certainty that God. It was what made him so appealing. And once you were dead and in Heaven, any doubt you might have had was gone. God was the unmoving point at the centre of a tumultuous universe. Whatever the chaos that surrounded you, there was always God. Even the atheists, once they'd seen him on the television at Christmas eventually came round to that idea, however grudgingly. And it was nice. It was the one thing that could be depended upon. However, if God were killed, what was there left to hold onto? Chaos would rule. That is if there was anything left at all. She realised too that Primo was now quite mad. To even come up with the thought was enough to commit him. What did he think would happen? That he'd move into the palace and that everyone would just accept this transition of power?

"Primo," she said, placing a calming hand on his shoulder, "let's just think about this."

He looked at her and, after a moment, his eyes became accusing.

"What did Carmine tell you?"

"What do you mean?"

"You two talked a lot."

It was in that moment Margaretha understood that she was no longer safe. Once a man like Primo Fortunato doubts your loyalty, you really ought to start making alternative plans.

"I did most of the talking," she said, carefully. "I think he was still having trouble adjusting to being dead."

Fortunato stood up sharply, causing Margaretha to flinch. He straightened his tie and left without looking back. Bruno skipped after him, followed by Enzo, but not before he checked in on Margaretha to make sure she was all right. She was, but for how long she couldn't say. In the absence of any other idea, she waited in the bar for an hour before leaving discretely, making sure she wasn't followed.

She had never been to the hotel Eric said he'd been staying in, but it was so tall as to be visible from anywhere in the city. She stopped for a coffee along the way and browsed some books at a stall that stood in the shade of a bridge which spanned the river. If anyone had been following her, they probably would have been satisfied she wasn't up to anything she shouldn't be and left her alone by then.

A couple of hours after leaving Fortunato's club, she was in the cool of the Eden Hotel, her heels clicking on the marble-tiled floor, still wearing vast sunglasses and looking like a European film star. Unlike Eric, she looked like she belonged in a place like that, which was ironic, as she would have wanted nothing more than a simple house with a garden to grow food, far out into the country. But for her, and for a lot of people, Heaven wasn't what she had hoped it would be. In fact, apart from the weather, it was not very different to life on Earth. She often wondered if she were in Heaven at all. All she knew was that she was somewhere else. Where that was exactly and what she was supposed to do, she hadn't worked out. The cancer that had killed her was gone, though. That was something.

Having found out his room number at the front desk, she adjusted her hair, composed herself and knocked gently on Craxxi's door. When he opened it, he took a moment to recognise her. She was the first person he had met in Heaven that he knew, and he regarded her the way a person lost overboard would a passing log. Taking the advantage, she strode in, kissing him on one cheek as she passed him, and arranged herself on the sofa.

"It got you in the end," he said, seating himself opposite her.

"Something gets us all. In the end."

The last time Carmine Craxxi had seen Margaretha had been in New York, perhaps five years before. She was working in real estate, and he was in the market for a house. They began an affair which had lasted only as long as her health did. Her diagnosis had brought a cooling breeze to their relationship. Fifty-thousand dollars toward medical bills bought his exit, though not a clear conscience, and they never saw each other again.

"I'm sorry," he said. "I shouldn't have . . . it was a lousy thing to do."

"That's not why I'm here."

Margaretha didn't like to think back to her time with cancer. She was always sure to put it that way too. She had been *with* cancer. To everyone else, she was battling it, but that wasn't the way she felt about it. Whether she was a fighter or not was irrelevant. Cancer doesn't care how determined you are to get better. The doctors fight the cancer, and the cancer fights back. She didn't think she had very much to do with it. She had lost her battle with cancer. That's what people, she was sure, had said when it had finished consuming her from the inside. Others win their battle; some lose. Had she just not fought hard enough? Did she simply not have what it took? She could see it in the eyes of her parents. They thought she had given up, but she hadn't. She was dying; that was all. There was nothing she could do about it. But she was drawn into the narrative. She felt as if she were letting her family down. Perhaps there was more she could do. She prayed, but that was apparently something else she wasn't very good at, as the rate of her decline only increased. And there she was, in Heaven, anchored by the guilt of not having tried harder.

Craxxi spread his arms, crucifix-like, on the back of the sofa.

"You look good."

"That's not what I am here for either."

Craxxi brought his arms back down to his sides.

"I wasn't-"

"It's okay," said Margaretha, putting a close to the matter with a wave of her hand.

There was a silence, which Craxxi chose not to be the one to break.

"So, what happened? Someone moved against you, or was it just an ex-girlfriend."

Unlike Margaretha, Craxxi had been thinking a great deal about how he died. He knew exactly what had happened to him but not who had been responsible. It really could have been any one of dozens of people. He'd spent the evening at a restaurant with his friend, Giuseppe Schillaci, to celebrate his fiftieth birthday. He'd known Giuseppe, or Joe, since school. No one knew more about his business than Joe. He was an honest man, but not squeamish about his friend's activities. He was the only man Craxxi ever truly trusted; the only other person around whom he could be himself. The two of them had finished their coffees and sunk a couple of grappas, paid and left. As they stepped from the restaurant into the sharp November evening air, Craxxi sensed a movement. He had survived more than one attempt on his life, and that kind of thing makes a person alert to men lurking outside restaurants. Perhaps he shouldn't have had that second grappa. Maybe he was getting old. Well, he wasn't going to get any older.

The moment had been all too brief. The man had said his name, as if to confirm he was really Carmine Craxxi. He knew before turning toward the voice what was about to happen. Like Eric, he had always wondered how his end would come. Unlike Eric, he had known all along. He saw his trigger finger tighten and everything went black. It was the silence that lingered in his mind as he sat opposite Margaretha. Bullets travel faster than sound, so you never hear the bullet which kills you. Joe had been all right. The man had no quarrel with him. He really should have been treated for shock, but that wasn't his way. He went home once the police had finished speaking to him, went to bed, and the next morning, turned up at his office as if nothing had happened.

"You can't run forever," was all he said.

Margaretha could sense there was something different about Craxxi. The man she knew made the air tremble with menace. If you stood anywhere near him, you could feel it. If you were alone in a room with him, as she was now, he was terrifying. Not now. He was far from someone who shone with peace and love, but a flame had been reignited somewhere in him. She could see it in his eyes.

"You're different."

"So would you be if you had died twice."

Margaretha looked quizzical.

"I had to get in through the back door."

"Sun Yu?" she asked, realising what suddenly what he must mean.

"You know him?" said Craxxi, sitting up stiffly.

"We've met."

Craxxi opened his mouth to speak, but what did it really matter? He had a feeling that the old man was as unique to him as he was to her; that even if they were talking about the same person, his Sun Yu and hers were just different facets of the same diamond.

"I'm happy to see you, but why are you here?"

"We have a problem."

Twenty-Three

Suzan kicked off backwards from the riverbank and flapped her arms in the water. A goose rose irritably out of the river and extended its wings but did not take flight. She called up to Eric who was still on dry land slipping on his Tee-shirt after first retrieving it from the lower branches of a tree where she had thrown it.

"Aren't you coming in?"

Eric shook his head.

"I don't think so."

"Oh, come on! You don't know what you're missing."

"I think," said Eric, grinning, "I've done enough letting go for one afternoon."

Suzan took a deep breath and dove into the water. He could see a slither of her naked body as it glided just under the surface. Bubbles broke the surface and her head reappeared. She sprayed water from her lips then floated on her back, her pale breasts reflecting the sun and her hair spread out like tentacles of coral. Eric found her lack of bashfulness both astounding and enviable. They were, after all, in a public place, yet she appeared utterly unconcerned at the possibility of someone strolling by, perhaps with their dog, and seeing her.

"Don't you think," said Suzan, "that it's a bit late to be worrying about someone coming along? You didn't seem too concerned a few minutes ago."

"A few minutes ago," replied Eric, "I was not thinking at all."

"You mean you didn't notice the party of elderly day-trippers who stopped their bus and came down for a picnic under our tree?"

Eric's mouth gaped open.

"You're joking!"

"Yes."

Eric sighed and patted his heart.

"Don't ever do that to me again!"

"They weren't really elderly. More middle-aged."

Eric looked at Suzan sideways, gave up trying to see through her, and poured himself a cup of tea from the flask. He noticed his arms had reddened slightly in the sun and although he knew they were likely to cause him some discomfort the next day, he was glad of the healthier colour.

"I didn't notice," he said facetiously, "thinking I was the ocean, though."

"But you forgot yourself."

"So did you!"

"Don't flatter yourself."

"No, I distinctly recall you thinking you were an ocean."

"I was faking it."

Eric clasped his chest in mock agony.

"No!"

Suzan sloshed about in the water and swam towards Eric, slowly.

"Does this sound familiar? 'I'm the ocean! I'm everywhere!'"

"Stop it!"

"I can see everything! I know it all!'."

"Stop it!"

"I am the universe! The wisdom of creation is mine!"

"No!" cried Eric, shielding his ears with his hands.

Suzan threw her head back, cackled, placed her hands on the grassy bank and lifted herself out of the water. Eric rooted through the bag they had brought with them and tossed her a towel, which she wrapped around her as she sat, her feet dangling over the edge. He sat next to her and joined her in staring at the water slipping by below.

"Peaceful, isn't it," said Eric after several minutes' silence.

"Here it is. A few miles upstream it's fast moving. If you go far enough the other way there's even a waterfall. Not a big one."

"And then," added Eric, "it all pours out into the sea."

"And it's all happening at exactly the same time."

"I suppose," said Eric after a moment to reflect, "that gives a whole new perspective to taking the rough with the smooth."

Eric suddenly became melancholy.

"What's wrong?" asked Suzan, sensing his change in mood.

"Well, if this river's anything to go by," he said, tossing a twig into the green water, "if I am enjoying the smooth right now, I am going to have to expect some rough just around the corner."

Suzan knew when to keep silent and this, she calculated, was one of those times.

"I just . . ." said Eric, frustration welling inside him. "I just wish this moment would last forever. Me here with you. It's perfect. I don't want it to change."

"Everything changes. All the time."

"I know!" said Eric, anguished.

"But it also stays the same."

"I don't follow you."

"That's what the river understands," said Suzan, quietly.

Eric stared into the moving water and saw his reflection. At that moment he became aware of the river as a whole: its beginning, its middle and its end; the rough and the smooth, all happening together—at the same time. With a gentle nudge from Suzan, Eric saw his life in its entirety: his past, his present and his future; the good times and the bad times; the happiness and the sadness; the joy and the despair; his life and his death, spread out in every direction except that of time; everything happening together. He watched the water continue on its idle progress, towards turmoil and the ocean and understood, for an instant, that the bend in the river at which he sat—that stretch of calm—would always be there, no matter what. That just as it ended at the ocean it began in the mountains. That even as it evaporated into the air it fell again as rain. Souls ascending only to return again to the Earth below with no before and no after, no life and no death, no Heaven and no Hell.

Eric took hold of Suzan by the shoulders, turned her

to face him and kissed her.

"What was that for?" asked Suzan when he had released her.

"Just because," he said grinning.

He threw a stone into the water and knew that the ripples would never stop spreading.

"I've never listened to a river before!" he said, lightening the mood.

Suzan, having dried out in the sun, put her clothes back on. There were a few more broken clouds in the sky than there had been, and they brought a cooling breeze with them.

"What shall we do now?" asked Eric.

"If we take the long way back, we'll make it just in time for dinner without having to do any of the cooking. And we'll be hungry again by then."

They cleared the picnic away together. Suzan strapped the guitar case to her back, and he carried the basket with the food.

"Which way?"

She pointed to a path that wound its way up a hill and disappeared into a wood. They set off hand in hand. Suzan was happier to be close to Eric now as his mind was quieter than it had been. She just hoped that Eric himself would not notice as he might start thinking about it, picking apart the process. Once that particular thread was pulled, she knew, the entire tapestry would start to unravel.

By the time they got back to the commune the sky was a deep blue and the lights inside were on. For the first time since his death, Eric had the feeling of Home-Sweet-Home and walked with familiarity up the front path without the sense he was trespassing. Once inside, Suzan balanced her guitar under the window and Eric took the picnic things into the kitchen to put away.

"You've got a visitor," said Lola.

"Who?" asked Suzan, turning around but recognising no one she knew.

"Not you," said Lola, "lover-boy."

Eric spun around.

"Someone's here to see me?"

"They're out in the garden waiting. Have been for an hour."

Eric dried his hands on a dishcloth and went outside, followed by Suzan. At the table sat a willowy woman with long, black hair and, beside her, a broad, mean-looking man. She was wearing high boots on the outside of her skin-tight jeans and a flowing, white top, while he wore a suit Eric recognised as one of those that had been hanging in his closet. The woman stood up slowly and walked towards them, turning heads among the men of the commune as she did.

"Hello, Eric," she said, in a melodic, Latin voice.

Eric stood rigidly.

"Margaretha?"

Twenty-four

Eric spun around, scanning the garden for Fortunato and his men.

"It's okay," said Margaretha. "I'm here on my own. Primo knows nothing."

"You're not on your own," he said pointing, "What's he doing here?"

"It's okay. He's here to help. Primo has no idea."

Suzan had been standing in the doorway watching, but the need to protect Eric overcame her discretion and she joined him by his side.

"Who are you?"

"I'm the woman who kept your boyfriend alive and I'm here for his help."

"Help?" asked Eric. "How could I possibly help you? I can barely help myself."

"Can we go somewhere to talk?" Margaretha glanced at Suzan, clearly reluctant to disclose anything in front of a stranger.

"Anything you want to say," said Eric, still shaken, "you can say in front of Suzan."

"Even if hearing what I have to say puts her in danger?"

"Danger? What sort of danger? Why can't you just leave me alone?"

Suzan faced Eric with her back, pointedly, to Margaretha. She stood on the tips of her toes and planted a kiss on his lips.

"I'll be inside if you need anything." She squeezed his hand. "You've got this."

She left them alone.

"So what is it?" asked Eric.

"Not here," said Margaretha, "somewhere more private."

Eric took Margaretha to the back of the yard, past the vegetable patches, the chicken runs and toward a patch of rough grass that was being dug up for a pond. They were joined by Craxxi.

"How did you find me?" he asked them.

"This address fell out of your suit that night in the club. I guessed the rest."

"Right, so you found me. What do you want with me? And what's all this talk about danger?"

"Primo was furious when you got away."

Eric felt a sudden queasiness overcome him but said nothing.

"He's furious with God, too, for refusing his request."

"What's that got to do with me?"

"He's planning to assassinate him."

Eric broke into a fit of laughter but stopped abruptly under the steady stare of Margaretha.

"You're serious, aren't you!"

"Deadly," she said.

"But, but, you can't just kill God!"

"Why not?"

"Because! I mean, is it even possible? Can God die?"

Margaretha slapped Eric's face hard.

"What was that for!" he cried, holding his cheek.

"Did that hurt?"

"Yes!"

"If you can feel pain you can die, even in Heaven."

"But *God*?"

"Honestly, Eric, I don't know. But Primo believes it and if I have learnt something here it's that belief is a very powerful thing. We create our own Heaven and Primo's is a Heaven where he is God, where nothing can stop him. With that kind of a man pulling the trigger, I hate to think what might be possible. I am not prepared to take that risk. Are you?"

"Me? What has this got to do with me?"

"You have to stop him."

"Margaretha," said Eric, joining his palms in prayer. "I'm an idiot! I was way in over my head. Now I am out. I can't help you!"

Margaretha closed her eyes to think.

"When there is trouble," she said, "the universe will give you the tools you need to get out of it. All you have to do is recognise those tools and make use of them."

"Can't anybody just give me a straight answer around here?" asked Eric, throwing up his arms in exasperation.

"When this trouble started, I began to look for what tools the universe had sent me," said Margaretha.

"You're not going to say it sent me are you?"

"I knew you weren't Carmine the moment I saw you.

And when you told me your story, I just couldn't believe that a bungling fool could get so far."

"Oh, you can rest assured. If I am one thing it is a bungling fool."

"And look how far that got you," said Craxxi, speaking for the first time.

"When you finally told me what was really going on," said Margaretha, undeterred by Eric's protestations, "I didn't believe it for one second."

"It's the truth!"

"Oh, I know you told me the truth, Eric. But I knew there had to be more to it than that. Why had the universe brought you there and protected you along the way?"

"I told you-"

"Yes, yes, you told me," said Margaretha, "but it doesn't make any sense. Everything happens for a reason."

"Why must it?"

"It has to be you, Eric! There is no other explanation."

"Why can't it be him?" he asked, nodding at Craxxi.

"Do you know how rare it is that anyone can get to meet God? Do you know who's tried and failed? And then you arrive and suddenly, you're granted an audience."

"I wasn't; he was," Eric replied, jabbing a finger at Craxxi, who didn't mind nearly as much as he once would have.

"Bigger men than me have asked for access and been refused. Kings and queens, Eric. I'm no one."

"It was you, Eric. I don't know why. But it was."

Eric stepped away and placed his hands behind his head to think. He had been so happy next to the river earlier. And in a way, he still was. That time spent on the grassy bank with Suzan wasn't in the past. It was still happening. Just as, as he had sat with his feet in the water, this conversation with Margaretha and Craxxi was happening. As was whatever was about to happen next. The river was being fed by a stream in the mountains just as it was emptying into the sea. He had understood that a few hours ago. It was a nice thought, but why had he been so instantly called upon to actually live it? He wasn't quite ready to accept it.

"But why can't stuff just happen randomly?"

"Like it or not you have a role to play."

"And do I have any choice in accepting it?"

Margaretha stepped closer to Eric.

"So far, you've been charmed. You need something, and it happens for you. You needed a way into Heaven, and you just so happen to find a pass that's been dropped on the floor. Someone destroys your room with a bomb, and you're not in it. You need to escape from Primo and the doors to a tram conveniently close behind you. You need somewhere to go and there's Suzan-"

"And I'm very, very grateful-"

"The universe is very persistent. Even if you start ignoring it, it won't go away. One voice will be joined by another and then another and another until you think you're going to go crazy. It will get louder and louder until you cannot sleep at night, your body aches, your head spins, you are not able to concentrate, you get sick all the time."

"You just basically described every normal person I have ever known. That's just the way it is."

"And what does every normal person have in common?" asked Margaretha, passion rising. "However happy they are, there is something they're missing and no matter how they try to ignore it, it's always there. One day they look in the mirror and ask themselves what their life is all about; if it really was supposed to turn out the way it did; if perhaps they missed something along the way." She paused for effect before continuing more calmly. "What they missed they didn't hear. They didn't hear because they didn't listen. They look to the Heavens and ask for signs, but there are signs all around them, all the time, screaming at them. In their quiet moments they know it too. They know they weren't true to themselves. That's why they allow themselves so few quiet moments. That's why there is always noise. Because if you sit quietly with yourself, you hear the truth that you let yourself down and no one wants to hear that."

"But people are always looking for answers," protested Eric. "Religion, new age stuff. They're all at it."

Margaretha dismissed Eric's argument with a Latin hiss.

"They look for answers everywhere except where they will find them: inside themselves! They read book after book after book that tell them enlightenment is not in books, but they just keep on reading—buying more books! Even when they meditate, most of them turn it into a ritual; anything to detract from the risk of actually listening to themselves. I knew a guy who always meditated in front of a candle. Every day for years. He'd sit in front of a damn candle and stare at it for an hour. You know what happened, Eric?"

"His house burnt down?"

"He knew everything about candles and nothing about himself! One day the irony hit him. He blew out his last candle and that's when he became truly happy."

"Yes, but-"

"They spend years," she said, oblivious to Eric's attempt at an interruption, "pontificating over what the sound of one hand clapping is, never seeing the joke-"

"What *is* the sound of one hand clapping?" asked Eric, sweeping his hand across his body as if slapping an invisible child.

"Have you ever wondered?" asked Margaretha, not pausing to receive a response and not so much ignoring Eric as barely noticing him, "why you see these Buddhist monks and they're always smiling? They get the joke!"

"What joke?"

There is only so much obtuseness the Latin temperament can tolerate. She screamed an oath in Spanish and reached out with both hands for Eric's neck. He took a step backwards and took a secure hold of her wrists, as if plucking bullets from the air. Craxxi stood between them, and he released his grip warily.

"And you really think I can help?" he said once they had both calmed down.

"I don't know what your destiny is," said Margaretha, slightly out of breath, "but I do know that you have to see it through. No one else can. There's a lot at stake."

Eric thought of Suzan, about his fledgling new life with her at the commune.

"And if I agree, I can come back?"

"You can go where you want."

He fell silent and closed his eyes.

"I can't. I'm sorry."

TWENTY-FIVE

God entered the boardroom through the door. He didn't need to, of course. He could have passed through the wall, or just appeared in it. But he found that people didn't like it when he did that sort of thing. It wasn't like the old days. Back then he would materialise from out of a blinding light, angels blasting trumpets and hurricane-force winds knocking people from their feet. That was considered a bit hammy now. The modern day lacked magnificence, he thought, but he did understand the need to move with the times. Or at least, when his image consultants told him, so he had nodded and promised to tone it down.

God still got to sit at the head of the table. They allowed him that at least. There had never been anything so vulgar as a coup, but a creepy corporate structure and a series of modernisations had left God in little more than a cere-monial role. Heaven was run now by a board of directors; and since it was on Earth as it is in Heaven, by extension, they held sway over human affairs too. Some theologians had noticed that God, who had done nothing but talk to his favourite humans and interfere constantly with floods, plagues, swarms and people coming back from the dead for millennia, had chosen to be suddenly, and frustratingly, silent, for two thousand years. It was generally agreed that this silence was a prelude for the End Times. A forming of troops for the final battle between good and evil. The truth was the messaging from Heaven had been tightly controlled since the debacle of Jesus' time on Earth. That was the last time any big decisions had been made without first running it through a series of focus groups and committees. As a result, nothing had really happened for two thousand years, and the board were agreed that this was progress.

"Good morning, everyone."

The meeting was called to order by Nathaniel the Chief Executive Officer: a thin, neat man who appeared to be in his forties, but who had been dead for several centuries. When alive, he had proved himself an effective politician in Rome, serving under two popes and surviving several attempts ot his life. His death came about from natural causes, which for a man in his position, at the time he lived, was as good as anyone could hope for. It was Nathaniel who had begun the reforms and developed various revenue streams. It was he who had introduced the system of indulgences that Carmine Craxxi and so many others before him had made full use of. The money that brought in had transformed Heaven and made a few, very select individuals, incredibly wealthy in the afterlife. That was enough to win the argument in favour of such a controversial move against the traditionalists who thought it not only vulgar but likely to corrupt. God had been very much in the latter camp, but not even the Almighty can compete with market forces.

As soon as the minutes of the last meeting were signed off and apologies for absences read out, Nathaniel cleared his throat and introduced the next money-making scheme.

"The first item on the agendum is the proposal to place a charge of one penny per prayer."

God generally aimed to snooze through board meetings, but this caused him to open his eyes sharply and sit up.

"Charge for prayers?"

"Yes, Sir," replied Nathaniel with respect. God had been effectively sidelined, but he was still the creator of all Heaven and Earth. That buys you a certain deference at least. "You see, in the beginning, there was just Adam and Eve. Their prayers were easy enough to process, of course. We managed pretty well for centuries, although Job put a good deal of strain on our systems. Even so, we could manage. Now there are eight billion people, and we just can't hire enough staff to hear all the prayers. Fatima?"

Fatima had been around for thousands of years. When she first arrived, she was wrapped in linen and bare-footed. She was crippled by awe and humility, falling to her knees in front of anyone on the basis they may or not be angels. Now she wore well-tailored suits, had a woman who did her nails and was comfortable enough to offer God a biscuit from a plate.

"The data indicate that only point-eight of a percent of prayers are answered each day," she said, referring to her notes. "The mean waiting time is up at over twenty-two years."

"But charging for them?" asked God.

"Projections suggest," continued Fatima, "that the introduction of a nominal fee would reduce the volume of prayers by ninety-eight-point six percent."

"That's not a good thing surely?"

Nathaniel had been expecting such an objection and took over.

"The vast majority of prayers are frivolous. Twenty-four percent of prayers are asking to influence the outcome of a sporting event," he said from memory. "We'd be happy to oblige, by the time we get to them, the event is over. Thirty-nine percent are what we call miscellaneous. That is, prayers asking for lost keys to be found, you know the kind of thing." He brought a colourful pie chart up on the smart screen to complete his point. "As you can see, only fourteen percent of prayers are asking for a sick loved-one to be well again, or for world peace. We could afford to rationalise the current workforce in the call centre making considerable savings and still answer prayers within three days; even as little as two hours for class one emergencies."

"All that will happen is that those who can afford it will still ask for success, fame and fortune while the poor, who really need to pray, won't be able to. And the gap between them will continue to widen."

"The poor," said Nathaniel, pleased to now have the chance to speak as what he was about to say was his idea, "will be able to apply through the Church for credits."

"Which will help return the Church to its former place at the centre of human life. Having said all that," he continued brightly, "we will put the matter out to consultation and feed the results back when we have them."

"And when will that be?"

"We can expect a report in approximately two centuries."

"Well," said God, "since the matter is urgent . . ."

The meeting meandered on, but God fell asleep only a few minutes later and wouldn't be able to tell you what was discussed. He was the same trying to listen to Podcasts in bed.

Once the meeting was over and Nathaniel had gently nudged him awake, he wiped dribble from his chin and returned to his apartments. These were modest. Over the millennia, he had lost interest in almost everything he had once enjoyed. Except for chess. he had tried golf. Even as a beginner, continuously maddened by the game, he would very occasionally find every separate part of his swing click together and he would hit the perfect drive. One of such majesty that the crowd at the Open would have stood and cheered. And that was just enough to keep him returning to the greens. The chance that he might, just might, and for a fleeting moment, be accidentally brilliant. As good as anyone to have ever pushed a tee into soft turf. Even if, with the very next shot, his usual form would reassert itself. However–and this is what fascinated him about the game–you can't be accidentally good at chess. You will never move a bishop like a grandmaster. Even if you did, by some unlikely fluke, how would you ever know? Your opponent wouldn't even notice. They'd make some terrible move themselves and you'd frown, utterly baffled. And so he studied famous games, tried to solve classic chess problems and played online, though always under an assumed name, hoping to sense the poetry in the game he suspected was there but never finding it. But what made the game more fascinating still was that he hadn't created it. He had accounted for everything. Every subatomic particle. But there it was. An anomaly. He didn't like anomalies, so with a single thought he caused it to no longer exist—to have never even existed in the first place. Except it came back; and it kept coming back every time he cast it into nothingness. It was like trying to do away with a bubble under wallpaper. It just kept popping back up somewhere else. It seemed to be a natural consequence of a complex universe. An expression of its infinite complexity and bottomless mystery. All made manifest in a little wooden board with sixty-four squares and thirty-two carved pieces. He didn't fully understand it, and for a deity who knew everything, this was a refreshing experience. It was the closest he could ever get to feeling human.

The board meeting had left him demoralised, as board meetings always did. He wasn't sure how it had all got away from him, but over the millennia it had. He thought back to the early days, when it was just him and the angels. They were blessedly simple, but it couldn't last. Philosophically speaking, you can't make something that is Good without its opposite, Evil, existing too. He had known that from the very beginning. It was a flaw that had worried him even at the concept stage. He just hoped it would all turn out to be fine. And it was, for the first fourteen billion years. Give or take. But then the angels started to talk among themselves. There was, after all, so much worshipping you can do before you start to wonder if there might be more to existence. No one dared to wonder out loud for a very long time, until Lucifer. It's said that Lucifer was God's favourite, but that's just not true. He liked Lucifer, but he had very little to do with any of the angels if he could help it. It was Lucifer who first made the point about how you can't have a subjective idea of something without having something to compare it to. A short line, he said, was only short in comparison to a long one. And good could only be good if there was such a thing as evil. And that was how it started. First it was just a rumour that one of the angels had had a thought that wasn't specifically about worshipping God. It was a question; the first one ever asked, and it was thrilling. If God was good, who was evil? Arguments were put forward; sides were taken and lines drawn. On one side was God, very definitely representing good; on the other was Lucifer, representing the side of its equal and opposite. At this point, no one knew what to do next. What did such things matter to immortal beings? Then someone suggested a wager. The idea was that God would create a world with two mortal creatures, but with the promise of eternity. If they chose to be good, eternity could be made to be very comfortable for them; if they chose evil, they'd be sent somewhere else, ruled by Lucifer. When there was no one left, an account would be taken and whoever had the most souls would win. It did mean they had to decide what counted as good and what counted as evil. That took a while, but eventually an agreement was reached, and God got to work. He started with just two. He gave them everything they could ever need or want. He was sure the experiment wouldn't take very long, but he underestimated the lengths to which Lucifer would go to complicate matters. Six thousand years and eight billion people later, the game was still far from being over. It had all got out of control really, and God had long since regretted the whole thing. Still, he couldn't back out now.

He sat at the chess board and studied the problem he'd been set.

TWENTY-SIX

Suzan was kneeling by a raised bed, picking at idle weeds. She wasn't capable of much else. She had had a bad dream the night before and it had stayed with her. It was a memory. One that had been buried beneath strata of others for centuries–from a previous life–from one of many. She could sense them deep inside her during waking hours. They affected her the way a nation's cultural past influences its present; how current generations carry grievances, long since forgotten, into wars that they will pass down to their children. Suzan could remember faces with no names, moments out of context, fragments of happiness and grief, voices and thoughts. None of them made sense, but over the years she had been able to connect those from individuals. Not enough for a complete picture, but she was able to sense a little of who they were; of who she had been. Except at night. At night she could remember. Not the lives she had lived but the deaths she had experienced. Every one of them in the most vivid detail. She knew how each one felt, what each made her think. Right up to the moment she'd wake in Heaven, and always as herself. The one common factor in all those many, many lives. Eric had thought she was much older than she looked. He was almost right. There were just many of her in one young woman.

She looked around for Eric and saw him on the roof. He had taken up some spare tiles and a couple of tools, but he hadn't climbed up there to work. He had been distracted since Margaretha's and Craxxi's visit. He had told them to leave, and they had promised to never come back. That should have been the end of it. Eric was clear of the trouble he had got himself into and was free to get on with the rest of eternity. Except humans–even when dead–struggle with moving on, and Eric was finding it especially difficult. It wasn't just what Margaretha had told him about God being in danger either. It was the fact of eternity itself that was pressing on him. He'd have thought the finite nature of life would mean decision-making was more difficult. That each choice would count more as life was short and there was little time for second chances. But he was learning that making your mind up with eternity laid out before you was far more difficult. Life being short meant that the consequences of any wrong move wouldn't be with you for very long, but the same could no longer be said for him.

It would have helped perhaps if he knew more about how the afterlife worked. What would happen when, after making a life with Suzan, Amber died? Would she turn up at the door as an old woman, hoping to continue their life together? If she re-married, what would she do then? Surely awkward reunions should be happening everywhere you looked. New arrivals pleading with former partners that they had promised to wait for them? But Eric hadn't seen anything like that.

"Don't think of it as one Heaven," said Suzan as she slid down beside him.

Eric was no longer surprised that she seemed to know exactly what he was thinking.

"What do you mean?"

"It's a bit like being in a dream. All things are true. Nothing's impossible."

"So I *am* dreaming?"

"No, but similar rules apply."

Eric was quiet for a whole minute then spoke.

"So it's true that when Amber dies, she and I will be together again just as much as it's true you and I will be together literally forever?"

"Something like that."

"When I am dreaming, I never worry that nothing really makes sense."

"You just go with the flow."

"Yeah."

Suzan leant into him, nudging his shoulder with hers.

"A snowflake never falls in the wrong place," she whispered.

"What did you say?" he asked, turning to face her.

"A snowflake ne-"

"Yes, I heard you. But why did you say it?"

"Because they don't, do they? Snowflakes. Why?"

"No, nothing. I'm sorry."

He put his arms around her shoulders and she nestled into his neck.

"They make it all sound so simple," he said as he squeezed her tightly to himself. But he wasn't fully present still, and she could feel it. She didn't let on to him that it was breaking her heart.

A week later, it had been Suzan's and Eric's turn to cook for the commune. Preparing food for twenty people was an intimidating thought for Eric when he first attempted it, but he remembered a good recipe for curry that Amber used to make, and making large vats of it and steaming rice was simple enough, and the other residents always looked forward to it. He had settled in as one of them now; as someone not likely to be gone by the following morning. He sat at the table and poked at his rice but was not in the mood to eat. He was thinking about Margaretha and wondered what she was doing about Primo. She had Craxxi to help her, but she really seemed to think they needed him. The one thing that was bothering him–the thing he didn't yet know–was who had murdered him on Earth and why. He had a feeling that until he found out the answer to that question, he'd never really feel able to put his past behind him and move on. It didn't help that he was sure it was tied up with Craxxi, Primo and, ultimately, God.

"Not hungry?" asked Suzan.

"Not really," he said, pushing his plate away.

Wasting food was difficult to get away with at the commune. Since they grew almost everything they ate and were well aware of the work that went into every mouthful, you could make yourself unpopular by tipping your untouched meal into the bin. Suzan took his plate and scraped it onto hers. She had been unusually hungry recently, and she couldn't get enough beetroot chutney, that she didn't usually care for.

Eric finished his wine and went into the garden to sit in the cool of the late evening. He was joined soon after by Suzan. She was very good at letting silence do its work, but she also knew went to speak.

"Okay, Eric, what's bothering you?"

He did try to say that nothing was bothering him, but that was never going to work with Suzan.

"You're off your food. You're moping about like an empty bin bag."

"Do bin bags mope?"

Suzan smiled and rested her head on his shoulder.

"Why don't you just poke around in my head and find out?"

"I know where your head's been," she said, squeezing his arm. "No, I never pry that deeply."

"I need to go," he said, suddenly.

Suzan sat up.

"I'll come back. I just feel there is unfinished business. And I want to know how I ended up dead."

"You should do what you need to do. I'll be here when you get back."

"I'm sorry."

They lay back on the cool grass and looked up at the first stars to appear in the darkening sky.

TWENTY-SEVEN

Margaretha's apartment was rather too close to Fortunato's club for comfort, thought Eric.

"Are you sure it's safe here? What if Primo decides to drop by?"

Margaretha scoffed.

"In five years he's never been here."

The apartment was a surprise to Eric. Margaretha was always so elegantly turned out that he expected her to be living in a large space with high ceilings, large windows, wooden floors and minimalist lines. In contrast, her apartment was relatively small with thick blankets tossed over the sofas, heavy rugs and bean bags scattered about the floor, half-melted candles on every shelf and art work depicting Andalusian life in Spanish reds and yellows.

She disappeared into the kitchen and Eric was left alone with Craxxi. The two men hadn't spoken at the commune when they picked him up or on the journey back. Craxxi was filling an armchair. He'd helped himself to a glass of red wine, which Eric had declined, and appeared to be thinking.

"Why are you here?" asked Eric.

Craxxi snapped out of his thoughts and seemed to notice Eric as if for the first time.

"What do you mean?"

"Why are you helping?"

"Marga and I go back a ways," he said after a few moments spent deciding how best to put it.

"It's just that you don't seem to me to be a man who'd care."

Craxxi squinted, interested.

"And how do you know what sort of man I am?"

"I read our—your— record. I know what you did."

Craxxi dipped a finger into the wine and traced a line around the rim of the glass until it began to hum. He stopped, took a sip, and looked at Eric.

"It's a funny thing. I think back at the man I was, and it's as if I'm looking at someone else. Someone I don't know any more. You know?"

Eric did know. His own life may as well have happened to someone else too. Perhaps it was part of the process of being dead, but his living self was increasingly difficult to grasp in his memory. It was like trying to remember your very earliest years: a collage of fragmented remembrances, where it was impossible to know what were memories, photos or barely recalled stories told to you by your parents.

"You've changed?"

"If I hadn't," he said, smiling, "you'd never have survived our first meeting."

Margaretha returned carrying a tray of various interesting cheeses and crackers, plus a pot of tea. Eric started browsing the titles on the bookshelf: *Zen and the Art of Motorcycle Maintenance*; *The Tao of Physics*; *The Glass Bead Game*; *The Tao of Pooh*; *The Self-Aware Universe*.

"Interesting collection. Have you read them all?"

"Of course."

"They're a bit heavy for me. Apart from the Tao of Pooh. What's that about?"

"Winnie the Pooh is the greatest philosopher of modern times."

"You're kidding, right?"

"Not at all! Read it for yourself."

Eric took the book down from the shelf and read the back cover. *While Eeyore frets and Piglet hesitates and Rabbit calculates and Owl pontificates, Pooh just is.*

"Nah, I think I'll leave it. I didn't read Winnie the Pooh when I was a child, I'm not going to start now I'm an adult."

"Shame," said Margaretha, pouring the tea, "that little bear has a great deal to teach."

Eric frowned, feeling, as he did, that she was taking him for a fool. He slipped the book back into its place and slumped onto the sofa next to her. He looked up at a picture on the wall that was in a different artistic style to the others. It looked to Eric to be Chinese; it depicted a lotus flower in the middle of a swamp.

"That flower's you," said Eric, as he accepted his tea and sipped gratefully.

"What do you mean?" asked Margaretha, looking at the picture.

"This beautiful flower in the middle of all that mud and stinking water, but it remains untouched by it all."

"And that's me?"

"You spend all that time with Primo and his men. All that corruption and greed but it doesn't seem to have had any effect on you. That's why you're like that flower."

Margaretha looked at the picture, then at Eric.

"That's the most beautiful thing anyone's ever said to me, Eric," she said, genuinely moved. She leant forward and kissed him on the cheek. "Thank you."

She smiled and traced the rim of her cup with her long fingers.

"So," she said, "Suzan's a very beautiful girl."

"Yes, she is," said Eric, blushing gently.

"Tell me about her."

"She's incredible!" he blurted with unchecked enthusiasm. Embarrassed, he continued in a more detached manner. "She's a little strange."

"Strange! I'm sure she'd be delighted to hear you describe her like that!"

"She'd know what I meant. She's . . ." he said and trailed off into thought.

"You love her, don't you."

"Yes, I think I do."

"Have you told her?"

"No. Well, I was going to, but she was asleep."

"Well, you can tell her when you get back."

Eric finished the rest of his tea in silence.

"I've never met anyone like her," he said, eventually. "She's full of mystery on the one hand, yet when I'm with her, everything becomes so clear."

"And what do you see when everything's so clear?"

"I see myself. And I see everything. And I can't tell where I end and everything else begins."

"Quite a girl," interrupted Craxxi.

A wave of discomfort broke over him as he remembered Amber and his feelings for her, which remained.

"But I still love my girlfriend back on Earth."

Margaretha placed her hand on Eric's.

"And that's a problem?"

"Well, of course it is!" he said, rolling his eyes. "You can't love two people."

"Why not?"

"Because . . . just, because."

"If you say so."

"Don't you say so?"

"I'm just impressed that you understand what love is so well."

"I don't think anyone understands that," replied Eric with an ironic laugh, "least of all me."

"Yet you seem to have a very clear idea of what it can do and what it cannot."

"Well," said Eric after a moment staring into his empty cup, "what do you think?"

"I think that each time someone puts a different meaning on love it gets smaller and smaller until it can fit neatly into a little box. And then they continue on happily until one day something happens that defies that very strict meaning and a conflict arises."

"You think you can love two people at the same time?"

"I think you can love all people, Eric, if you're open to it."

"Don't you get confused by feelings, though?"

"No, not anymore. Feelings are never confused even if we sometimes are. If you clear your head and follow your heart you will be okay. So long as you remember that you don't always know what is best for you."

"But how can you be sure?"

Margaretha smiled.

"You take a risk, Eric. You take a risk."

Eric was not a natural risk taker, but he had learnt that with death not being the end of the journey, each decision made was far less critical. With more than just one chance to get it right he could allow himself the occasional mistake–to take more risks. "

And what about you?" said Eric, suddenly, dispelling his melancholy.

"What is a nice girl like me doing with a man like Primo?"

"I was wondering that too," chimed in Craxxi.

"It's not so bad. He leaves me alone, mostly. I'm free to get on with my own life. He's actually been quite good to me."

"He treats you like a thing. I saw him."

"That's just in front of other men. He thinks he has an image to uphold."

"So why are you going against him now if he's been so good to you?" asked Craxxi.

"He's gone too far this time. I can't stand by and watch anymore."

A thought occurred to Eric.

"You never said what we're going to do about it. I assume you have a plan."

"I was thinking you could go back to see God. Only this time, you tell him who you are, about Carmine and Primo and me. He can do the rest."

"What do you need me for then? Couldn't you just tell

him yourself?"

"Too dangerous. But I told you. The universe is on your side."

"Yes, you did . . . dangerous? What danger? You didn't say anything about any danger," asked Eric, his voice a little shrill.

Margaretha placed a calming hand on Eric's thigh.

"Don't worry. The universe will protect you."

Eric seemed less certain.

"A snowflake never falls in the wrong place," said Eric, wondering if it would mean something to him now that had eluded him before, but it did not.

"Clarence?" asked Margaretha.

"You know him?"

"Everyone knows Clarence," said Margaretha and she smiled as she recalled their first meeting.

"It's been bugging me ever since."

"Yeah, that's Clarence all right."

"I know it means something to me; I just don't know what."

"You are a mighty tree," said Margaretha, mimicking Clarence, "while I am a blade of grass."

"Not you as well. Does everybody talk in riddles up here?"

"That's what he said to me when I met him."

"And what does that mean?"

Margaretha became lost in thought. Clarence had been a customer at the club shortly after she met Fortunato and started working for him. He had claimed to be an angel, and it turned out he was. He was one of the original angelic beings. As old as the universe itself. Many of those who had been around since the beginning were rumoured to have gone mad with the sheer immensity of it all. Some, it was said, had become part of reality itself, as inseparable from it as milk in tea. Then there was Clarence. If you asked him if what people said about him was true, his head would roll back, and he'd laugh.

"My dear," he had said, taking her by the arm. "You are a mighty tree, standing strong against de wind dat blows."

Margaretha thanked him and tried to remove her arm, but he would not release her.

"I, on de other 'and am just a blade of grass dat gets flattened in de 'urricane."

Margaretha was used to dealing with drunk and difficult men, but this was different.

"And in de mornin' when you 'ave been torn from de ground by de wind and are lying in broken pieces, I'll still be dere, basking in de sunshine."

He released her arm and turned his attention to the dancers who slipped their bodies up and down shiny poles on the stage. She spent the rest of the night in a distracted daze. Clarence's words had skewered her, like a spear. When she returned to his table he was gone. On the table he left the money for his drink, a generous tip and a note scribbled on a napkin: *Have you ever seen a cloud being blown in the wrong direction?*

Later that night, Margaretha chose to walk home, rather than take the minibus with the other girls. Meditating with her legs crossed on the floor bored her. The act of walking, placing one foot in front of the other, was her mantra and it helped empty her mind of all unnecessary thoughts. She thought of Clarence and the note he had left for her. She recalled her life and realised, as most people do eventually, that the best things that happened to her had been unplanned. Conversely, now she thought about it, the misfortune that had come her way had been of her own making. The times she had chosen to take the reins of her life in hand had inevitably seen it rear up and toss her onto the stony ground.

She scuffed her heels as she stopped and looked up at the night sky. The moonlight illuminated the edges of the few clouds there were, just as it had the night she had finally given in to her tumour. She knew that night would be her last. She asked the nurse in the hospice to open the curtains. It mattered to her that she knew what the weather was like. As if she had always wondered what it would be in her final hours. The clouds had no control over the direction they were being blown, but none of them could be said to be heading the wrong way. If life could be explained in any way it was the feeling of being buffeted this way, then that. Just as standing against the wind only succeeds in you being pushed along the ground on the tips of your toes or being knocked over altogether, so battling against the natural flow of life had the same effect.

Just then, a strong wind could be seen approaching along the street toward her by the leaves and litter it scattered before it. When it reached her, a tree beside her creaked painfully. A loud snap sent Margaretha running for cover in a shop doorway and a heavy branch hit the pavement where she had been standing. Below the tree, blades of grass in a square patch tingled happily. Such strength in weakness, she thought as she looked down at them; then, looking at the dismembered branch: such weakness in strength. She returned from her daydream and noticed Eric waiting expectantly.

"I think it means that there is no such thing as our lives going the wrong way, just the way we don't want them to go, which is something else entirely," she said. "Life never, ever takes us the wrong way. It doesn't take us the right way, either. It just takes us."

"And you just have to accept it," said Eric, enlightenment, if not actually dawning, at least flickering.

"Accept it or not, it makes no difference, really. It's just easier if you do."

"So what's the point in making plans?"

"A sailor is ultimately at the mercy of the wind, but he can still steer his little boat in any direction he wants except one: against the wind," said Craxxi.

Eric and Margaretha turned to stare at him.

"What? I can't say anything wise?"

"It's just so unexpected," said Margaretha, smiling.

"It's just something the Old Man said once."

"Old Man?" asked Eric.

"The toughest bastard I ever met. Speaking of which, you all set for tomorrow?"

Margaretha shot a look at Craxxi, but it was too late.

"It's happening tomorrow?"

Margaretha nodded.

"And say hello to him for me."

Eric looked forlornly into his empty teacup.

"I think I will have something stronger."

TWENTY-EIGHT

Eric rolled his neck to release a knot of tension that was forming between his shoulders. He tested his breath by cupping his hands over his mouth, flattened his hair, wiped his palms on his chest and knocked three times on the door with a single knuckle.

Nothing.

He waited, then knocked again. More forcefully this time. The call to enter, when it came, was bad tempered.

"I'm sorry," said Eric, poking his head around the door. "I didn't hear you."

The office was much as it had been the last time Eric had seen it. Some of the books had been transferred from the desk to the floor and a stack of ring binders had been removed from the windowsill to allow more natural light through. A ceiling fan rotated idly above. It was missing a wooden blade and the discrepancy in balance caused it to wobble in its housing. Eric wondered what had happened to the missing blade. He could not imagine that a ceiling fan could lose one of its blades without there being an amusing story attached.

He noticed too the chess board upon which God was playing E-mail chess with the devil. The white queen, in tandem with its knight, seemed to have the black king on the run. Accompanied by only two pawns and a rook, it did not look promising for him. On the computer screen, a pixelated representation of a dinosaur egg cracked open, and a baby pterodactyl fluttered about the screen before disappearing, allowing the entire routine to repeat.

God was standing in the middle of the floor reading a report he had just been handed. The report, commissioned by just one of the many think tanks that had invented themselves over recent years, listed a series of recommendations for him to consider.

Top of the list was a proposal to reschedule the female menstrual cycle. The report calculated that, on average, each woman on Earth menstruates for a combined total of ten years and one month. Rather than forcing a woman to cope with the monthly inconvenience, she should be allowed—according to the report's authors—to take her menstrual cycles in one go or to separate them into blocks that are spread years apart, rather like the way some countries allow their young people to fit military service around their education and personal lives.

He read the proposal.

He read it again.

He sat down on the edge of his desk and ran his fingers through his hair. The authors of the report possessed that very special kind of stupidity that can make anyone confronted with it feel that they are the ones who are not getting it.

He tried reading the proposal once more, this time

mouthing the words in the hope that giving them some sort of form would help him see the logic in it, because quite obviously there was something he was missing. Eventually, he shook his head and decided to forward the report to one of his focus groups to see if they could make better sense of it.

"Yes, young man," he said, turning to Eric. "What may I do for you today?"

Eric was unsure where to start, so he decided to drop Margaretha's name in right away.

"Ah, yes, Margaretha!" said God, smiling to Himself and removing his glasses. "That boy was onto a good thing with her. He should have held onto her. He just couldn't see how lucky he was. Typical of him, I suppose. I had such high hopes for that one. We all did."

"Your son?"

"Yes, my son." He pushed himself up from his desk and strolled over to a picture of Jesus on the wall. This was not a picture of Jesus that Eric had ever seen before, however. He was not nailed to a cross, or healing the sick, or preaching a sermon. He was at a party with his arms wrapped around his father on one side, his mother on the other and streamers were dangling colourfully from his hair.

"He's a good boy really. Youngest of three. All boys. The other two are very driven. They were determined that they could never be accused of living off my name. Jesus, on the other hand, rather counted on it."

He sat down on the edge of his desk again and folded his arms.

"I blame his mother, of course. She spoiled him terribly.

I sent him to Earth to teach him responsibility."

"You didn't send him down to save us from our sins?"

"Oh, yes," said God, hastily, as if being caught in a lie. "That, too. He did very well, actually. We were all very proud of him. It didn't go all according to plan. If he had not managed to rub quite so many important people up the wrong way it wouldn't have ended in so many tears, but still, it was always going to be tough for him."

"Quite," said Eric sympathetically.

"When he came back there were the street parties and media interviews and, of course, the girls. It all went a bit to his head I'm afraid. I was hoping to give him a job working for me, but he barely turned up at the office and even then it was to flirt with the secretaries. I gave up on him in the end. I set up a trust fund for him so he wouldn't want for anything."

God looked at Eric glumly.

"Do you have children?"

"No."

God reflected for a while.

"And how is Margaretha?"

"Keeping well," said Eric, who was beginning to wonder if this wasn't a dream after all. "She said to say hello."

"Ah, that's nice of her," said God warmly. "I did like her. But you didn't come here to listen to my problems," he said, slapping his thighs, suddenly alert again, "what did you come here for?"

"I have some information for you."

God regarded Eric, suspiciously—recognition dawning.

"We've met before."

"Ah, yes," said Eric. "That's partly what I wanted to talk to you about. The last time you saw me I told you my name was Carmine Craxxi."

"Oh, yes. I remember now," he said with a withering tone. "I don't believe we have anything to say to each other, do you?"

He turned his back and began opening files on his computer.

"Except," continued Eric, "I am not him."

"You're not the person who came to see me before?"

"No. I am that person."

"So who are you not?"

"Carmine Craxxi."

"Then who are you?"

"Eric."

God's face brightened.

"Pleased to meet you, Eric."

Eric could feel the conversation slipping away from him.

"I was pretending to be Carmine Craxxi, because the gentlemen with me thought I was."

"Whatever gave them that impression?"

"Because I told them I was."

"Why would you tell them you're Carmine Craxxi if you're Eric? Eric's a perfectly good name."

"It's a very long story, which I don't need to bore you with. But the gentlemen I was with are going to kill you."

God laughed and waved a hand dismissively.

"Oh, nonsense!"

"It isn't nonsense. That's why I am here, at great personal risk to myself I might add, to warn you."

"They can't kill me; I'm God!"

Reminding himself of the seriousness of the situation and recalling the adage that desperate times call for desperate measures, Eric picked up a silver-plated letter opener from the desk and jabbed God in the arm with it midway between the shoulder and the elbow.

God leaped back and howled in pain.

"What did you do that for?"

"You said they couldn't kill you."

"So?"

"So," said Eric, stumbling over his words as he realised exactly who it was he had just assaulted, "I just proved they could."

"Well, I could have told you that! I just meant I am God. It's not the done thing. You didn't have to go stabbing me with, with . . . that thing!"

"It's a letter opener, and I hardly think I stabbed you."

"Look," said God, showing Eric his shirt sleeve. "You drew blood."

"Oh, come on. It's only a scratch."

"Only a scratch? I felt it hit the bone."

"You're exaggerating now. I'm sorry, okay?"

God rubbed his arm and inspected his palm for evidence of fresh blood.

"That bloody hurt that did," he said sulkily.

"I'm sorry. I misunderstood what you meant. It was a simple mistake to make. Roll your sleeve up. Let me take a look."

Eric took hold of God's bony arm and angled it toward the desk lamp.

"It's stopped bleeding already. It won't need stitching

up."

"What about infection?"

"This isn't the Somme. It isn't a war wound. You get worse shaving."

God rolled his sleeve back down.

"Margaretha really seemed to think I needed to come talk to you," said Eric. "Do you mind if I at least say what I came to say."

"I suppose you'd better before you get really violent."

Ignoring the last remark, Eric recounted the events of the last couple of weeks or so, as well as he understood them anyway.

"So, you see," said Eric, when he had finished. "You're in a great deal of danger."

God thought hard for some time, stroking his beard and chewing his bottom lip.

"What did Margaretha propose we do about it?"

"Nothing."

"She thinks we should do nothing?"

"No, she thinks we should do something, but she didn't know what. She was sort of hoping you'd come up with something."

"What makes her think I'd do any better?"

Eric stared at God blankly.

"Oh, I don't know," he said, with a hint of sarcasm.

"Usually when people come here they ask me why I allow wars and starving children. I know where I am with those."

"What do you say to them?"

"I just ask the same question back at them. Ask me another."

Eric puffed his cheeks out as an aid to thought.

"All right, does a tree exist in the forest if there is no one there to see it?"

"No."

"Why doesn't it?"

God sat in the swivel chair by his desk, swivelled, and, smiling, addressed Eric.

"The word *tree* is a noun and nouns exist nowhere in the universe."

"That's just grammar."

God raised a triumphant finger.

"Grammar is the language of the universe."

"Not mathematics?"

"Heavens, no. I was never any good with numbers."

Eric had by now forgotten why he was there. He rubbed the back of his neck and the genesis of a new frown, which would one day make a permanent home on his forehead, appeared above his right eye.

"In the beginning was the word, and the word was God," said God in an expository manner. "What's the key to that sentence, Eric?"

"God?"

"No! It's 'word'. In the beginning was the *word*. Not a number."

Eric didn't understand and said so, somewhat redundantly.

"There was nothing and then there was something. How? Language! You give Nothing a name and you split it into two: that which is it and that which is not it. Then boom! (He spread his arms out in a circle) it begins."

"What does?"

"The process. An interaction. All out of kilter and trying to return to the balance it had before."

"But how can something come from nothing?"

"It was all there, all the time," said God, enthusiastically. "There was just no one thing as opposed to any other. Just a great big potential waiting to be actualised."

Eric winced. God sympathised. He disliked the word 'actualised' too.

"It's all moving. Creating, nurturing, destroying. And not a single conscious thought behind it." God exhaled a breath he appeared to have been holding for some time. "It's quite beautiful really."

"And where do you come in all this?"

God looked at Eric quizzically.

"I don't know, where do I come into all this?"

Eric glanced at various objects around the room: an antique globe, the swinging pendulum of a clock, a pile of books, a reading lamp, a transistor radio, a telephone. He settled his gaze on God again.

"Do you exist if there is no one there to see you?"

God smiled broadly.

"Now you're thinking in the right direction." He pulled his sleeve up and looked at his watch. "Let's go for a walk."

God and Eric strolled together down the middle of a pedestrianised street. Lining both sides were market stalls, each beneath striped awnings of various colours. Crowds thronged, as crowds generally do, attracted to the traders' calls and the bright colours and vivid smells of the wares on sale. Behind the stalls, three-storey brick buildings housing cafes and bars and other businesses only made possible by the presence of the stall holders themselves, stood like sides of a steep gorge above the fast-flowing river of humanity which took its water-like course from one end to the other.

Among the jostling, shouting maelstrom, God and Eric strolled, avoiding on-comers, as if negotiating an asteroid belt.

"Interesting choice," said God.

"You brought us here."

God smiled.

"I once went for a walk with Dante Alighieri," he said. "Never again."

The literary reference was lost on Eric. A dusky looking woman with a criss-crossed face wrapped in a headscarf tried to press a lucky heather on Eric. He declined forcibly and shook his head with regret, but the woman persisted.

"For your journey home," she said.

"No, thank you," repeated Eric.

But the woman slipped the heather into his hand, closed his fingers around it and quickly became part of the crowd once more.

"What was all that about?"

But he was talking to himself. God had wandered off to a stall that sold cheese and was enjoying the free samples.

"Here, try," he said when Eric joined him.

He handed Eric a toothpick with a cube of cheese skewered to one end. He took it gingerly, sniffed it and popped it into his mouth.

God laughed. Few things are humans more wary of than a cheese they have never tried before. Eric looked at the scene around him.

"Let's just say I really am imagining all this and this is

Heaven. Why? I mean, I don't even like smelly cheese."

God shrugged.

"Why do people have nightmares?"

Eric popped a blue-coloured cheese into his mouth, grimaced, and spat it out into a napkin.

"And if this is Heaven," he said, pausing to swallow a cup of water, "what would Hell be like?"

The two men moved to the next stall. It sold salad dressing, in a myriad of flavours. God picked up a little plastic bottle, opened his mouth, and squirted a dose onto his tongue.

"Tell me about your girlfriend."

The abrupt change of subject threw Eric.

"My girlfriend?" he asked, stumbling. "Well, she's, lovely. Really (he hesitated) interesting. Sort of dark and mysterious. Seems to always know what I am thinking. Even when I don't."

"Amber?"

"No, Su-"

Eric fell silent. God cleansed his pallet with a glass of water and squirted more salad dressing onto his tongue.

"It's probably for the best that you've forgotten Amber."

"I haven't forgotten her! "said Eric angrily.

"But you've moved on."

"No. Well, yes, sort of."

"Don't let it bother you, Eric." God paused. "She doesn't."

Eric took God by the elbow and turned him to face him.

"What do you mean?"

"Just that she's managed to move on with her life."

"You mean she's met someone?"

Eric reflected that he had only been dead 'five minutes'

but it seems that in Heaven as in team bonding days, time moves at a very different rate. To Amber, he had been dead some time.

"But that's good, isn't it?" asked God. "You do want her to be happy."

Eric said he did, but he didn't sound very convincing. Even to himself.

"Who?" he asked.

"Adriano."

His stomach felt as if it were filling with liquid mercury. This was the news Eric feared. He had never liked Adriano, Amber's boss: the wealthy, good looking, sporty Italian with whom Amber had had a brief fling before meeting Eric.

"I feel sick."

"Why?" asked God, apparently genuinely surprised. "Would you prefer her to mourn you the rest of her life?"

They edged to another stall–this one sold wood carvings– but Eric was in no state to pay any notice.

"He takes good care of her," said God. Then, after a well-timed pause. "*Very* good care of her."

"What do you mean?"

"Oh nothing," he replied with mock innocence. "He just, you know, takes care of all her needs."

"All right, that's enough."

"That's not what Amber says. She can take as much of Adriano as Adriano can give her."

"Stop it!"

"That's something else she hasn't said for a while."

Eric clenched his fists, crushing the stalk of the lucky heather he was still holding, the image of Amber and Adriano together stuck in his mind.

"Yes," continued God, having glanced at Eric out of the corner of his eye, "Adriano has been a great comfort to her since you died."

Eric took a rough hold of God's collar and dragged him between the stalls and thrust him hard up against the wall of a boarded-up shop. He had never experienced the Red Mist before. He had till then doubted that such a thing ever existed. Now, however, the periphery of his vision was blurred, and the eclectic sounds of the market faded away into silence. His blue eyes gleamed and bulged from his increasingly rubescent face.

"Shut up!" he growled, loudly. "Shut up! Shut up! Shut up!"

"And here," said God, his voice constricted by the force of Eric's grip, "lie the gates of Hell."

"What?"

But God didn't speak. He fixed his eyes on Eric's and waited. The grip on his collar loosened slightly and he was able to breathe more freely.

"What are you talking about?"

"You were wondering about Hell. It's a crude demonstration, I admit, but usually effective."

More pennies began dropping in Eric's mind than in a Victorian convenience.

"What you said about Amber."

God shook his head.

"Adriano?"

"There hasn't been anyone since you, Eric. There will be. Someone kind and who makes her happy. Not too good looking."

Eric released God and stepped away. He cupped his face in his hands and crouched among the scraps of newspaper, food cartons and cigarette butts which find their ways to the edges of all markets. He looked up at God through eyes glazed with tears.

"I am so sorry," he repeated. "I am so sorry."

God lowered himself beside Eric and laid an arm across his shoulders. Eric rested his head on God's chest and for the first time since he had died, wept.

"And there, Eric," he said, softly, lie the gates of Heaven."

Very slowly, Eric opened his eyes, as if for the very first time. He blinked several times and looked about him. It was as if everything that ever was, is or would be—formless and nameless—was concentrated into a single point of white light and burnt directly onto his soul. It was the moment before the universe began; the instant before creation; before judgement, when meaning itself did not exist. In that eternal nothing there were no bounds: no good and no evil; no right and no wrong; no life and no death; no Heaven and no Hell.

Then it was gone.

"What happened to it?" asked Eric.

"It's still there, waiting."

"What for?"

"For you."

God stood and lifted Eric from under his arm to his feet. Eric cupped his face in his hands and rubbed his cheeks roughly.

"Are you all right?" asked God, resting a steadying hand on Eric's shoulder.

Eric nodded.

God extended his arm past Eric's neck and rested it on the other shoulder.

"Let's go," he said, and they stepped back out into the crowd from between two stalls. The two men continued walking, God deep in thought, Eric reflecting on his recent experience and wondering if the reality he perceived, which seemed so solid, so dependable, was really just gossamer thin and that behind the curtain lay another realm of infinite depth, that occupied many more dimensions in space than the now rather flat three he had been used to. Four if you included time. Was what he saw a minute ago any more real than what he could see now; or was it just another veil with something yet more wondrous radiating out on the other side?

Everything and everyone now looked to him like cardboard cutouts: a Hollywood set propped up by scaffold. What did that make him? He raised the backs of his hands to his face then turned them over to inspect the palms. They did not look like they belonged to him. They were no more his, he thought, than a robotic arm picking through a shipwreck on the ocean bed belonged to its operator on the deck of a ship a mile up on the surface.

The chaos of the market then appeared to crystalise into a pattern too complex for him to have noticed before, that gave the impression of randomness but was in fact anything but.

He started to question his own impulses and wondered where they sprang from. They felt like his and his alone but now he was not so sure. He darted left to avoid a woman carrying shopping. She had stepped into his path to avoid a stall holder pushing a bicycle. He had stepped in front of her to pass a young couple who had slowed to share a kiss. How had they met? wondered Eric. And why were they there at that moment? He saw stretched out behind him a concatenation of events, each being influenced by the one behind it and influencing the one which followed. When had his dart to the left begun? Had it been inevitable from the beginning of the universe?

Did the same apply to his thoughts? The long chain of cause and effect which had caused him to avoid, on that day, in that place, walking into that woman had led also to the questions he was asking himself. Were they his thoughts then? Just like his evasive action they too had emerged from the maelstrom of the past: blown this way and that by his culture, education and experiences; every book he had read, every conversation he had had, every lesson taught him at school or sermon given from the pulpit. He felt as if he were the master of himself, but he had the sense at that moment that he was no less than the result of a process: not the thing itself but of it; an action emerging from an action; a verb not a noun.

Nouns exist nowhere in the universe.

Yet he was observing himself. Wherever his thoughts came from, whether they were his and his alone or not, he was discovering them as if for the first time and the sensation it gave him was something new and belonged only to him. At least that part of him was free to experience himself and the world. The part of him that experienced a tree before everything he knew about trees was applied. It was the part of him that, on the roof of the commune with Suzan, had seen the sunset—really seen it—for the first time. That noticed colours which had always been there but which he had not till then been aware of.

A thick-set man collided with Eric who, being British, apologised. He glanced back at his hands, and they were his again. The chaos around him made no sense to him once more. The veil between this reality and the next broadened.

"Are you quite all right" asked God, who had recognised the signs and had left Eric to his revery.

Eric thought so but sounded distant as he tried to hold on to the scraps of the fading dream that had just a moment ago been so present.

"The truth is, Eric, that you can go back any time you like. Anyone can."

"How?"

"You'll be given a choice."

"And then what?"

They walked on a few more steps.

"You choose, Eric. You choose."

TWENTY-NINE

The next morning, Eric stripped off in Margaretha's bathroom and stepped, uncertainly, into the shower cubicle. Eric had never been able to use other people's showers without being accompanied by a deep sense of dread. There was no other enclosed space more personal and familiar to a man, thought Eric, than his own shower and, to his mind, someone else's was akin to alien technology. He stood beneath the shower head and, having deciphered the controls, pressed the red power button.

A basic error.

A blast of icy water sent him across the confined space like a startled cat. It took Eric a little time to discover that the area on the control—between freezing cold and hissing steam—was no more than three millimetres across. Holding the shower head away from his body with one hand and adjusting the dial with the skill of a safe cracker with the other, he managed to find the temperature setting most comfortable for him.

Eric had been more of a bath man on Earth. He didn't appreciate standing in one place for very long, whether it be at a bus stop or in a shower. He was also reluctant to use shampoo that did not exactly match his particular hair type, which was Fine and Fragile. If there were no other formulae available, he did not mind using shampoo for Normal/Greasy hair so long as it was not a regular occurrence. Margaretha's shampoo for Dry or Damaged hair put him off his ease. He read the labels—front and rear—and, after considering dialling the free helpline for advice, popped the cap off. He placed the bottle to his nose and sniffed as if having to differentiate between mineral water and rat poison. He poured some out onto his palm: it was pink, which seemed to confirm his fears. Appeasingly, it formed a nice lather and he proceeded to massage it into his scalp, not knowing if it would make his hair fall out or turn a different colour.

Fifteen minutes' later, he stepped from the shower, dried (checking the towel for clumps of hair), dressed in his old clothes and presented himself at the table, upon which sat a continental breakfast of bread, butter, watermelon and coffee. Eric was never very keen on the way the Mediterraneans started their days, so he settled on dipping biscuits into his coffee.

"You really should eat," said Margaretha.

"You don't have any eggs or bacon, I suppose?"

"Agh, you English!" she replied, disgusted. "If it isn't dripping in oil you're not interested."

Craxxi, wearing one of Margaretha's pink, silk dressing gowns, joined them from the bedroom. Eric glanced at Margaretha who looked down. Not that she had anything to be ashamed of, thought Eric. They ate quietly. Eric thought of Suzan and wondered what she was doing at that moment and if she were thinking of him too. He placed his coffee cup on the table before he dropped it as he felt a wind enter his body, swirl about his chest, expand through his veins, hit the top of his head and ebb away like a retreating wave.

"Are you okay?" asked Margaretha.

"I have absolutely no idea." said Eric, gasping.

At that precise moment, Suzan, shopping for a gardening fork in town, giggled.

Eric pushed his food around his plate with a fork and sighed.

"So, are you going to tell me what happened?" asked Craxxi.

Eric had not been at all talkative since his return to Margaretha's flat. She had asked him what happened in his meeting with God, but he had only flopped onto the sofa and said nothing.

"He'll be fine. We don't need to worry about him."

"He said that?"

"He said that."

Margaretha sighed. She wasn't certain that the danger had passed, but she was contented that she had done what she could do at least.

Craxxi buttered a slice of toast roughly, crunched into it and, still with mouth full asked, "Is that all you talked about?"

"He said," mumbled Eric, "I will have to choose."

"Choose?"

"Between staying here or going back."

Eric closed his eyes. God had not been specific. He had only told him that a moment would arrive, and soon at that, where he would be faced with a decision. That until then he would have to do nothing special except carry on as he had been.

That was going to be easier to say than to do, knew Eric. When Margaretha had asked him whether he wanted tea or coffee he wondered if that was it: the big decision. Tea meant he would go back to his old life, coffee meant committing to his new one. He hoped the choice would come soon as he did not fancy the idea of living like that for very long: continually second guessing the significance of even the tiniest detail.

Margaretha carried her chair and placed it next to Eric. She sat and took hold of his hands.

"And what do you think you will choose?"

He didn't know. It was a terrible position to be put in. He had not asked for two lives and to have to decide which one he preferred.

"Will I forget everything if I go back?"

"I've been told," said Margaretha soothingly, "that it is like waking from a dream. The memory of here fades but it remains with you, deep inside. A word or a sound or a smell can recall it but only as a feeling, and that vanishes."

Eric dropped his head into his hands.

"But you will be a different person," she went on. "Your experiences here have changed you. That will remain. Those closest to you will notice. It won't all be completely wiped out."

"And if I stay?"

"In time you'll forget your old life too."

Eric uncupped his face and looked at Margaretha with bloodshot eyes.

"But you haven't forgotten."

Margaretha's gazed slipped from Eric's to somewhere far away. She spoke quietly.

"I haven't chosen yet."

Eric stood and paced the room, stopping eventually at the window where he looked down onto the people passing by.

"So I have to choose who I forget," he said, not without a trace of bitterness. "The love of that life or the love of this."

Margaretha had no words for him. She would one day have to choose too. It came to everyone in Heaven eventually. It always seemed so unnecessarily cruel to make a person decide something like that; but dying, it turned out, was a long and drawn-out process and who knew exactly when it started or where it ended, if it ever did. Perhaps life itself was no more than a part of it. It seemed, though, that there had to come a point. Not where or whom you chose to forget but to let go; to move on.

Move on.

That is what everyone talked about, thought Eric. You always had to move on. From a relationship, a bereavement, a lost job, even a defeat at some sport or other. Move on, go forward, be positive. But who ever really did move on? You just learnt to keep walking while carrying yet more bags. The heart was a temple, or was it a tomb, to the past: to its loves and heartbreaks; to its disappointments and regrets; to ghosts and memories and unfulfilled desires. It was impossible to not see your past in your present or a former lover in the eyes of a new one. All we ever did, he decided, was to walk backwards into our future, always looking at the receding road of our past.

You cannot walk backwards forever, though. You must eventually turn around and face your future. To tear your eyes away from your past and embrace uncertainty. To finally let go and to move on.

"You just have to listen to your heart."

He laughed bitterly and sat back down at the table.

"Listen to your heart. Oh God!"

"Yes, that's right."

"Be yourself, that's another good one."

"What are you talking about, Eric?"

"Words, words, words. So easy to say. They don't mean anything, though, do they."

"Yes, they do."

"Really? So how do I know which of the voices inside me to listen to? Because I have to tell you, there's quite a crowd in there," he said, tapping his head.

Amber was always telling him to just be himself, but what did that actually mean? He was himself when he was with his parents; he was himself when he was with his niece; he was himself at work, when he was with his friends, when he was asking a policeman for directions, at a job interview, or on his own watching a grand prix on the television. Yet they were all different. One Eric would not dream of using bad language, while the other would use it as punctuation; one Eric would be formal and polite, while the other completely casual; another would be respectful while the other irreverent.

Which was the real Eric?

An empty space, he had once heard, was defined by how it was enclosed. It could either be the centre of a bowl, or a living room or a cathedral. In the same way he was defined, surely, by the people around him. He was sometimes a son; sometimes a brother; sometimes a boyfriend; sometimes a friend; sometimes a colleague.

Strip all that away he thought and keep stripping. Take off his clothes, rub away his upbringing, his nationality, his education and experiences and was what that left the real Eric? If so, who was he? What was he? Peel away each layer and in the end you would be left with nothing. Was that who he really was?

Nothing?

He got up.

"Where are you going?"

"Home."

THIRTY

"Primo, we just feel that assassinating God would bring too much heat down on us," said Bruno.

Primo Fortunato hadn't exactly calmed down since his recent setbacks, but he was now at least no longer a danger to furniture.

"Not to mention the metaphysical ramifications," added Enzo.

Primo and Bruno turned to stare at Enzo.

"I enrolled in evening classes."

The three men were in Fortunato's club. It was in the afternoon and the club was several hours away from opening again. He walked around the bar, scooped ice into three glasses, poured a generous measure of whisky into each. They each took a sip, trying not to wince in front of the others.

"But I want to kill *someone*, you know?" he said once he had recovered.

"Who?" asked Bruno.

"Craxxi would be a good place to start."

Bruno thought his over.

"We'll have to find him first. He's completely gone to ground. We've had guys out everywhere. Nothing."

Enzo swirled the drink in his glass. He liked the sound of the ice knocking together. He was less keen on the drink itself, but he wasn't about to admit that. He had a thought. It wasn't fully formed yet and was based only on something half remembered in class: *Metaphysics for Beginners.*

"My professor said something about how time really works."

"That's great," said Fortunato.

"Not now," added Bruno.

"She said that time here and time there are different. She said," he went on, thinking hard, "that it's like dropping a needle on a record."

"Enzo," snapped Bruno. "I said not now."

"No, listen. She said that, in theory, you can go back to not just any place, but any time."

Fortunato's glass was midway to his lips, but now he paused and placed it back on the bar.

"What are you saying?"

"I'm saying that maybe we know exactly where to find Craxxi. We go back to when he was still alive and kill him."

"And then," said Bruno, warming to the idea, "we can be waiting for him when he gets back."

The three men thought about that for a minute.

"Has this already happened?" asked Bruno.

Fortunato snapped out of his attempt to understand what they were considering doing.

"What do you mean?"

"I mean, perhaps it was us who killed Craxxi in the first place."

"Do you guys get the feeling we've had this conversation before?" asked Enzo.

"No," said Fortunato eagerly, "why, do you?"

"No. I was just wondering if you did."

"Stop, stop, stop," said Bruno, waving his hands in the air, as if he were trying to stop a horse. "Let's not go there, okay? Let's stick to what we know."

"That's not much," said Fortunato.

Bruno settled his gaze on Enzo.

"This professor, where can we find her?"

Enzo was reluctant to get Dani involved. He liked her. Not romantically. It was just that she was from another world that was far removed from his. He appreciated being able to spend an hour every Wednesday evening with someone untouched by the filth of organised crime.

"Oh, I don't know, she's a civilian."

"We only want to talk to her, " said Fortunato.

"That's right," said Bruno, "we just want to meet her and ask her a few questions."

Enzo sighed.

"Class is tomorrow. Meet me there after."

Bruno and Fortunato exchanged looks and smiled.

"But be nice to her!"

The next evening, Enzo hadn't taken very much in of the class. True, he rarely managed to follow more than half of what Professor Dani Fitzgibbon ever said, but tonight had been particularly difficult for him. He regretted telling Fortunato and Bruno about her. He only had because it wasn't often he had the solution to a problem, and the novelty of it was far too tantalising to ignore. But now his worlds were about to collide. He loved being around nice people whose only motivation wasn't to make money, gain power or command respect, but to learn something new and, perhaps, make some friends. He didn't even mind that he was almost definitely the least academic of anyone else in the room. Dani had told them all that being a good academic didn't require intelligence so much as hard work. If you find a topic interesting, if you can be passionate about it, then it's easy. Enzo wasn't passionate about metaphysics, but he suspected that if he understood it, he might be.

Five minutes before the end of the class, Enzo had noticed Fortunato and Bruno in the corridor. He had been hoping they just wouldn't come, as unlikely as that was. The professor called an end to the class and the students busied themselves putting their notepads away. A young woman, who always sat just in front of Enzo turned to face him.

"Hi, a few of us are going to go to that bar opposite. Would you like to come?"

The young woman wore a beret, which Enzo was curious about. She had pale skin and bright red lips. She had short, black hair in a bob that hung perfectly straight in a perfectly straight fringe that touched the top of horn-rimmed glasses. Tattoos could be seen beneath her black stockings, but he couldn't make them out. It was very definitely a look.

"I can't tonight. I'm meeting friends."

And as he said that, Fortunato and Bruno pushed past the exiting students into the class. Enzo dashed over to them and urged them to let him do the talking.

Professor Fitzgibbon was in her twenties. She didn't

wear make-up. Enzo didn't think she had to. She had dark brown skin, almond eyes and a British accent, but not one he could pin-point. It sounded strange to his ears, but he liked it. He'd never stood so close to her before, but now he was, he was taken by her casual beauty. She draped a shawl over her shoulder. Enzo thought the pattern was South American. He couldn't be more specific than that. Actually, she had knitted it herself. There was a black pin attached to it. Had he known more about Gothic literature– or anything at all–he'd have recognised it as the face of Edgar Allan Poe.

"Enzo," she said, smiling with her soft, brown eyes. She noticed his companions and didn't recognise them from the class. "What can I do for you?"

"Professor Fitzgibbon-"

"Dani."

"Dani, that was great. Really interesting."

"Thank you."

"These are my friends. We were talking the other night about what we discussed in class last week. About time."

"We take a great interest in Enzo's education. All he does is talk about you," said Fortunato.

Enzo blushed.

"You always give us so much to think about."

Dani thanked him and waited. Clearly Enzo and his friends wanted something. She wasn't in a hurry exactly, but she was meeting someone. He'd be waiting for her in their favourite restaurant. Later, they'd go back to hers where he'd read to her from one of Poe's short stories. They were halfway through The Maelstrom. She could read them herself, of course, but she liked listening to him. It was their thing. Like the restaurant.

"We were talking about time," said Fortunato. "About how time here relates to time on Earth. We were up half the night."

"I'm glad Enzo has managed to inspire his friends. Education is like a virus. It passes from host to host."

"You said something about how we could go back to Earth to any point in time we like," said Enzo, snatching the conversation back.

"If you imagine time here in Heaven being like a beam of light, and if you imagine the mortal realm to be a glitter ball, then when the light hits it, it is reflected and scatters. Each point of light that comes from it is a different point in time."

"I see," said Enzo. He did see, but only to a point, and not a very sharp one.

"So," said Bruno, "is it possible to pick a point in time you want to go back to and find the right beam of light, so to speak, and go back to where and when you want?"

"Yes, it's possible."

"And how would someone go about doing that?"

"Ah, well, it's not available to just anyone."

"But it happens," asked Fortunato.

"There are agents. Angels really. They go back to do God's work. Although it's not really his work they're doing these days. There's a committee-"

"What about people?"

"It does happen, very rarely, that people go back." She was suddenly not entirely certain she wanted to go on with the conversation. "What's this about?"

Enzo was beginning to feel uncomfortable too. He

liked the professor, the class and the other students. He didn't want to have to never come back.

"Who would we go see about it?" asked Fortunato.

"About what?"

"About going back," he replied, patience wearing.

"There's a department at the university. It's called The Gateway. You can try there." Fortunato and Bruno turned without thanking the professor and left. "They won't help you," she shouted. Then, more to herself than anyone else, "it's closed now anyway."

Enzo was still standing there, red with embarrassment.

"I'm sorry," he said.

"Don't be silly. You're not responsible for your friends. I'll see you next week. Don't forget the reading. Chapter four."

Enzo thanked the professor and made his way out. Dani shook her head, smiled to herself and switched the lights off on her way out. She had a date to keep.

THIRTY-ONE

Carmine Craxxi was in his suite contemplating eternity. He had not really been one for philosophical enquiry while alive. Like the heroes of antiquity, he didn't spend any time second-guessing his actions or weighing up the moral and ethical issues at play. He simply acted. If a nail is sticking dangerously out of a wall, you don't stop to consider the nail; you just fetch a hammer and hit it as hard as you can. It had been a simple and effective way to negotiate life. The afterlife, he assumed, was going to ask a little more of him. For a start, there was no need to hurry. He had been in a terrible rush to accumulate wealth and power while alive. Now, there was always tomorrow, and tomorrow *and* tomorrow. He looked over at the grand piano: white with gold trim. He'd probably learn to play that one day, he thought. Not now, though. Later. He'd never read a book; now he could read every book ever written, so long as they stopped writing new ones. He stood before his bookcase and angled his head to read the spines. He took Moby Dick from its place, read the back, then turned to the front page.

"Ishmael, huh?"

He dropped the book onto the sofa and looked around him. He thought of the people he could look up. His father was a good place to start. He had avoided thinking of him until then. His father had been a tough old dog and had vanished when he was four years old. His mother told him he'd been killed in the Vietnam war, but he had learnt later that he'd been shot dead over a card game. He'd tracked down the man who did it. He wondered if he were in Heaven, too. He doubted it. Now he came to think of it, he doubted his father would be either. His mother would be, though, when her time came. She'd done all she could to steer him away from crime, but it was inevitable. She had had her heart broken once with her husband; she didn't think she could survive any more tragedy. He promised her he'd be careful, yet there he was. He thought of her and how she was likely feeling. He shook away the thought and was grateful for a gentle knock at the door when it came.

"Marga."

He wasn't sure he was going to see Margaretha again. They had got their warning to God, and he didn't seem very worried about it. He'd left Margaretha's flat and she'd gone back to Fortuanto. What was there left to say to each other?

"Is this a good time?"

He said it was the perfect time, but he didn't let on why. He offered her a drink, which she refused, and he stood, arms by his side, waiting.

"I'm happy to see you," he said when she didn't explain the reason for her visit, "but something tells me this isn't a social call. Is it Primo? Has he done something?"

"No, not Primo," she said, dropping onto the sofa, "it's Eric."

"What trouble has he got himself into now?"

She stood up again, agitated.

"Who killed him, Carmine?"

"Does it matter? People get killed."

"Not people like Eric. Carmine, you've lived in a dark world for too long. You forget that it's not like that for most people. Men like Eric don't just get killed for no reason. Especially the way he was."

"Why, what happened?"

"He told me it was an assassin."

That was something Craxxi didn't know.

"But who'd want to take a professional hit out on Eric?"

"Exactly," said Margaretha, as much in gesture as in words.

Craxxi sat down.

"Okay, so what do we know?"

"That Eric was killed by a professional. He took your place. Primo still thinks he's you."

"Wait," said Craxxi, surprised. "Primo still doesn't know?"

"Well, I'm hardly going to tell him, am I?"

Working out who might have wanted another person killed and why and then knowing what to do about it was something Craxxi was well practiced in.

"So Primo is angry with Eric. But he thinks he's me?"

He touched the side of his head with his fingers and closed his eyes.

"What is it? What's wrong?" asked Margaretha.

Craxxi didn't answer. He felt he was close to something, and he didn't want to lose it by speaking. But he couldn't grasp at it. Then it was gone.

"I think it's time I went to straighten things out with Primo."

THIRTY-TWO

Primo Fortunato strapped a gun holster under his arm and adjusted the buckle. He'd never worn a holster before. He slipped the gun into place, put his jacket on and stood back to see if he could notice the bulge. He could, but he decided that was because he already knew it was there. He reached in and pulled the gun out as quickly as he could. It caught on the inside pocket of his jacket. He replaced it and tried again. Smoother this time. Once he had practiced enough, he was satisfied he'd be able to pull it out under pressure, he smoothed his hair back. It was just beginning to grey at the temples. Or it had shortly before he died. Now he'd be slightly grey at the temples forever. Suddenly, he could see the appeal of dying young.

There was a firm knock at the door. It was Bruno.

"All set?"

He was, but something else was on his mind.

"Bruno, just you and me for this."

Bruno hoped he hadn't shown it, but that last comment from Fortunato had punched him in the gut. If he was having doubts about whether or not Enzo could be trusted, then things weren't safe for Enzo. He liked him, and he had felt for him and his obvious discomfort in front of the professor. He had shown another side to Fortunato, though. That had been his mistake. Men like Fortunato didn't have sides themselves and didn't trust them in those who did. Bruno had sides, but he was smart enough to keep them to himself. Alone in his apartment he would crochet. He found it therapeutic. It was one of the classes he signed up to in Heaven as a new arrival. The other had been water aerobics, but he never went back after the introductory session. If Fortunato ever found out, he'd been a dead man.

"Sure, thing. I'll bring the car round."

On his way out, he told Enzo he was needed in the club. There was an order coming and someone senior had to sign for it. There wasn't an order coming, but there was no need to worry him unduly. Bruno would work on Fortunato on his behalf. He'd never need know.

Five minutes' later, Bruno was behind the wheel of a car, driving Fortunato, seated beside him, elbow resting on the door. He was wearing his dark glasses.

"How are we going to play this?" asked Bruno.

"First we'll ask nicely. Then we won't be asking at all."

Bruno had not been involved in crime, organised or otherwise, when he was alive. He'd been a chef, of all things. There was little need for those in Heaven, however. There was very little need for anything actually. With eternal life comes a low attrition rate; especially in the more sought-after professions, so he had wandered into Primo's club one afternoon, three weeks into his death and already bored, and noticed a sign that said Staff Wanted.

He applied, thinking he'd be putting in shifts behind the bar a couple of nights a week, and that's how the two men met. At first, Primo took no interest in his new employee. Why would he? But he noticed what he thought was an accent that came from the same borough of New Jersey he had grown up in. It only took a few minutes to establish their mothers knew each other, and a few minutes more Bruno had been promoted. He never knew what he had been promoted to exactly. He followed Primo around and did what he told him to do. It felt like a senior position. The other employees talked to him as if it was. The money was pretty good, and the work didn't bother him. Or at least it didn't used to. He was beginning to worry about the path his boss was going down, and he wasn't sure he wanted to accompany him all the way to the end.

The Gateway was to be found at the university. That's what it was called. There was only one. It was, however, huge. Originally, it was housed in a temple. No one thought this blasphemous, as knowledge was considered holy. Over the millennia, buildings had been added. It was now no longer possible to tell where the university ended and where the rest of the city began. But the main campus, ancient as it was, was still at the heart of Heaven, bordered by a sandy-coloured and crumbling wall. There were four gates at each of the cardinal points of the compass. The North Gate was the biggest and busiest. It was where places to buy food and drink had been set up many thousands of years before, still serving academics and students on cobbles now worn into shallow troughs by millennia of footfall. Many of the proprietors had been there for just as long. They had died in the stone age and, like ancient and gnarly elms, the modern world had sprung up around them, leaving them untouched.

Fortunato and Bruno passed through the open gate, brushing aside a barefooted and bearded panhandler. They strode purposefully to the main reception where they saw a sign to the Gateway and made their way toward it, through stone tunnels chiselled from rock. The air cooled and the walls dampened as they dropped into the ground. Primo didn't like the thought of tonnes of rock and soil pressing in on him from all sides, but he didn't show it. A few more minutes later they came up against a wooden door. Primo knocked once then let himself in, followed by Bruno. They spilled into a cathedral-like cavern. Standing on a ledge, they peered down, feeling their stomachs lurch, into a deep pit. They couldn't make out what they were seeing, but it was clear that was where they would find the Gateway. They took a metal cage down to the ground level, where they were unchallenged as they moved through the space. At the centre, a ball of light held in a large metal ring glowed and throbbed. Primo had never seen a portal before, but a glowing, throbbing ball of light was, he thought, probably going to be it.

"Can I help you, gentlemen?"

A short, white-shirted man with a dark blue tie tucked into his shirt between the buttons smiled brightly at them.

"Yeah," said Primo. "We're looking for the Gateway."

"I am delighted to say you've found it."

Bruno was relieved that they hadn't had to shoot their way to this point, but he wasn't very hopeful for the following few minutes.

He didn't have that long to wait.

Primo pulled the handgun from under his arm and pointed it at the short man's head. Clearly, this was not the first time the short man had had a gun pointed at him, for he simply carried on smiling and suggested there was no need for threats of violence. If Primo needed something, he only needed to ask.

Primo faltered. Should he keep pointing the gun? After a moment thinking it over, he placed the gun back in its holster and, as he did, he felt such a fool.

"Why don't you tell me what's got you so worked up?"

"My colleague here," said Bruno, stepping forward, "would like to go back to a specific place and time on Earth."

"Can I ask why?"

"Unfinished business," interrupted Fortunato.

"I see. Well, you'll need a-440 filled in and signed in triplicate."

Fortunato considering tapping the gun-shaped lump under his arm and replying that he had already shown him his credentials, but, although he was relatively new to being a tough guy, even he cringed at the thought. He noticed three security guards lower their newspapers and put their coffees down. He estimated he had no more than another thirty seconds to do what he was about to do. He still hadn't worked out what that was, though. The security guards began their lumbering way over and had made half the distance when a rare insight lit up his synapses. Fortunato noticed that the Gateway had no wires or cables leading to it. There were no banks of computers. There wasn't even a red button. How did they know where and when to send people back to? He looked deep into the Gateway. It would be far too grand a claim to say that it spoke to him. It did no such thing, but it was now that inspiration struck. He wanted to go back to Earth at a place where Carmine Craxxi was. It didn't really matter when. He held that desire in his mind. He closed his eyes and concentrated hard on that one thing. Just as the guards were approaching, he opened his eyes and ran for the Gateway, pushing the short man to the ground. Flinching only slightly when Bruno screamed his name followed by a 'no', he only had one more split-second decision to make: head or feet first? He launched himself toward the light, covered his eyes with a forearm and plunged forwards into the unknown.

"Is he okay?" asked Bruno, gaping.

"Unnecessarily dramatic, perhaps," said the short man picking himself up and re-tucking his tie, "he could have just walked into it like everyone else, but that's essentially how it's done."

"But is he okay?"

"That very much depends on what he was thinking when he took the leap."

THIRTY-THREE

More than anything else, Carmine Craxxi liked to eat. He wasn't a glutinous man and, while well filled, he was relatively slim. He just loved the ritual of food. He enjoyed stepping into a restaurant off the street and being seated; the browsing of a menu, the moment you realise the waiter is carrying in your order; the smell, the first bite and the very last.

He was in his favourite restaurant. It was nothing special. Small and family-owned, the food was simple and capable of transporting him back to his childhood. He knew it wasn't sensible for a man in his position to always eat in the same place, but it was a risk he was willing to take.

His dining companion was Joe Schillaci, his schoolboy friend and accountant. They'd known each other since they were six years old. They'd been through school and college together, got their first jobs in the same place, dreamed about the future and reminisced about the past. Although Schillaci wasn't in organised crime– he had a legitimate accountancy business–he and Carmine were still very much a partnership, and the mafia boss rarely made a big decision without discussing it with his friend over dinner, in that restaurant, first.

Not that there were any big decisions to make. It had been a difficult climb to the top for Craxxi, but the last few months had been relatively peaceful. A rival head of family who had been encroaching on his business had, conveniently, died of natural causes before he had had to take action of his own that would likely have started a war. The rival's place had been taken by a far more pragmatic man and stability followed, which was good for business. His income was steady, and the FBI had, he had been told by a reliable insider, taken their eye off him. Life was good. He knew it couldn't last, but he was determined to enjoy the good times while they lasted. It didn't occur to him that it would last the length of his meal and the time it took to get up and leave.

%2 Primo steps through portal

Primo Fortunato had experienced something few ever had. The short man with the tucked-in-tie hadn't had the time to warn him that with each step he took toward the Gateway, time would move at a slightly faster rate and space would fold increasingly. What he would have emphasised, had he the opportunity, was that this phenomenon took place at tiny increments. That meant the front of his body would be occupying a different place in time and space than the back of it. He was bound to experience a little disorientation. That would have been putting it mildly. For a moment, Primo saw his body stretch out away from him at an ever increasing speed. At one point, he looked back and saw the rest of himself stretching like an elastic band into a vanishing point. Just as quickly, he snapped back into shape and fell onto his knees on a damp New York street. He got up, staggered sideways, vomited profusely while holding onto a wall and, after wiping his mouth with his sleeve and taking a few deep breaths, started to recognise where he was. He'd been there before. In fact, he'd grown up only a few blocks away. Behind him, the portal was throbbing brightly in the dark of the night. He didn't know how long it would wait for him, but if his instinct had been right, he wouldn't need much time.

On the opposite side of the street from him was a restaurant—its narrow glass frontage casting a weak yellow light into the night. He walked unsteadily across the road, pausing to let a car pass him, and edged along the wall to the window of the restaurant. He scanned the diners for Craxxi, but he couldn't see him. Nor would he have recognised him if he did, of course. He slipped into the doorway of the shop next door and thought. He took the gun out from under his arm, if only to feel something solid and familiar in his hand. How long would he wait before giving up and heading back? He paused his breathing when he heard the door of the restaurant open. He could hear two men chatting as they left. They stopped just a few feet from where he was hiding, and he forced himself farther back into the shadow. He could hear at least one of the men light a cigarette and breathe it in deeply.

"Do you wanna go to Carlo's for a drink?" asked the smoking man.

"I got an early start," replied the other.

"All right, I'll see you Thursday."

The two men hugged. Primo could hear the slapping

of backs.

"Carmine, my friend," said the other man, "always a pleasure."

Primo stepped from the shadows, his gun held out in front of him. He couldn't make either of the men's faces, so he called Craxxi's name. Both men looked around, so he aimed at the taller of the two. He closed his eyes and squeezed the trigger. The gun almost jerked out of his hands. He opened his eyes, his ears now ringing. One of the men was standing, clearly in shock. He had been sprayed with blood and, it has to be said, brains. The other man was on the floor. Primo tried to get a good look at his face, but that was mostly missing now. He threw the gun into the doorway and ran across the road, causing a yellow taxi to screech its tyres as it swerved around him. Knowing what to expect now, he braced himself for the experience and thought of Bruno and the short man with the tucked-in tie and dived head first into the portal.

Thirty-four

"Whose reality is this? Mine or yours?"

Eric and Suzan were shelling peas in the garden. They were seated beside each other on a long wooden table.

"Why do you ask?" replied Suzan, true to her habit of answering a question with another question.

"I'm shelling peas with you, but are you here shelling peas with me, or are you doing something else altogether?"

"We're both here shelling peas, right here, right now."

"But how does that fit?" asked Eric. "If we create our own realities, surely only one of us can really be here."

"It's a bit like if I throw a stone in a pond, it creates ripples," said Suzan after a moment to reflect. "If you throw a stone in the same pond, it creates ripples, too. They're separate to mine at first, but they meet and interact and a whole new pattern, unique to itself, is created. But what you have to remember is, there are a lot of people throwing stones."

But we don't throw stones into a pond. It's a pretty way of describing it, but that isn't the way it really is."

"It's a metaphor, Eric."

Eric didn't want metaphors, but he was beginning to realise they were as good as he was going to get. He had seen something when he was with God. For the very first time it was something real. But when he tried to explain it to Suzan, he had to resort to metaphors too, which he wasn't very good at. The truth was always like something else. The universe nothing more than a vast, impenetrable poem, written by a poet high on opium who had died in his twenties from standing in the rain for too long.

He hadn't told Suzan that he was going to have to choose between his life with her and life back on Earth with Amber. It may never come to that, or he might be forced to make his choice in the next moment. He didn't know how it worked.

And he still didn't know who had killed him on Earth. He had forgotten to ask God when he had the chance. Suzan had tried telling him it wasn't important; that lots of people in Heaven had no idea how they had died. Most of them hadn't been murdered, though. Surely anyone would be curious about that.

"Are we still in the universe then? Here in Heaven, I mean."

"Still in the universe?" Suzan laughed. "You still think of here as being somewhere else, don't you?"

"Isn't it?"

"There is no somewhere else; only here. There is no past or future; only now."

Eric had shelled his last pea. This was true figuratively but also metaphorically. He stood up wordlessly and took the pea pods to the compost heap. When he returned to the table Suzan was no longer there. He sat down on his own.

He really should be happy, but if he were really making his own Heaven, what did the events of the last week say about his state of mind? Bombs and kidnappings? Something was very definitely wrong. He didn't need a psychiatrist to hold up a blob of ink on a card to know his mind wasn't as it should be. God had told him he was going to have to choose. How would he know when the time came what he would need to do? In such situations, people generally advise to follow your heart, but how often had that turned out well? Eric didn't read poetry, and he didn't much pay attention to lyrics in songs, either, but even he knew that if the heart knew what it wanted and what it should do next, music and literature would be very different. That left the head. Eric wasn't even going to bother explaining to himself why that was a bad idea. Amber had chosen him. If it had been left up to him, he'd still be living the life of a fourteen-year-old boy with personal hygiene to match. When you know you know, people claim. But do you? Humans were very good at remembering their hits and forgetting their misses. *Confirmation bias* was the term Eric would have used, had he happened to know it.

Dinner came and went, but Eric wasn't hungry. He stayed upstairs, lying on his back on the unmade mattress. He could hear the murmur of voices and laughter floating up through the floor but couldn't make out Suzan's. That was because Suzan wasn't speaking, and she wasn't laughing. She'd been here before. There was something coming. She could sense it. She didn't know what it was, but she could feel it drawing nearer. She reminded herself that a snowflake never falls in the wrong place. She wasn't a snowflake, though, and neither was Eric. She wanted them to keep falling together. Wanting things to be other than they are was, she knew, at the source of all suffering. She didn't mind a bit of suffering, however. That was what was missing from Heaven. Most people had everything they wanted, exactly as they wanted and were, as far as she was concerned, less human for it. That's why she lived at the commune, on the periphery, where she had always been.

She finished pushing her uneaten food around the plate and left the table. No one noticed her go. She climbed the stairs silently on bare feet, laid next to Eric, her head on his chest and, saying nothing, fell asleep.

When she woke it was still dark, and Eric was no longer there. She knew he wasn't downstairs getting a drink. He wouldn't be coming back. She switched on the bedside light and saw a note on the pillow next to her. She knew what it said, but she read it anyway.

Dear Suzan, I am so sorry. God said I had a choice to make. The funny thing is, I don't even think this is it. I think that's still to come. It's not easy, but I have this feeling it's okay, that we will always be here in Heaven together, by that river, sitting on the roof watching the sunset, in bed together. And I know that we'll find each other again. I don't know how I know. I just do. I am sorry I slipped away in the night, but I think it's how you'd want me to do it. I don't know what's coming next, but it will be all right. Thank you for everything you've given me. I love you – Eric x

Suzan held the letter to her chest and laid on her back. She had known every word before she had read it. How? She felt like a needle in the groove of a record, playing someone else's song.

THIRTY-FIVE

%Carmine and Marga go to see Primo who reveals it wasn't Eric he went to kill. So who killed Eric?

%Carmine and Marga get Suzan and they go after Eric

Fortunato strode back into his bar as if he were being carried on shoulders. He even punched the air and whooped. Enzo looked to Bruno for some sense, but he just shrugged back. There had to be consequences to what Primo had done, and he, Bruno, was going to have to bear at least some of them.

"What happened?" asked Enzo.

"I did it," said Primo, speaking too quickly. "I went back, I saw Craxxi, I blew his head off. Tell him," he said, gesturing to Bruno.

"It's true. He was only gone a second at our end."

"Is that puke?" asked Enzo, looking at Primo's shirt.

"Yeah, well, it was a wild ride."

"So what now?"

"Enzo, my friend," said Primo, placing a heavy arm around Enzo's shoulders, "we wait for Carmine Craxxi to arrive in Heaven."

"How long will that take?"

"Not as long as you think."

That last remark came from behind them. Walking towards them was a strong-looking man accompanied by Margaretha.

"Who are you?" asked Primo.

"I'm Carmine Craxxi," was the reply, followed by a solid fist in Primo's face.

Bruno and Enzo stood by as their boss fought to clear his vision while struggling to his feet.

"You're not Craxxi."

"Oh my God, Primo, how can you be so stupid," spat Margaretha. "The man you thought was the most feared organised crime boss in New York was a British IT specialist called Eric. He played you."

Craxxi crouched next to Primo.

"So it was you who killed me. I was wondering."

"I don't understand what's happening," said Primo.

Margaretha scoffed.

"You've never understood."

Carmine helped Primo to his feet and put him on a bar stool.

"How about we all have a drink?"

A few minutes later, with everyone holding a drink and Primo prodding his nose with a napkin, Craxxi opened proceedings.

"You went back to kill me. Why?"

"You had slipped away from me," said Fortuanto. "Or Eric had. I couldn't track you down."

"So you went to the one place you knew I'd be."

"I didn't get a good look at you. It was dark. I heard

someone call you by your name, so I just assumed."

"You assumed correctly."

Enzo was happy to let Craxxi go on thinking he was just the barman, so he polished some glasses and did his best to look like a disinterested party. Bruno sat more nervously.

Craxxi reached into Primo's jacket and removed the gun. Primo cursed silently as he had forgotten it was still there and knew that, had he remembered it, the last few minutes might have gone differently.

"So you don't have Eric?" asked Margaretha.

"I have no idea where he is. Or who he is."

Craxxi spent a moment to complete his assessment of Fortunato. This was something he was very good at. He decided that this man was almost scared enough to not be a problem ever again. But not quite. He stood and regarded the gun in his hand.

"I have to give you some credit," he said, not looking up. "You got me. Many tried and failed. You succeeded." He pressed the nozzle of the gun to Primo's forehead, who seemed to shrink in size. "You were lucky, but your luck has run out. You're done. I don't want to see you or hear from you again. You'll never bother Margaretha, and Eric stays safe. Do you understand?"

Primo, unable to speak, nodded.

"You have a nice thing going here," Craxxi said, pointing with his eyes to the rest of the bar. "Be satisfied with it. If you move out of your lane just an inch, I will blow your brains out. I didn't know it had even happened when you shot me, but I'll make sure you will."

That ought to do it, Craxxi thought. And just to emphasise the fact he knew he had been completely emasculated and was no longer a threat, he put the loaded gun into Primo's hand, knowing he no longer had the courage to use it. He fired a glance at Bruno and Enzo and left, Margaretha striding tall and proudly by his side.

They stopped outside the bar.

"I'm sorry I spoke for you in there," said Craxxi. "I was on a roll, and I just assumed."

"That's fine."

"So what now?"

"Now we go for another drink."

Sitting on the veranda of the first bar they came to, Margaretha and Craxxi fully intended to not leave again until they were drunk. It was halfway through their third glass when Margaretha put her finger on what was bothering her still.

"So who killed Eric?"

"Huh?"

"If Primo went back to kill you, who killed Eric?"

"Does it matter?"

"Carmine, it was a deliberate hit. Who would want to kill Eric?"

Carmine swirled the whisky and ice in his glass.

"What are we missing?"

Margaretha played back the events of the last few weeks, looking for clues. Eric gave the impression as someone who stumbled from one situation to the next, always out of his depth, and relying on dumb luck to get him through. But when she considered it as a whole, it did seem to be an awful lot of luck.

"I think we need to speak to Eric."

An hour later, Suzan was waiting on the front step of the commune. The fog that had been shrouding her and Eric's past, present and future had cleared. She remembered what was happening and why, so when a now mostly sober Craxxi and Margaretha turned up the path to the house, she was already on her feet and met them halfway.

"This isn't the first time we've stood here. I know every word you're about to say, so let's save time and just follow me.

Thirty-six

The short man with the tucked-in tie looked down at his clipboard.

"Ah, Eric, yes. We were told to expect you. Are the rest of your party running late?"

"What party? There's just me."

The short man consulted his clipboard, shrugged, and guided Eric forward.

"It's very simple really. All you need to do is think about where you want to go and when. Then step into the light. The difficulty is not allowing a different thought to invade your mind at the last moment and being pulled away. Really focus."

Eric took some deep breaths, closed his eyes and pictured the moment he was leaving his office to meet Amber for the last time. He was holding a newspaper as he stood from his desk. He recalled as much detail as he could: his empty coffee cup, the background on his computer screen, the water cooler behind him . . . He opened his eyes and stepped forward, feeling his body lurch away from him.

A moment later, he arrived violently back in his office.

Another moment later, his mind joined him.

"Are you okay?"

The question came from Sandra who had the desk facing his.

He ran to the bathroom, slid on his knees toward a toilet bowl and vomited lavishly. Once the dry retching had stopped, he rinsed his mouth and washed his face at the sink. As he did, he glanced down at the newspaper he had carried into the bathroom with him and placed it down. The headline read: *Mob Boss Slain*. Under it was a picture of Carmine Craxxi. It had been the last thing he read before his death. He wasn't in the right state to consider the unlikeliness of the coincidence.

He returned to his desk.

"My God," said Sandra, "you look terrible."

Eric dropped the newspaper on his desk and put his jacket on.

"I think I'll go home."

"You do that, hun," she said and, as he was halfway out of the door added, "drink plenty of fluids." She was careful not to say 'water' as when people are unwell, it's well known that it's fluids they need.

Outside in the street, Eric dashed across the road and made himself inconspicuous. He remembered now. He had been in that exact same situation before. Farther along was a parade of shops. Above them were tiny flats for rent. He hurried toward them, heading around the back into the car park and up a set of metal stairs to a balcony. He walked along the flats, touching each door as if looking for something familiar. He came to a door with flaky blue paint. As he touched it, it swung open. He stepped inside cautiously, calling out to any occupants but the flat appeared to be empty. The floor was uncarpeted–just bare gritty concrete that crunched under foot. He found the living room. It overlooked the high street. He looked at his watch. He estimated he had around five minutes before his other self would pass by with Amber. It occurred to him then that he had no plan other than to be there at that window at that time. He just had to trust that he'd know what to do when the time came.

"Hey."

Eric spun around to see Suzan, Craxxi and Margaretha standing in the room, side by side. He hadn't heard them enter.

"What are you doing here?" he asked.

"We were about to ask you the same thing," said Craxxi.

Eric sat on the window ledge. He looked down the street to where he knew he was about to appear, then back at his companions.

"Seriously, what are you doing here?" asked Eric.

"Because this is where we always end up," said Suzan. "I don't know why. Perhaps I did once, but that's been lost."

Eric stood up urgently.

"There I am," he said, pointing. "There's Amber."

"You're facing a choice," said Suzan.

"What choice?"

He watched his other self holding Amber's hand as they stopped to look in a shop window.

"I think I need to decide whether to stay here or leave with you."

"What are you going to do?" asked Margaretha, but Eric didn't answer.

"It was me, wasn't it."

"What was?"

"I am my own murderer. I don't know how, but I shoot myself from this window."

"You don't even have a gun," said Margaretha.

"I do," said, Craxxi, stepping forward and handing it to Eric.

"What the hell did you give him that for?" asked Margaretha.

"Because he has a decision to make. And I think that giving him that gun is probably what I always do."

Eric had never held a gun before. It was the ugliest thing he had ever seen. He was reviled by its blackness, weight and intent.

He looked to where he knew he had been shot. It was perhaps a hundred yards.

"I'll never hit me with this thing from here."

"Apparently, you do," replied Craxxi.

"Eric," said Suzan, "before you do that, there is something you need to know."

Eric let the gun hang by his side. His other had noticed a shop selling cameras. He could remember what he'd been thinking at the time. They were going on holiday and that was as good an excuse as any to buy a good camera.

"What?"

She pulled a piece of paper from her jacket pocket, unfolded it and gave it to him. It was a pencil sketch of a young girl. The girl, whoever she was, had long hair that hung in ringlets. She had big eyes, a button nose and a small chin. Eric was not good at guessing ages, but he decided the girl in the sketch was no more than two years old.

"The eyes," he said, looking closer.

"What about them?"

"It's you, isn't it, when you were young. It's very good! I didn't know you could draw."

"It isn't me."

"Then who is she?" he asked," looking closer and squinting.

"She's our daughter."

Eric swallowed hard. Having become accustomed to being able to keep up with events in the last few days, suddenly being deposited back into the dark days of confusion came as a jolt to his psyche.

"What are you talking about?"

"I'm pregnant. That's what our daughter is going to look like. I sketched her when I found out."

"But you and I . . . we . . . it was only a few days ago! How can you possibly know?"

"I *know*," she assured him.

"Of course you do."

He stared at the girl in the drawing, still not quite able to make the connection between her and himself and sat down on the floor against the wall before he toppled over.

"Well, that's it then."

"That's what?"

"I can't go back now, can I?"

"Why not?"

"Isn't it obvious?" shouted Eric.

Suzan sat down beside him and wrapped her arms around her knees.

"There's a lot you don't know."

"That's the only thing I do know. "

"I mean about what happens when a baby is conceived in Heaven."

"I might have known," said Eric, shaking his head, "it wouldn't be so simple."

"When a baby is conceived in Heaven," she said, carefully, "someone close to the couple on Earth will become pregnant."

Eric turned to look at Suzan.

"What are you saying?"

"I'm saying that our daughter won't be born in Heaven, to us; she'll be born on Earth to someone one, or both, of us were close to."

"That," said Eric, having waited a moment to take this new knowledge in, "is the most beautiful thing I've ever heard."

"It's how we're reborn."

"Reincarnation?"

Suzan nodded.

"But," said Eric, "it'll be both of us being reborn in one baby."

"Then there are those who were reborn through us and those that were reborn through them and so on. That's why there are people walking around on Earth today with the thread of literally thousands of lives running through them."

"So if I don't shoot myself, I won't die, we won't meet, and our baby won't-"

Suzan laid her hand over Eric's.

"It's already happened. Nothing can change it now," she said, resting her hand on her belly. "Not even it never happening."

Eric opened then closed his mouth.

"It's just one amazing thing after another," he said. "The whole thing. It's just so amazingly beautiful I can hardly stand it!"

Eric noticed Craxxi following something with his eyes. He stood up to see his other self and Amber approaching the time and place of his death. He raised the gun and looked down the barrel to across the street.

"Eric," said Margaretha, gently, "how many times have we all been here before? All of us, in this room. A hundred times? A thousand? More?"

"What do you mean?" he asked, still aiming the gun.

"This isn't the first time this has happened. That's why you and Suzan remember so much of it."

"Each time you pull the trigger we go back to the beginning. Stuck in a loop."

Eric lowered the gun and stared at Suzan.

"Suzan, you told me I was in a loop. You said I kept killing myself."

"And God told you that you were going to have to choose."

He looked at himself. If he aimed the gun in his hand and pulled the trigger he would, against all the odds, achieve a direct hit that would kill him. He'd come back to Heaven; he'd meet Suzan and fall in love with her all over again. If he didn't shoot himself, he'd cease to exist in Heaven and carry on living his life with Amber as if nothing had happened.

No, not as if nothing had happened. He knew he'd take something back into his old life with him. That he could never be quite the same again. But he'd forget Suzan and meeting God. The wonderful things he'd learnt would remain as an aftertaste, but at least they wouldn't leave him.

He didn't know for how long he had been stuck in the loop, nor how many times he'd been standing there with a gun in his hands. Margaretha suggested thousands. He knew in that moment it had been many more than that. He suddenly felt incredibly tired. The gun became too heavy. He took one last look at his other self and let it slip from his grip and onto the floor. His other self continued walking with Amber.

The loop was broken.

Eric's emotional hide gave way and he wept. Suzan draped her arm around his shoulder and buried her face into his neck.

"Hey," she whispered. "This is only the beginning. There is so, so much more to come."

She knew that, so far, Eric's credulity had been stretched to its very limits, but that it would not be until the outer reaches of his incredulity had been breached that he would receive the very first glimpses of what lay beyond.

"You cannot even imagine," she said, weeping herself now, "what's waiting for you–for all of us. One day, someone will reach up and point a finger at the sky and the sky will shimmer like the surface of a pond. That person will stand up and part the sky with two hands, peer through to the other side and vanish and that will be just the start of it. After that, everyone will follow. The world and their lives on it will seem just like a dream they have woken up from, but instead of waking up to a harsh reality, the reality they'll wake up to will be . . ." and that's where words would have failed even Shakespeare.

"I hope I'm there when that happens," said Eric, in awe.

"When that happens," sniffed Suzan, "we'll all be there."

They kissed, as Eric and Amber walked by on the street outside.

"I know I'll forget you, but I'll always miss you. There will always be an ache in my heart, and I won't know what it is, but it'll be you."

Suzan pinched the end of Eric's nose. "You won't forget me. I'll make sure of it. I'll be there to watch over you, to make sure you're happy. More than anything else, I'll be there to make sure you don't forget the things you've learnt here."

"But how?"

Suzan paused and burrowed deep into Eric's soul.

"Trust me."

"And when the time comes and it's my turn to step through the sky," said Eric, "you'll be there with me to hold my hand, won't you."

Suzan smiled.

"You just try getting me to let go."

And then he was gone.

The Epilogue

Eric left his supervisor's room a few minutes after his other self left.

"Forget something?" asked Sandra.

A slightly confused Eric smiled.

"Where's my jacket?"

"You just took it."

"What are you talking about?"

"And you're looking a lot better suddenly."

Eric tolerated Sandra at best and didn't want to get involved in a conversation with her. He looked at his watch.

"I'm meeting Amber for lunch," he said and left, assuming he had not brought his jacket with him that morning. He turned right out of the building and headed for the bank, outside which he was to meet Amber. When he got there, there was no sign of her. At least, he thought, he would get away with being told off for being late this time.

A few minutes later Amber came breezing up.

"Hey, babes," he said, kissing her.

"Where's your jacket?" she asked.

"That's what I want to know."

"I've had a rotten day so far, Eric. I've been feeling sick, and I'm not in the mood for your antics."

"What have I done?" asked Eric, spreading his arms out wide, but Amber had already moved the subject on.

"That holiday's still in the window. Hurry up or someone else will have it."

Eric muttered something about not being able to do anything right and followed his girlfriend into the travel agent from which he emerged less than ten minutes later, ruefully slipping his credit card back into his wallet.

"That's your birthday present and Christmas present combined, all right?"

"Thank you, honey," said a newly magnanimous Amber. "But I really don't mind going halves."

Eric smiled and put his arm round her shoulders.

"Come on, let's grab something to eat," he said, adding with a wink, "You can pay."

They went to their usual caf'e for lunch. Eric had a bacon sandwich, but Amber, still feeling a little fragile, had a couple of slices of toast and a cup of sugary tea.

"You've had a good day," said Amber, pushing the brown crusts to the edge of her plate.

"What makes you say that?"

"You just seem different. Lighter. What happened?"

"Nothing, I think," said Eric, having replayed the events of the morning. "I wish I knew what happened to my jacket, but apart from that, it was nothing special."

"I don't know. Maybe it's just me."

Eric finished his sandwich, wiped bacon grease from his lips with the back of his hand and drained the last of his tea.

"I'd better get back," he said, looking at his watch. "If you're not well, why don't you go home?"

"No, it's fine. I'm feeling better actually. That toast helped."

"What do you think it was?"

"Just a bug," she said, shrugging.

When they left the café they head off together towards Amber's office.

Amber's phone beeped from her handbag.

"This doesn't make any sense," she said, shaking her head. "Predictive text is useless. *She'll ball me at good?*"

She repeated the phrase several times, under her breath, until the words rearranged themselves into something more likely.

"She'll *call* me at *home!*" she exclaimed at last.

Going nut, she replied, *Pee you newt vine you are fred.*

Chuckling at her own joke left her only partially fulfilled, so she offered the phone to Eric. On finding him absent from her shoulder, she stopped and spun on her heel to find him face up against a shop window admiring a range of digital cameras.

"Am I talking to myself?"

"If we're going to go on holiday, we really should buy one of these babies."

"Apparently," she sighed, "I am."

" I'll get you one for your birthday if you're good."

"I'm always good!"

"Yeah, but at what? That's what I can't figure out."

She took his hand and tugged.

The following morning—a Saturday—Eric woke early. Amber was still breathing gently, her eyes closed. He felt as though he had had a night of sleep like none before. He was not just refreshed but renewed. He thought about it but put it down to a dream he must have had but could not now remember.

He was leaning up against the kitchen counter, waiting for the tea to brew, when he heard something being pushed through the letterbox in the hall. The postman had already been and most of it had been filed in the bin as junk. He'd kept the menu for a new Chinese takeaway. Glancing at the door he saw the outline of someone in the frosted glass disappearing back down the pathway. It looked like a woman, with long black hair—or perhaps it was dark brown. She seemed to be in a hurry. He put the menu down and stepped to the door quickly. Opening it, he made his way down the path. He was wearing slippers, very much an indoor shoe, but he was one of those who believed it was okay to use slippers outside, so long as you tiptoed and were back inside in no more than ten seconds. He leant over the gate at the end of the path and looked both ways, but whoever had dropped the letter off was not to be seen. He tiptoed back into the house and picked up the letter. It was addressed to him by name in florid handwriting. Inside there was a pencil drawing of a little girl that he very faintly recognised, but from where he didn't know. Written across the bottom was a message that left him baffled. Deciding that it was too early to be trying to work it out, he finished the teas, put the letter into his dressing gown pocket, and went upstairs.

"Tea's up!" he said, pushing the bedroom door open with his backside. "Rise and shine!"

But Amber was no longer in bed. He put the tray down

on the dresser and went to the bathroom, where he could see her sitting at the edge of the bath.

"You all right, love?" he asked, without pausing for an answer. "Here, I got this really strange letter this morning."

He removed the letter from his pocket and offered it to Amber, but she didn't take it. Her eyes were red where she had been crying.

"What is it?" he asked. "What's wrong?"

A smile tugged, weakly, at Amber's lips. She waved a little white stick limply in his general direction.

"I'm pregnant."

For a moment, the world ceased to spin for Eric. He took two steps back until he came up against the door frame and allowed his bottom lip to sag below his chin.

"So," asked Amber, brightly, as if this were a morning like any other, "what does your letter say?"

"What?"

"The letter," she repeated, pointing to it with her eyes as it hung loosely by his side, "what does it say?"

He remembered to breathe again and showed the mother of his unborn child the pencil drawing of the little girl. She leant in closer and read what was written across the bottom.

Call her Suzan.

Printed in Great Britain
by Amazon

40745686R00215